THIRTEEN
CONFESSIONS

THIRTEEN CONFESSIONS

- STORIES -

DAVID CORBETT

MYSTERIOUSPRESS.COM

OPEN ROAD
INTEGRATED MEDIA
NEW YORK

Cover art by Mauricio Díaz

978-1-5040-3595-8

Published in 2016 by MysteriousPress.com/Open Road Integrated Media, Inc.
180 Maiden Lane
New York, NY 10038
www.mysteriouspress.com
www.openroadmedia.com

For Mette, *hjertet mitt*

CONTENTS

STRAY

Christmas patrons thronged the bank. Outside, rain fell, third day running.

All these bodies should warm things up, Marybeth thought, but no. Still, there were festive touches about—harp and dulcimer carols piping softly in the background, twirled bunting draping the walls, ribboned wreaths the size of tires. She caught a hint of pine, drifted into memory. Sacrament of childhood, she thought, this time of year.

She stood in the teller queue, trembling. Be calm, she told herself. Calm as a mutt by a midday fire—Jamie's turn of phrase. He had so many expressions, most of a darker sort: vivid as a cat's ass, face like a bulldog licking piss off a nettle, cold as my dear mother's heart. That bitter turn of mind, so Celtic, but that was why she loved him.

From the very start the attraction lay precisely in what others might call his failures. Success held little appeal for her. Always something brittle about success, something garish, too lucky. She preferred her men wounded but resolved. Solemn determination had greater purchase in her heart than confidence. A man who knew the edge was only a footfall away and who was thinking of how to grab you back from it, protect you, not because he was scared but because he'd made that fall himself once or twice, loved you too much to wish it on you—that was the fella for her.

The queue advanced a step, everyone trudged forward, squeaky boots, soggy shoes. Not much in the way of merry in the faces, she thought, eyeing the others in line. Despite herself, she glanced over her shoulder at the guard near the door.

He was hardly more than a boy. His uniform draped on his bone-thin body like a hand-me-down on a rack—a Latino, face dotted with acne, hair gelled into a black shiny wave frozen in time, thumbs tucked in his belt—no gun, just pepper spray. Good, she supposed, feeling a bit less afraid.

Sensing her gaze, perhaps, he turned toward her and met her eyes. Unable to help herself, she smiled.

He returned a smile of his own, self-effacing and slack, then reconsidered, averting his face toward the door, but in that instant she detected not one of those sullen, antsy, me-first young men she so despised and feared. Instead she caught a little of the lonely, the lost.

What is it with me, she thought, and strays?

She looked down at the purse she'd brought, one of those shapeless sack-like vinyl things you could get so cheap along Market Street, the Salvation Army bells ringing all around you as you browsed the vendor racks and stalls. Would it be big enough, she wondered, was it too big? She nudged it with her foot along the floor as the line inched ahead.

She'd met Jamie two Januarys past, at the Horn & Whistle, her neighborhood pub, the holidays well behind them, just the bleak cold wind and metal-gray sky outside, the empty promise of a new year. But then there he was, and promise beckoned.

He was a charmer, yes, the sandy-colored hair, the milky Irish skin and rust-brown freckles, the chesty laugh and the endless string of slightly cruel jokes.

A pint of stout, that's what he ordered for her, like a black liquor soup, topped with creamy foam. She nursed it as they got acquainted, she a teacher at city college, remedial composition— a tragedy, how poorly most young people read and wrote these days—and he was in sales, something involving computers, she never did grasp it completely.

Ireland was the new promised land for the digerati then, and he'd worked in Dublin for a while, earned his degrees and certificates, then come over with a cousin, acquired one of those visas Silicon Valley was sponsoring right and left a decade back.

He soon tired of the whole mega-corporate slog, went off with a few cohorts to start their own venture, a freelance affair, striking that right balance, enough coin on hand to keep the wolves at bay, enough freedom in his heart to feel like a man.

There were setbacks, sure, and he told her about them and they broke her heart. He knew what it meant to fail, then pick himself up, have a pint, share a laugh, get on with it. Leave self-pity to the Russians and Mexicans, he said. Dreams get dashed so new dreams can take their place. They drank to dreams. And she knew in the pit of her heart they would marry.

A mere four weeks later, they did. Valentine's Day. The courthouse, two strangers for witnesses.

She suddenly found herself at the head of the queue, and a queasy lightheadedness came over her. She bit back the nausea, dabbed at her face with the back of her wool glove.

The house was Jamie's idea. No better investment than property, he'd said, San Francisco property in particular.

What about the recession, she'd said, and he'd answered that's why the timing's perfect. Buy low, sell dear.

There's still no way we can manage it, she'd told him, but he'd taken rein of the finances—a husband's mortal obligation, his words—and he knew a man who knew a man and said trust me and how could she not?

And then there they were, a two-bedroom bungalow bordering Noe Valley, a fixer-upper for sure, but home.

She left her job with its benefits to manage the most essential repairs, emptied her savings to pay for them—the kitchen and bath had to be gutted, rebuilt from the floor joists up, so much dry rot, and she blamed the ache in her joints on all the physical labor, pitching in with the workers—while Jamie, suit and tie and freshly shined shoes, went out each day to slay the beast. Solemn determination. Protecting her.

It took until Thanksgiving for him to confess the truth. There was no job, hadn't been for over a year. He just rode the bus from one end of the city to the other, or sometimes he'd get on the train, ride down to San Jose or out to Walnut Creek, the suburban outposts, all those majestic hills and bustling malls, all the traffic and the nouveau riche.

The mortgage lender, in truth a den of crooks Marybeth could hardly believe existed, filed their notices, moved to foreclose and evict—a scam from the start, and she wondered if Jamie had been duped or complicit.

Regardless, two days after the last papers were served, she had her consult, learned her joint aches were not arthritis but something much worse.

The teller near the end came free and beckoned Marybeth forward. She reached down, snatched up the giant floppy purse, trundled over.

The teller said something festive in greeting but Marybeth barely heard, it was like she was underwater, rustling around in the bag for the envelope and remembering what Jamie had said the day he'd left: You deserve someone better, I can only drag you down, I'm nothing, a wretch, a failure. I know, she'd thought, I'm a lover of failures, it's my curse, wanting to tell him—I have cancer, it's in my bone marrow—but the words wouldn't come.

Finally, she felt it, the card, brought it out and, hand shaking as though from palsy, slipped it across the counter to the teller.

A plump girl, heavy-lidded eyes, flat nose, chestnut hair. She lifted the flap on the envelope, withdrew the Christmas card, inside of which Marybeth had written: *I have a gun. Do not trigger the alarm or make a sound. Give me all the money in your cashier tray or I will shoot, one-by-one, the customers standing in line behind me.*

Her heart bucked inside her chest as she hefted the huge bag onto the counter for the teller to fill. A note job, they called it—in truth there was no gun, and she hoped she'd get consideration for that when they prosecuted her. Glancing about to see who was staring—no one, it turned out, not yet—she listened to the fluttery thump of the banded stacks of bills as the teller stuffed them inside the purse.

Then a sudden flare of pain shot through her, ripping through her bones like black fire. No, she thought, not now, and she steadied herself, grabbed the purse, then glanced at the teller whose eyes were scared and resentful.

"I'm sorry," Marybeth whispered as she turned away, shouldering the purse, surprised at its toppling weight, then staggered toward the young Latino guard.

A few of the other patrons finally seemed aware of what had happened, there were whispers and stares but Marybeth paid no heed. Her eyes remained fixed on the guard with his stiff wavelike hair, his expression first puzzled then alarmed as she plodded closer.

"I've just stolen this." Grimacing from the pain, she dropped the purse at his feet. They both stared at it. "You need to arrest me, or call the police, if that's how it's done."

Last week, in a magazine that someone had left behind in the bus shelter, she'd read that women could get chemotherapy in prison. And a bank robbery meant federal custody, better care. By no means good care, she thought, but a small hope is still hope, almost collapsing as the young guard glanced down into the bag, saw the money, then looked back at her, panic in his eyes. So young, she thought. Christmas is for the young.

"I'm not crazy." Her voice was clenched. "Sick, yes, you can probably tell. But not mad."

He still seemed paralyzed. Fearing she might faint before he understood, she took his hand, clutched it tight. "Please," she said softly. "Help me."

THIRTEEN CONFESSIONS

—1—

Best as I can, I've told what I know. Told the police, in fact, which my lawyer no doubt finds inconvenient.

I murdered John McMahan, my friend, my neighbor. Killed him with my own bare hands, strangled him in his own living room, dug my thumbs deep into his windpipe, watched his eyes get cloudy, staring up into mine, then go blank.

He didn't fight, not much. Sure, he'd been drinking. So had I. Drink wasn't it.

He gave up.

The truth? He'd given up long before I got there.

This was New Year's Day two years ago, during the Rose Bowl.

So there's no question, not one, as to who, or how, or when, or what. Only question remaining: why?

Still can't answer that, exactly. Wish I could. God knows I've tried.

In the end, I keep coming back to this: I wanted to see justice done. For once.

Not justice for John, the man everybody now seems to prefer calling the Victim. There was nothing "just" in what I did to him. No one deserves to die any more than he deserves to live.

I wanted to see justice done between me and anybody willing to step up and do the job. Wanted to see We-the-People carry out the demands of the law. Mostly because I doubted they were up to it. And so far they've bent over backwards to prove me right.

Christ, not even a confession matters. My lawyer won't let me plead guilty. That'll trigger some strange procedural square dance where I have to be found mentally competent by three independent shrinks who agree I'm not suffering from schizo-paranoia or suicidal mega-depression or whatever the hell. It'll just slow the whole thing down even worse, which is unimaginable. Damn thing's already at a standstill.

Lawyer said (he is so damn sick of me): "You really want to throw yourself in front of the train? Trust me, you've done enough already." Clicking his briefcase shut. "Sit tight, Mister Craig. One thing you can always bank on: You want to watch the ending, all you have to do is wait."

Not like he's the only irritation in this. Honestly? Just about everybody involved seems to be going through the motions—a shuffling herd of nobodies doing everything in their power to look away. Like I'm the sun, and they'll go blind or their eyes will melt in their heads if they so much as turn my direction too long.

John didn't have that luxury. Right up until those final seconds, he locked his eyes tight on mine. And strange as this may sound, the expression on his face was almost one of gratitude. Not that I'd killed him, or that he was dying. Something else, something he'd been waiting for, a sense of completion that'd been hanging around in the back of his mind, waiting to come out and stretch its legs.

Like some question that had puzzled him for a long time finally had an answer. Or some nagging fear dissolved, and he could feel peace.

Me? I woulda fought. I woulda kicked and bit and clawed at his eyes, reached for something close, a lamp, an ashtray, crashed it over his goddamn skull.

John didn't do that. He let me go ahead. Like I was scratching some itch that had been driving him crazy for ages. Thanks to me, his friend, it was gone.

Know what's scary? I mean, even to me, after all this time. The scary part is that I not only knew all that, I was part of it, if that makes sense. We were in it together. Because once it was done, once I knew he was dead, I leaned down, put my forehead against his, and whispered, "You're welcome." I mean, just like that. Out of the blue.

So come on, it's time. Somebody show me justice. I dare you.

—2—

I'd call it an ambush, sure.

One minute I'm folding laundry, TV on in the background, something to keep me company, the next the doorbell rings. I open up and there's, like, a throng, I'd guess you'd call it. Reporters pushing microphones toward the screen, shouting my name, cameramen behind them, TV vans at the curb.

Pushy one up front, enough hairspray on her head to wax a car, says, "You're Peter Craig's ex-wife, is that right?"

I hadn't heard yet, see? But right there, right then, I knew.

Thank God I was smart enough to close the door and hunker down, wait them out. Some went around the sides of the house, rapping on the windows. Another knocked on the back door, like that would make a difference. Took about a half an hour, but finally they packed up and left.

No way, no how, was I going to give those jackals the satisfaction. No secret what they wanted, and it sure as hell wasn't the truth. They wanted to show the world the awful look on my face when they gave me the lowdown. They wanted a reaction.

Well, that's funny, all things considered. They should try that with Pete.

You spend enough time with him—I spent two years, felt like two hundred—trust me, last thing you want is a reaction. Came to where my happiest days were when he was gone, out of the house, off at work or whatever, and it dawned on me finally: time to go.

Did I see this coming? That's the point of the exercise, I suppose. Did I *know*?

What kind of question is that?

Here's the thing. I saw Pete fly off the handle, sure, a thousand times. Pete always had the idea nobody was stepping up to the plate except him. I wouldn't call him violent, though. I'd call him stormy. Yeah, yeah, I know, storms can be violent, aren't you clever—hear me out, okay? Yes, Pete could blow his stack. Yes, it happened a lot. But once he finally got it out of his system, he settled back down and seemed normal. That was my experience anyway.

Model husband? No. Nice guy? Sure, at times. The "quiet type"? Don't make me laugh.

What he was, was a lot of work. And that can wear you down.

Did I love him? Yes, I did. Still do, in my way. But there comes a time in life, after the stars fall from your eyes, when you realize there are limits to things. Even love. Can't be helped. Just the way it is.

I still don't know the details of what happened, the man who died or any of that. Don't want to know—there, I said it.

And it'd hardly knock me down to find out Pete did this, killed the man, just to make a point. Like he was drawing a line in the dirt: *prove me wrong.* Man had a chip on his shoulder big as this house.

But if you're trying to imply that I knew something I should've shared with the world, like I could gaze into the crystal ball and see all this coming, you're out of line. You can't lay this on me. That's just not fair.

—3—

Hard to believe I'm beginning a new journal, but all of this, every single bit of it, is hard to believe. What better excuse, though, to start up again, than what happened? What better time than now?

I've always been better at working things out when I can see the words in front of me, rather than having them stir around endlessly inside my head. Not because they become less abstract, quite the contrary. Abstraction has long been my element. It's the truest thing anyone can say about me.

I know what people will want me to say, that I abhor what happened to my father, his death—his murder—that my life has been changed forever. I wake in the night screaming at the new, shocking terror I feel, the sinister cruelty of this existence, the monster we must band together to fight.

They will want me to say my capacity to go about my daily business, to live and love, has been ruined forever, that I miss my father terribly and feel an aching emptiness in that territory of the heart where my fondness for him used to reside.

But I can say none of these things. To be honest, I'm not sure my father was ever really here.

That's not the philosophy professor talking. Don't look for footnotes referencing Aristotle's refutation of the Ghost in the Machine, or Hume's denial of the self, or its modern reformulation as Bundling Theory, or neuroscience's elimination of the mind.

I mean, honestly and concretely, that my father made as little impression on me as humanly possible in the years he was alive. And it feels like I've been waiting to say that all my life.

I remember what Mother said, as we were scrambling about the house in such a panic, packing so hurriedly. "I have to get out before I disappear along with him."

It wasn't just Mother who felt afraid, of course. Why else would I need to write all this?

I think I felt it most strongly that time he told me, when we were discussing my studies, that he'd long had a secret fascination with Nietzsche, in particular his theory of eternal return. "Every moment of our lives will repeat in exact detail for all eternity," he said. "What do you make of that, Stephanie?"

I tried to explain that Nietzsche's point wasn't to state a cosmological conviction, but to propose a way of life: we should live each moment in such a way that we would be happy to revisit it over and over and over for all eternity.

He didn't seem to hear, or perhaps had drifted off, or once again simply wasn't listening. He seldom cared what I had to say.

But from that day forward it seemed to me that he was rehearsing for how he should behave if that particular moment, the one he was currently experiencing, ever occurred again—that in fact he'd been rehearsing his whole life. But that would suggest an actor playing a part, and I never felt any genuine conviction anything existed but the role. No actor resided behind the mask. Just a kind of quivering emptiness.

And yet perhaps I suffer from the same affliction. If there's anything I dread, that's it. My genetic heritage: invisibility.

As for Nietzsche and eternal return, I suppose that means my father will be repeatedly strangled to death in the same disgusting way for all of time. Presuming, of course, he was ever actually here.

I wonder what Natalie would say about all this. Or, as Darling Daddy liked to call her: Naughtily. Except she's in Africa, doing what she does, delivering medical aid to Darfur. She's engaged in the world.

Freudian slip: I almost miswrote that last sentence as: *She's engaged with the word.* But that, of course, would be me.

—4—

Every day in court I been watching that man, the so-called killer, watching him real close, wondering if he was gonna jump up and do something.

Let me tell you, there's an anger in him for sure. Sensed it in him like I sense it everywhere around me every day.

Some folks think like, you know, anger's just a lie. A "masking emotion," one of them fellas on the stand, the so-called expert, called it. Way to hide the fact you're scared, or hurt.

But maybe we're just angry. What about that?

Truth be told, I come to hate every damn soul in the courtroom, judge and jury both, even the pretty little slip of a thing taking it all down on her machine. So smug, so la-di-da about how above it all they is. They ain't above nothing. Phonies. Hypocrites. Pharisees.

Jurors act like just because we all sit together in that box we some kinda family. Come up to me and compliment my shoes, my hat, my suit, "Oh I just love that shade of violet," like I can't see the ugly meanness behind those smiles.

Didn't much care for the lawyers, neither. Prosecutor was one of those slick, put-together jobs thinks he got it all, and I mean all, figured out. Defense lawyer, sad-and-brainy type, trying not to talk down to everybody but he couldn't help himself.

There's the truth, you want any of it.

So if I feel this anger inside me, every minute, every day, like water just about to boil—who am I to judge that man? Can't make me do it. Could be me sitting over there, him sitting here. Am I the only one here with an honest bone in his body?

—5—

I understand the other jurors view me as an outsider. My speech, my manner, so much is different. And I know I am expected to be one of them, to think like them, to come to some agreement with them in the end. But I fear this is not possible. Not yet. Not given what I have heard and seen so far.

It feels as though I have been given something to fix, but a crucial part is missing.

As anyone who has seen me knows, I sit here every day, listening intently. I have taken careful notes—I will gladly share them with anyone who asks. I have performed my task seriously and done my best to fulfill my duty.

But doubts remain.

I am new here. When not in court, I spend my time, or most of it, catching up with work at my repair shop. I live modestly, a small apartment, few possessions. It is important to be honest, reliable, clean, polite—this I believe. I try my best to do what is expected of me. I have done that here, to the best of my ability, with the seriousness of a student, paying close attention because, after all, how can we know which detail will prove crucial?

But despite everything I have heard, the evidence, the testimony—the facts, as the lawyers say, or refuse to say—I still do not understand why the victim, Mister McMahan, died. Why the accused, Mister Craig, killed him.

Anger is a reason. Greed is a reason. But there was no argument—the neighbors who came forward confirmed this, they heard no shouting, not on "the day in question," as I've heard the lawyers say. There are no bruises or marks on the victim's body to suggest he tried to defend himself. The police have testified nothing was stolen or even disturbed. They arrived at the house and found one man dead on the floor, the other sitting calmly in a chair, waiting. And all he said was, "I'm the one who called. I'm the one responsible."

Yes, I know, he said more at the police station, his so-called confession, but am I the only one who finds all that a bit fantastic? Could not all that be the result of shock, or despair, or some subtle influence the police exerted in their desire to, as they say on TV, "close the case"?

Let me suggest an alternative. Imagine the shock of stumbling upon your neighbor, your friend, lying dead in his house. Picture it in your mind, as we have been obliged to picture the events of that day in our minds throughout this trial. Imagine thinking: If I'd only come by a few minutes earlier, I might have saved him. Imagine the terrible sense of helplessness, of insignificance. Would you not want to do something, say something, anything to reclaim a sense of power, of purpose?

I do not want to be a problem. I do not want to disappoint or cause difficulty for the other jurors. But a man's life is at stake, and I cannot afford to be wrong.

As I said, I repair things. It is my job, my reason for being. I am supposed to know when an item can be fixed and when it cannot. Nothing is more humiliating than to discover I do not know what to do. Nothing more humbling than to stare into the puzzling, infuriating machinery only to ask: but why?

—6—

I should, perhaps, explain why I did not come forward. I don't feel proud about it, of course, but I don't feel overly guilty, either. Just how it is.

I live across the street from both John and Pete and know both men rather well. Knew, I guess I should say, in John's case at least, though I wonder at this stage how much I really know Pete.

Regardless, in my opinion—and, admittedly, I wasn't there—but in my opinion, and it's only an opinion, they'd probably been drinking (again) and arguing politics (again).

By politics, I mean everything—the world, work, money, people, government, guns, you name it.

John, I suppose you could say, took an expansive view of matters. Every question suggested another question. And that is precisely the sort of thing that drove Pete up the wall.

Let me give you an example. John said the reason people believe in the Apocalypse is because they're terrified by life's uncertainty. They want to believe in fate and victory. They want to be shown the way out, but there is no way out. We're wandering a labyrinth in the fog, he said.

To this, Pete replied somewhat predictably, "You want out? Build a ladder."

"But Peter," John responded, in that tone of his, "everybody knows that if you climb out of one labyrinth, all you do is land in another."

The more they drank, the worse it got. John saw the joke in everything, life was a gray haze, and there was no finish line except death. Pete believes in materials and tools, jobs to do and payment for work performed. Leave the middle ground for the cowards. It's black or it's white. Take a stand.

Another example: the poor. John always took the side of the down-and-out. He said if you spent five minutes honestly trying to see things from that end of the stick, it would change how you viewed the world. Pete considered that kind of thinking, to use his terminology, unmitigated crap.

He had nothing against poor people, he said, who worked hard and played by the rules. But being poor was no more an excuse for anything than being an astronaut. History can't be blamed for your sorry life—we're all born into the same mess. We all come out of the womb a little lazier, a little weaker, a little needier than we'd like. And who honestly thinks he has enough money? Sooner or later you just have to suck it up, admit you're on your own—no one is going to bail you out and nobody else is to blame—and get on with your business.

To which John, with almost pathological irony, would say something like, "And what exactly is our business, Petey?"

But as I've said, that was just one thing among dozens that stirred them up. They were on opposite sides of virtually every issue, and yet they also seemed, to the rest of us in the neighborhood, to be fast friends. In the end they always just poured another drink and slapped each other on the back. Which is why none of it makes any sense.

It also brings me back to the reason I kept all this to myself.

New Year's morning, the day John died, he rang me up and asked if I'd come over and watch the game with him and Pete. He said things had ended a bit rough the night before and he felt the afternoon would go more smoothly with a referee of sorts in the room. "Pete tends to rein it in when he feels outnumbered," he said.

Well, I'll admit, I couldn't have been less interested. I mean, if you'd ever watched them go at it you'd understand. The thought of sitting there as they played Down the Hatch and eviscerated each other had about as much appeal as watching someone cut out his own liver.

So I begged off. I made some excuse, a trip to my sister's. "I'm afraid I'm obliged to wander my own labyrinth today," I said.

John found that humorous, actually.

You can imagine my shock, then, when I learned what happened. And everything else I felt. If only this, if only that, and so on. But I saw little point in speaking with the police. What purpose would it serve? It can't bring John back. And Pete confessed. What more does anyone need to know?

—7—

I have served on the bench in this county for twenty years, in civil and criminal and probate divisions. I have listened to thousands of arguments and issued as many rulings. I have come to accept that, despite all the trappings of the law, there is no justice. There is, in the end, only a decision.

Permit me to explain myself.

I have had the same court clerk for almost my entire tenure, and have come to rely upon what others might belittle as her fussy exactitude. She wears high-collared blouses and mid-calf skirts, nothing more than a one-inch heel, flesh-colored hose. Her jewelry consists of her wedding band, a wristwatch, faux-pearl earrings with a matching necklace, nothing more. Ever. Her footfall is quick and hard—you can hear her coming from half-way down the corridor. She can, admittedly, come across as a bit of a martinet.

And yet any belief that her life is pinched or dry or unloving would be wildly off the mark.

I've met her husband—an ample, balding, rumpled sort, the kind of cog-in-the-wheel who passes unnoticed, I'd imagine, all day every day. But make no mistake: the man adores that woman.

And yet their marriage is, to be kind, a trifle strange. They barely converse—no, it's more than that, they hardly utter a word to each other, as though whatever once needed to be said was long ago ritualized into habit: a gesture, a smile, a nod.

Once, early on, when they invited me over for dinner, I'd barely spent five minutes in their house before feeling like I'd been trapped in amber. And yet, as the evening wore on, I came to recognize in the silence between them the kind of stillness one encounters in the desert. And like the desert, it secretly abounds with life.

I have come to envy that. Who doesn't hope to discover some-day that the emptiness isn't, in fact, empty?

This is what I was thinking, sitting there in my robes, perched at the bench, when, right in front of me, the defendant rose from his chair in the middle of the medical examiner's testimony, took the bible he'd been holding, and slammed it down onto the floor, bellowing, "Why are we wasting all this time? Why piss away good people's tax money? Get on with it!"

I've had disruptions in my court before, of course, but this was unique. The man began to laugh. And with that it felt as though

time had opened up and swallowed us all. I don't know how else
to explain it.

Still laughing, the man latched his gaze onto my bailiff and
began marching toward the bench. Toward me. "This what it's
gonna take? Am I gonna have to do this?"

My bailiff exhibited commendable restraint. He drew his sidearm but did not fire. The defendant, he would later explain, did
not yet pose a credible threat, and was unarmed. You can't kill a
man for mockery.

In that moment's hesitation, to kill or not kill, I recognized the
whole of justice. A decision was made.

—8—

See it all the time. Suicide by cop. Told myself, don't give him the
satisfaction.

He took one look at my weapon and all thought of harming the
judge must've melted away, because he turned from the bench and
came straight at me. Daring me to shoot him. Instead I waited till
he came in close and just coldcocked him, hard, blow to the temple,
my gun hand. Man hit the deck like a magnet dragged him down.

No trouble after that. I got him cuffed while he was still dazed
and on the floor, and pretty quick a swarm of deputies showed up.
We took him away and put him in the holding cell we have here in
the courthouse, called medical staff to see to his head, which was
cut and bleeding a little. Let him sit there awhile, I thought, cool
off, though by that point he didn't look all that riled up anymore.
More just baffled and kinda impatient, seemed to me, like he had
some appointment to keep and we were all in the way.

Just as I was turning away to get back to court, his eyes met mine
and held for a second. And I remembered this one time with my
granddad on our way back from church. We'd taken a different route
home that day, and were walking down a street in the nicer neighborhood that bordered ours. Big old houses with screened-in porches,
giant oak trees shading the lawns—and all the good people staring

out at us from behind their curtains, like even in our Sunday suits we might rush in, steal everything we could get our hands on, rape the women, kill the men.

Granddad said, "I want you to remember this day. Remember it good." Then he took my hand and held it, real gentle. Felt like my fingers were wrapped in leather. "You live up to your own expectations, young man. Not down to theirs."

— 9 —

Let me tell you how it is. I was a trustee here at the jail, worked the food cart. There ain't no dining hall in here like they got up at Quentin or Folsom. Here the inmates all eat in their cells, two hots and one not, though "hot" is kinda relative, if you follow me.

Routine went like this: I come by with the cart and deliver the trays one at a time through a thigh-high slot in the door, which is solid, thick, made of steel, okay? If there's a specialty menu to consider, like diabetic or gluten-free or kosher, I identify that tray when I'm sliding it through. Otherwise they all get the same food, so there ain't no fights—trust me, some of these nitwits will kill over a goddamn cupcake. There's usually four to five inmates in a cell, and a small table in there where they all eat.

That's the system, okay?

After whatever happened in the courtroom, some outburst or whatever it was, they moved NK, the Neighbor Killer, to the Isolation Pod and put him on suicide watch. Iso means you're in there all by your lonesome, and they check in on you every half hour, but from my 'spective it meant there ain't no issue about whose tray belongs to who.

And that, if you follow me, means, let's say, that if somebody in here wants to deliver a little something to a specific inmate in Iso Pod, there's a way. Understand?

Okay, so come lunchtime I'm stacking trays on my cart and one of the other trustees, inmate who works in the kitchen (I'd prefer to keep this no-name for now), he takes me aside.

"You hear what that fool did up in court yesterday?"

He means NK. I tell him I heard in general, no particulars.

"Tried to get the bailiff to take him out. Like just by raising a little fuss he gonna get his sorry ass killed."

I agreed that sounded slight.

He says, "Man gotta understand you need to go big or go home you wanna make a weak-ass bailiff, does nothing but collect dust most days, shoot you dead."

Then he looks around, make sure ain't nobody watching, and he slips this toothbrush been honed to a point, wrapped in a note. "You tape this up under his tray, slip it to him."

I try to tell him it ain't that simple, guard standing right there as I pass along the tray, watching me like a hawk.

"Then you better make it simple. Ain't just the damn guard watching now."

See what I'm saying? No choice in the matter. Do what I'm told or I get done.

Well, I had a chance to duck inside the toilet and check out the package. Standard-issue shiv, plastic probably softened with a cigarette lighter then shaped and sharpened against a brick or cinder block. It was the note that was non-standard, if you know what I mean.

Use this on your lawyer.
Stab that no-count Public Pretender in the neck.
Be a hero.

Ain't that just it, I thought. First kill all the lawyers. Or get somebody else to do it for you.

I wrapped it up again, stuffed it in my pocket, then headed to the metal shop, got me some tape, and went back to the kitchen, did what I'd been told.

Guard that day is a Raider's fan, so I chatted him up about Amari Cooper being maybe the new Biletnikoff and it was like I'd pulled a plug. He starts jabbering about the good old days, Snake and Ghost, how jazzed he is about the new regime, first time he's felt pumped about the team in years, and he musta gone on like that nonstop for the next half hour. Gotta understand how boring the job is most days, damn near ex-static to have something to talk about. So no problem slipping NK his love letter.

Now I just wanna get off the pod, before the man discovers his tray's got a little something extra attached. Maybe he'll call out for the guard—no telling with his kind. But we make it out okay, wheel my cart on out through the pod door. Damn near cry when I hear the lock click shut behind us.

I'm thinking I've done my bit. Anybody got a gripe, ain't with me.

Comes time to collect the trays, I'm back in Iso Pod, another guard this time. I call out for NK to do the usual. Instead of the tray, though, he slips the shiv and the note through the slot. Says through the opening to the guard, "Tell whoever gave me those they need to keep looking for their hero."

In case you're wondering: No. I ain't a trustee no more.

—10—

Defense counsel filed his motion for mandatory mistrial by the end of that afternoon, which conformed to the relevant sections of the code of civil procedure for timely submission. I checked to make sure the motion was signed with proof of service attached, date-stamped both documents, made copies for my personal case file, another for the judge's (he likes to keep his own for reading in chambers so the original stays at the clerk's office, available to the public).

By the next morning the prosecution filed its response. I repeated the procedure with those papers, then calendared the hearing for the following day. As a courtesy, I called both lawyers to let them know when arguments were scheduled.

Late in the day I took a moment to read the motions. The defense argued that the disruption in the courtroom substantially and irreparably prejudiced the defendant's case, making it impossible for him to receive a fair and impartial verdict. The prosecution responded that only outbursts by counsel, jurors, or the judge present clear grounds for mistrial; as a matter of law, outbursts by the defendant himself, especially of an "intemperate or profane nature," are not to be given great weight.

Knowing the judge as I do, having worked with him for so many years, I doubted the motion stood much chance of success. But I'd had difficulty reading his mood during this trial. He'd seemed unusually distracted and lost in thought, and after the incident in court—especially when violence became necessary to subdue the defendant—he seemed particularly sullen and remote. I honestly had no idea how he would rule as I packed up at day's end and headed home.

I prepared a simple dinner, steamed vegetables with a teaspoon of lemon juice in the water to perk up the flavor, and a poached salmon with dill and mustard. My husband and I ate in silence, as we always do, for we agree that needless conversation disrupts the digestive process.

After dinner we read, my husband his history (he's currently making his way through Livy's account of the Punic Wars), and I a seventeenth-century Chinese classic titled *The Craft of Gardens.*

Come ten o'clock we moved to the bedroom and put on our pajamas. Before turning out the lamp on my side of the bed, I pulled back the covers, rose to my knees, and straddled my husband, placing both hands on his throat. I pressed my thumbs into his larynx, a slight pressure at first, then increasing. He put up no resistance, a response I expected. He simply looked up at me with a gaze of calm bemusement, even as my efforts quite clearly began causing him pain, and he could no longer take in air.

Finally, his hands shot up and took hold of my wrists, a reflex gesture, but even then he did not struggle or protest so much as simply try to connect. His grip felt accepting, even as my hands remained on his throat, pressing harder, harder.

When I finally let go and climbed off him, he sat up, sputtering and heaving for several seconds, trying to reclaim his breath. Our eyes met.

I said, "How did you know I would stop?"

That struck him as funny. "Seriously?"

"Yes. How did you *know*?"

He took that in, as I knew he would. No one has ever truly seen me the way he has. He gave it considerable thought, his eyes never straying from mine as his breathing settled. Finally he said, "I suppose, in fact, I didn't."

"You hoped I would," I said. "Stop, I mean."

"I presumed you would."

I reached over and stroked his soft, stubbled cheek. "Is there a difference?"

—11—

I personally resent being denied the opportunity to render a verdict.

When the judge called us back from the jury room and let us know he'd declared a mistrial—we were dismissed, thank you for your service, blah blah, go home—it felt like a goddamn insult. Apparently, we're just too unsophisticated, too small-minded, to put aside what we'd seen and come to a fair conclusion.

Look, I know the difference between losing your temper and strangling somebody. Give me some goddamn credit already. I see a man flame off in frustration, I don't automatically think he's a killer. I mean, come on. Seriously? Nothing that happened that day added or subtracted from what any of us already knew about the guy.

That's not to say deliberations would've gone off without a hitch. Maybe a mistrial was inevitable—because of a hung jury, I mean. You could tell there were traitors in the room.

The mope who seemed to be writing down damn near every word anybody said—what was up with that? Always had this look on his face like he needed somebody to slap him, bring him to his senses, clue him in. I dunno, he bothered me. But I think I could've brought him around.

But the old lady in purple with the bows on her shoes and the little veiled hat—she was going to be trouble, you could just tell.

Came from a different planet. One where gravity doesn't exist. Never looked anybody in the eye. If you said good morning, she put on this saccharine voice so damn phony you could tell, down in the darkest pit of her soul, she'd get off watching rats eat your face. Woman had poison in her veins. She'd refuse to convict just to spite us.

But there's ways around that. You can bump a juror who refuses to deliberate honestly, call in one of the alternates, start over. But we never got that chance.

Free men and women deserve the right to deliberate on the facts as they see them, render the fairest verdict they can. That's nothing more or less than the law. We were deprived of our right to carry out our duty. And you ask me, that makes those responsible criminals, whether they wear an orange jumpsuit, black robes, or purple.

—12—

Once the first trial was vacated, I thought I should visit the defendant. He'd refused to see me every time I'd tried before, but chaplains grow accustomed to that. We're trained never to surrender hope, never to stop trying. Besides, for whatever reason, I had a feeling this time might be different. It turned out I was right.

His outburst in the courtroom seemed to me indicative of impatience. And that in turn suggested remorse. The soul, fouled by sin, hungers for light and clarity, which is to say judgment. Contrition is the gateway to acceptance and mercy.

I intended to let these thoughts guide me as we talked.

When I entered his cell, I detected an atmosphere of resignation, and his posture and expression amplified that. I felt he might be ready to yield to God and make himself whole.

And yet he said nothing, not even hello. I realized it would be up to me to get things rolling.

I'd read up on his case, and had some idea of how to ease my way into his good graces. I began by noting that the issues that seemingly divide us—Christian versus Muslim, believer versus atheist, innocent versus guilty—ironically are often ways to forge bonds. Discord rewards our fear of the unknown. And faced with the hatred coming from both sides, we choose one camp or the other, if only because it's simply too terrifying to be alone.

He looked at me with a weary smile. "Last man who talked to me like that," he said, "I strangled."

Our knees were almost touching in the small cell. I did my best to return his smile. "Well, how about this time we pray instead?"

That seemed to amuse him. "No thank you." He began rubbing his hands together. "But would you mind if I told you a story?"

This had a hint of progress to it. "Not at all."

"Great. Good. Here we go." He smiled with genuine warmth. "There's this shepherd watching over his flock, okay? And one day he becomes aware of a wolf lurking nearby. So come nightfall the shepherd gathers all his stragglers into the center of the pasture, then takes out the giant knife he's been sharpening for just this moment. With me so far?"

I will admit to being uncomfortable, but managed to say, "Of course."

"See, the shepherd knew that protecting his livelihood meant more than just keeping the sheep alive one more day. What about the next day, and the day after that? He had to remove the threat. The wolf had to die. Agreed?"

I said nothing.

"The wolf, on his end of the equation, knew the key to staying alive long-term wasn't to attack the sheep. He had to take out the shepherd."

"If you're trying to justify—"

"I'm just telling a story. Okay?"

It is difficult to convey in words the intensity of his stare. "Fine, but—"

"Come midnight, the wolf sneaks into the pasture and goes for the shepherd. The shepherd draws his knife. At the very same moment, he sinks the blade deep into the wolf's chest, the animal's fangs rip open his throat. Both bleed to death as the sheep just stand there, dazed, watching."

Again, I chose to say nothing.

"The sheep stay like that, unable to move, for three days. Finally half the flock wanders off in search of a new shepherd. The remaining sheep trail away in hope of a new wolf. Except for one. Care to guess what he did?"

It took a second for me to gather my thoughts, but eventually I managed to say, "You're confusing a paradox with a parable."

"Yeah," he said. "That's me all over." He patted his knees like bongos. Then: "Tell you what, before you go, I'd like to ask a question."

Despite myself, I sighed. "Certainly."

"I assume you came here to talk to me about God's love and such."

I nodded cautiously. "It's why we're never truly alone. God will not abandon us."

"Far out." He flashed me a peace sign. "Well, if that's true—if God loves me—why won't he kill me?"

—13—

Happy New Year!

Thanks so much for the most recent letter, Naughtily, for a number of reasons, some of which I'll get to in a moment.

First: you continue to amaze your useless father. What you're doing out there where no one else wants to go (most people don't even want to think about it, to be honest), handing out rations and medicine, risking your life—government on one side, the militias the other—it makes me wonder sometimes if you're really my child. But you always took after your mother. Unlike your sister, who all too sadly resembles me.

Steph continues to keep her distance. And yes, you're right, it's probably due to the ancient law of Like Repels Like. The Narcissism of Minor Differences. One day, perhaps, we'll mend the fence. Maybe this year! I hope so.

Getting back to your work—I was particularly impressed with the fact you'd helped drill two new boreholes and repaired the hand pumps for the town's wells. You're getting to be a regular Jill of All Trades, if that's not too sexist a way to put it.

It reminded me of the neighbor I told you about, the contractor, Pete. Once again he helped me with some small chore around the house—repairing some of the grout in the stonework on the porch this time—because, as you know, I'm worthless in such matters. As always, I invited him in for a drink—this was last night, by the way, New Year's Eve—and since we're a pair of pathetic divorcees we sat for a while and shot the breeze, licked our manly wounds, waiting for midnight.

I'm not sure why, but he seemed unusually restless and caustic. The turn of the year can do that, of course. I've told you about his bitterness, the anger that never slips too far beneath the skin. He's one of those classic middle-aged men who feels victimized by life, sees threats to everything good and pure at every turn and can't help but dip into the usual grab bag of buzzwords: *freedom, strength, values.* Talks a lot about "them," a predictably moving target. Wish I had a nickel for every time he's stared at the TV and said, when something particularly mindless pops up, "Christ Almighty, have some pride."

And yet he can also be incredibly generous. He never seems happier than when he's helping me out, and he's hardly unaware or uninformed, though he could choose his sources a bit more judiciously—a smidgen more fact, a pinch less rant—something I've told him more than once. And got my head handed to me for the privilege.

His slant, though, last night, seemed unusually extreme. And personal. Like I'd said something particularly offensive or reprehensible or just clueless. Can't even remember what we were discussing, to be honest. Sometimes I think it's the mere fact I exist that he finds inexcusable.

Anyway, he called me a few names, nothing I haven't heard before, and to be honest, there was a moment when I couldn't tell if he was talking to me or to himself. His eyes went from a dead stare one minute to out-of-focus the next.

"What woman worth a postage stamp would give you second

look?"—he said that, I remember. And: "If I had to get up every morning and see you in my mirror I think I'd slit my wrists."

Like I said: New Year's Eve. Sometimes the ghosts come out even worse than Halloween. The loneliness can really kick you in the teeth.

But there was something else, too, a sense that he wanted someone to pay, be held to account for some crime. But who? For what? I didn't know whether to apologize for something I'd inadvertently done or ask him if he wanted to get something off his chest.

Regardless, the point became moot when he slammed down his glass and stormed out. It's happened before. I called out through the doorway, "Sleep it off, Pete. Come on by tomorrow, we'll watch some football."

Maybe he heard me, maybe not. We'll see, I guess.

But the point is, the way he was acting? It reminded me of something you said in your letter.

I've spent a lot of time trying to apologize for what a lousy father I was—how, in virtually every way, I wasn't there. Apologies never seem to carry the full weight they need, though. Easiest words to say in any language: *I'm sorry.* Know the hardest words? The ones you wrote: *I forgive you.*

I can't begin to tell you what that meant to me. It's like a thousand chains have dropped away and I'm finally free.

Thanks. If I said it over and over until the day I die, it wouldn't be enough.

Maybe that's what I should say when Impossible Pete comes over today to watch the game: *I forgive you.* Wonder how he'd react to that.

Anyhow, that's what I wanted to say. You're an amazing person and I'm so grateful you're in my life, even half a world away. Be safe.

IT CAN HAPPEN

Pilgrim watched as, just outside his bedroom door, Lorene handed Robert fifty dollars and told him she wanted to visit personal with her ex-husband for a spell. Robert was Pilgrim's nurse. He'd been a wrestler in college—you had to be strong to heft a paralyzed man in and out of bed—and worked sometimes now as a bouncer on his off-hours.

Robert glanced back toward the bedroom for approval and Pilgrim gave his nod. The big man pocketed the money, donned his hat and walked out the door in his whites, not bothering with his coat despite the cold.

Pilgrim liked that about Robert—his strength, his vigor, his indifference to life's little bothers. Maybe 'liked' wasn't quite the word. Envied.

He lay back in bed and waited for Lorene to rejoin him. His room was the largest in the cramped, dreary house and bare except for the twenty thousand dollar wheel chair gathering dust in the corner, the large-screen TV he was so very tired of watching, an armchair for visitors with a single lamp beside it and the center-piece—the mechanical bed, a hospital model, tilted up so he didn't just lie flat all day.

Lorene took up position bedside and crossed her arms. She was a pretty, short, ample, strong woman. "Don't make me go off on you."

Pilgrim tilted his head to see her, eyes glazed. Every ten minutes or so, someone needed to wipe the fluid away. It was a new problem, the tear ducts. Three years now since the accident, reduced to deadweight from the neck down, followed by organs failing, musty skin, powdery hair, his body in a slow but inexorable race with his mind to the grave. He was forty-three years old.

In a scratchy whisper, he said, "I got my eyes and ears out there."

"Corella?" Their daughter. Corella the Giver, Lorene called her, not kindly.

"You been buying things," he said.

"Furniture a crime now?"

"Things you can't afford, not by the wildest stretch—"

"Ain't your business, Pilgrim. My home, we're talkin' about." She pressed her finger against her breastbone. "Mine."

Lorene lived in a renovated Queen Anne Victorian in the Excelsior District of San Francisco, hardly an exclusive area but grand next to Hunter's Point, where Pilgrim remained, living in the same house he'd lived in on a warehouseman's salary, barely more than a shack.

Pilgrim bought the Excelsior house after his accident, when he came into his money through the legal settlement. He was broadsided by a semi when his brakes failed, a design defect on his lightweight pickup. Lorene stood by him till the money came through then filed for divorce, saying she was still young. She needed a real husband.

Actually, the word she used was "functional."

The divorce was uglier than some, less so than most. The major compromise concerned the Victorian. Her gave her a living estate—it was her residence till she died—but it stayed in his name. He needed that. Lorene would have her lovers, the men would come and go, but he'd still have that cord, connecting them—his love, her guilt. His money, her wants.

He got $12,000 a month from the annuity the truck manufacturer set up. Half of that went to pay Lorene's mortgage, the rest got eaten up by medical bills, twenty-four hour care, medicine, food, utilities. He had no choice but to stay here in this ugly, decrepit, shameful house.

"Know your problem, Pilgrim? You don't get out. Dust off that damn wheelchair and—"

"Catch pneumonia."

"Wrap your damn self up."

"Who is he, Lorene?"

She cocked her head. "Who you mean?"

"The man in the house I pay for."

Lorene put her hands on her hips and rocked a little, back and forth. "No. No, Pilgrim. You and me, we got an understanding. I don't know what Corella's been saying—"

"I know you got men. That's not the point here. You take this one in?"

"You got no say, Pilgrim."

"Even folks at Corella's church know about him. Reverend Williams, he calls himself. Slick as a frog's ass."

"I ain't listening to this."

"All AIDS this and Africa that. But he's running from trouble in Florida somewhere, down around Tampa."

"That's church gossip, Pilgrim. Raymont never even *been* to Tampa."

"Now you spending money hand over fist. That where it's coming from, Lorene? Phony charity, pass the basket? *Raymont?* No. That wouldn't pay the freight, way I hear you re-done that house. What you up to, Lorene? You know I'll find out."

Finally, fear darkened her eyes. He wanted to ask her: What do you expect? Take away a man's body, he still has his heart. Mess with his heart, though, there's nothing left but the hate. And the hate builds.

"Pilgrim, you do me an injustice when you make accusations like that." The words came out with a sad, lukewarm pity. She sighed, slipped off her shoes, motored the bed down till he lay flat then climbed on, straddling him. "This what you after? Then say so." She took a Kleenex from the box on the bed and wiped his puddled eyes, then stroked his face with her fingers, her skin cool against his. She cupped his cheek in her palm and leaned down to kiss him. "Why do you doubt my feelings, Pilgrim?"

"Send him away, Lorene."

"Pilgrim, you gotta let—"

"I'll forgive everything—don't care what you've done to get

the money or how much it is—but you gotta send him away. For good."

Lorene looked deep into Pilgrim's eyes then got down off the bed, slipped her shoes back on and straightened her skirt. "One of these days, Pilgrim—before you die—you're gonna have to accept that I'm not to blame for what happened to you. And what you want from me, and what I'm able to give, are two entirely different things."

Robert returned to find Lorene gone. How long she leave Mr. Baxter alone, he wondered, chastising himself. He checked his watch, barely half an hour since he'd left but that was plenty of time to have an accident. And he ain't gonna blame her, hell no. That witch got the man's paralyzed dick wrapped around her little finger tight as a yo-yo. He's gonna lay blame on me.

That was pretty much the routine between them. Bitch rant scream, beg snivel thank. Return to beginning and start again. Even so, Robert knew he had the makings of a good thing here. He didn't want it jeopardized.

Mr. Baxter wasn't long for this life, every day something else going wrong, more and more, faster and faster. The man relied on Robert for all those sad, pathetic, humiliating little tasks no one else would bother with. If Robert played it right, made himself trusted and dependable—the final friend—there could be a little something on the back end worth waiting for.

Everybody working in-home care knew a story. One woman Robert knew personally had tended an old man down in Hillsborough, famously wealthy, and he scribbled on a napkin two days before he passed that she was to get forty thousand dollars from his estate. The family fought it, of course—they were already inheriting millions but that's white people for you—claiming she'd had undue influence over his weakened mind.

The point was, though, it can happen. Long as you don't let the family hoodwink you.

Venturing into the bedroom doorway, Robert discovered Pilgrim trembling. His breathing was ragged.

"Mr. Baxter, you all right?"

Edging closer, he saw more tears streaking down the older man's face than leakage could explain. His lip quivered.

"Good Lord, Mr. Baxter? What did that woman do?"

Pilgrim hissed, "Call my lawyer."

Marguerite Johnstone had gone to law school to escape Hunter's Point but still had clients in the neighborhood—wills and trusts, conservatorships, probate contests, for those who could afford them. She sat parked at the curb outside Pilgrim's house, waiting a moment behind the wheel, checking to make sure she had the address right.

The place was small and square with peeling paint and a flat, tar-paper roof. In back, a makeshift carport had all but collapsed from dry rot. Weeds had claimed the yard from the grass and grew waist-high. How in God's name, she thought, can a man worth three-quarters of a million dollars live in a dump like this?

It sat at the corner of Fitch and Crisp—Fish & Chips, they used to call it when she lived up the hill on Jerrold—the last residence before the shabby warehouses and noxious body shops rimming the old shipyard.

The Redevelopment Agency had big plans for new housing nearby but plans had never been the problem in this part of town. The problem was following through.

And if any locals, meaning black folks, actually got a chance to live in what the city finally built up there it would constitute an act of God. Meanwhile, the only construction actually underway was for the light rail and that was lagging, millions over budget, years behind schedule, the muddy trench down Third Street all anyone could point to and say: *There's where the money went.*

The rest of the neighborhood consisted of bland, crumbling little two-story houses painted tacky colors, with iron bars at the windows. At least they looked lived in. There were families here, holding out, waiting for something better to come—where else could they go? And with the new white mayor coming down all the time, making a show of how he cared, people had a right to think maybe now, finally, things would turn around.

But come sunset the hoodrats still crawled out, mayor or no mayor, claiming their corners. Making trade. Marguerite made a mental note to wrap things up and get out before dark.

Robert led the lawyer through the bedroom door and Pilgrim sized her up. A tall, freckled, coffee-skinned woman with her hair pulled back and tied with a bow, glasses, frumpy suit and flats. Be nicer looking if she made an effort, he thought.

"Nice to meet you," he croaked. "You come well recommended. This here's my daughter."

Corella sat at the end of the bed, dressed in black, down to the socks and shoes, her hair short like a man's. His other daughter, Cynthia, was the pretty one but she wasn't Lorene's child. Cynthia lived with her mother far away, St. Louis the last anybody heard.

Corella would never move away. She was daddy's little princess, homely like him.

Marguerite extended her hand. "Pleasure."

"Obliged," Corella said.

Pilgrim shooed both Robert and his daughter from the room. Robert went quick, Corella less so. Clingy, that was the word he wanted. But bitter. He waited for the door to close.

"Got the feeling," he said, "way your voice sounded over the phone—"

"You were right, there are problems." Marguerite removed a thin stack of papers from her briefcase, copies of documents she'd discovered at the County Recorder. "With the Excelsior property."

She explained what she'd found. Six months earlier, the IRS had filed tax liens for over three hundred thousand dollars in back taxes against a Raymont Williams—who came with a generous assortment of aliases. Soon after that, Lorene, who worked at a local credit union, recorded the first of three powers-of-attorney, forging Pilgrim's signature and getting a notary at the credit union to validate it. Then, acting as Pilgrim's surrogate under the power-of-attorney, she took out a loan for a hundred-twenty thousand dollars, same amount as the oldest of the tax liens, securing it with the Excelsior property.

But no release of lien was ever recorded. Apparently, when Lorene realized how easily she could phony up a loan, she got the fever. The IRS could wait for its money. Two more loans followed for increasingly shameless sums from hard money lenders. The house was now leveraged to the hilt, the total indebtedness over six hundred thousand dollars and that was just principal.

Worse, though Lorene had made a token effort to cover her tracks, keep up with the payments, she'd already slipped into default.

"Expects me to come to the rescue," Pilgrim guessed.

"It's that or lose the house to foreclosure," Marguerite said.

"All that happen in just six months?" Pilgrim chided himself for not seeing it sooner. Hadn't even known about this Raymont fool till recent. Why hadn't Corella told him earlier? She went to see her mother from time to time—not often, they didn't get on, but often enough. Daddy's homely, clingy, bitter little princess was playing both sides. But she'd pay. Everyone would pay.

Marguerite said, "You've got a very strong case against the notary, pretty strong against the lenders, though the last two are a step above loan sharks. I don't know what Lorene told them—"

"Woman can charm a stump."

"But they'll want their money. They'll know they can't go against Lorene or this Raymont individual for recovery. And they could say they had a right to rely on the notary and turn on her but her pockets most likely aren't that deep, either. So they'll come after you. And my guess is they won't be nice about it."

"How you figure?"

"It'll suit their purposes to stick with Lorene and her story, at least for a while. She'll say she had your full authority to do what she did and now you're just reneging out of jealousy. It's not an argument that'll carry the day in the end but the whole thing could get so drawn-out and ugly they could grind you down, force a settlement that still leaves you holding a pretty sizable bag."

"Maybe I'll just walk away from the house."

"If you're okay with that, why not do it now? Save yourself my legal fees."

Pilgrim cackled. "You don't want my money?"

"Not as much as some other people do, apparently."

Pilgrim blinked his eyes. He could feel the water building up. "And this Raymont Williams, this phony preacher, he walks away clean."

"I call it the Deadbeat Write-off. Meanwhile, for you, this could all get very expensive, particularly in addition to the other work you mentioned."

Pilgrim glowered, trying to shush her. He figured Corella had an ear pressed up to the door, trying to hear his business.

"Expensive is lying here doing nothing. I can't move. Don't mean I can't fight."

That night Pilgrim dreamed he had his body back. He and Lorene were in the throes, the way it used to be—give some, not too much, take a little away then give it back till she's arching her spine and making that sound that made everything right. Damn near the only good he'd done his whole sorry life, pleasure that woman— that and turn himself into a quadriplegic piggy bank.

But no sooner did she make that gratified cry in his dream than the whole thing changed. He heard another sound, a low fierce hum, then the deafening broadside slam of the semi ramming his pickup, the fierce thrum of the diesel inches from his bleeding face through the shattered glass of his window, the scream of air brakes and metal against metal then the odd, hissing silence after. His head bobbing atop his twisted spine, body hanging limp in the shoulder harness. The smell of gas and smoldering rubber and that *tick-tick-tick* from the radiator that he mistook for dripping blood.

Raymont Williams, dressed in pleated slacks and a cashmere V-neck, Italian loafers and silk socks, heard the doorbell ring and glanced down from a second story window. A fluffy little white fella, baggy suit, small hat, stood on the porch.

Something wrong with this picture, he thought. White people in the neighborhood didn't come to visit.

Raymont lifted the window: "Yeah?"

The man backed up, gripping his hat so it wouldn't fall off as he tilted his head back to see who was talking. "Reverend Raymont Williams?"

No collar, Raymont thought, touching his throat. "You're who?"

"Name's William Montgomery. I live down the block. I received some of your mail. By mistake. The names, I guess." He tugged on the brim of his puny hat. "Kind of similar in a backwards sort of way."

"Shove it through the slot."

The man winced. "There's a bit of a snafu." He looked at the wad of mail in his hand, like it might catch fire. "One of the letters is certified, I signed by mistake. I don't know, I didn't look carefully, I just . . ." He scrunched up his face. "I called the post office. I have to get your signature, too, next to mine, then take the receipt down to the main office on Evans. It's a hassle, I realize—"

"That don't make sense."

"They were very specific. I'm truly sorry, reverend."

The hairs on Raymont's neck stood up. *You mocking me?* "Hold on."

He closed the window, walked down the carpeted stairs to the entry.

The crystal prisms on the chandelier refracted the sunshine streaming through the fanlight. In the dining room a bouquet of lilies and irises exploded from a crystal vase on the Hepplewhite side table. Lorene had this mania for Waterford lately, in addition to a number of other decorating obsessions. Out of control. They'd need to talk on that.

He flipped open the mail slot from inside. "Okay, slip it through."

The little man obliged. Raymont took the bundle of paper, at which point the voice through the mail slot said, "Reverend Raymont Williams, a.k.a. Raymont Williams, a.k.a. Raymond White, a.k.a. Montel Dickson—you've been served with a summons and a complaint in accordance with state law and local rules of the California Superior Court. You must appear on the specified date or a default judgment may be filed against you. If you have any questions, you can call the number that appears on the summons."

Why you schemey little bug, Raymont thought.

He pulled himself up, booming through the door: "How dare you. Coming here, full of hostile intent and subterfuge. I am a man of the cloth. What's the difficulty, tell me—the difficulty in simply ringing the bell like a decent man with honest business."

Beyond the door's beveled glass, the white man grinned, his eyes hard. He didn't look so fluffy now. "Yeah, right. Straight up, that's you." He turned and started down the steps, saying over his shoulder, "You're served."

Raymont threw the door open, came after him, one step, two. "You listen—"

The little man spun around. "Go ahead. I'll sue you for every cent you're worth."

Raymont cocked his head, perplexed. "Will you now?" He reached out, lifted William Montgomery or whoever the hell he was off his little white feet and tossed him down to the sidewalk. His head hit with a hollow, mean-sounding thunk. The man groaned, curled up, clutching his hat.

"Sue me for every cent I'm worth? Joke's on you."

The phone started ringing inside the house. Raymont slammed the door behind him, went to the hallway and picked up. He could hear Lorene, sobbing.

"So. Lemme guess. They got you at work."

"We got ten days—to *get out*. That's *my house*—"

"What did you do? What did you say?"

"I tried, Raymont, I swear. But he is a stubborn, spiteful—"

"You best try again, woman. Try harder. Try till that horizontal nigger sees the motherfucking light of God damn day."

"Mr. Baxter says I'm to stay in the room this time."

Robert opened the bedroom door so Lorene could go in. She put away the fifty dollars she'd planned to pass along, tidied her hair, gathered herself.

"Fine then." She strode in like a shamed queen.

Pilgrim's voice stopped her cold. "You come here to try to weasel your way into my good graces, don't bother. You got ten days to quit. You and that hustling no-count you taken in. The two of you, not out by then, sheriff kicks you out."

Lorene gathered her pride. "From the very beginning, Pilgrim, you promised—"

"Promises don't always keep, Lorene. You crossed the line."

Lorene sat down and tried to collect her thoughts. *Crossed the line.* Yes. And what an interesting world it became, across that line. The things you never thought you could have, right there. But here and now she was running out of options. Still, she reminded herself: *I know this man.*

With the nurse there she couldn't be as bold as the moment called for. All she could do was lean forward, tip her cleavage into view, bite her lip. "What is it you want, Pilgrim?"

Marguerite sank back in the chair and tapped her foot. "I don't agree with this."

"Not your place to agree or disagree."

"That's not entirely true. I can withdraw."

"Just find me another lawyer, not so particular."

"Mr. Baxter, it may not be my place, but you might want to think of your estate plan as way to take care of your loved ones, not settle scores."

"I want that kind of talk, I'll turn on Oprah."

"All right. Fine." Marguerite took the papers out of her briefcase. "I've drawn things up the way you asked. Both sets." She glanced up. "Are you all right?"

Pilgrim blinked. His face was wet. "Damn eyes, is all."

Corella came that evening to visit and found her father sleeping. His breathing was faint, troubled. She put her hand to his forehead. Cool. Clammy.

Hurry up and die, she thought.

He'd always made no secret of his feelings. If her mother was in the room, Corella did not exist. Children are baggage. How much time had she wasted, pounding her heart against his indifference—only to melt at the merest *Hey there, little girl.*

As fickle as the man could be, he still had it all over her mother. That woman was scandalous.

Corella had tried to be gracious, turn a blind eye to the parade of men through that big old house—even this Raymont creature— but then the woman started spending money like a crack whore on holiday and Corella had to draw a line.

Woman's gonna burn up my inheritance, she thought. That can't stand.

She pulled up a chair to wait until her father woke up. A manila envelope peeked out from under the bed covers. Carefully, she lifted it out. The lawyer's address label was on the front, with the notation: "Pilgrim Baxter—Estate Plan—DRAFT."

About time he got to this, she thought.

Corella had earned her teacher's certificate just as the new governor was talking about taking pensions away and basing sala- ries on "merit"—meaning your career lay in the hands of bored kids cut loose by lazy parents. Schoolwork? Not even. Not when there's curb service for rock and herb on the street, Grand Theft Auto on the Gameboy, streaming porn on the web. The American dream.

She was sorry for what had happened to her father but the money was luck and she'd need all she could muster. Otherwise the future just looked too grim.

She checked to be sure he was still dozing then opened the envelope quietly, removed the papers inside.

There was a living trust, a will, some other legal documents captioned "Baxter v. Williams et al." Not like I don't have a right to see, she thought. He'll need me to make the calls, transfer accounts, consult with the accountants and all.

She read every page, even the boilerplate. By the time she was done her whole body was shaking.

Raymont, wearing his preacher collar under a gray suit, stared out through the beveled glass of the Victorian's front door at Corella on the porch. Girl's nothing but a snitch for her father, he thought, and felt like telling her to just go away.

But Lorene hadn't come home the night before. He'd rattled around all night alone in their canopy bed, like a moth inside a lampshade, wondering if he shouldn't call the police. But, given his troubles, that could turn tricky. Besides, he figured she wasn't missing. She was hiding.

He cracked open the door. "Your mama's not around."

Corella had her hands folded before her, prim as a nun. "I didn't come to see her."

She might as well have thrown her shoe. "Say that again?"

"Turns out, you and I have something in common." She looked him square in the eye. "We need to talk."

They sat in the kitchen, Raymont sipping Hennessey with a splash of Seven-Up, Corella content with tap water as she told him what she'd learned.

"The lawsuit and eviction remain in place—against you. Everything against my mother is dismissed in exchange for her cooperation and truthful testimony."

Girl sounds like a bad day on Court TV, he thought. "Your mama says I forced her into anything, that's a damn lie. I may have *suggested*—"

"She gets the house, too. He's quitclaiming it to her. But the debt comes with it."

Raymont shook his glass, the ice rattled. "There's his pound of flesh. Payments too steep. She can't keep up, they'll foreclose."

Corella shook her head. "She'll be able to hold them off for a while. And the insurance annuity that pays for my father's care? It has a cash payout when he dies. Half a million dollars. He's giving half of that to my mother to pay down the debt. That should make it manageable but still steep enough it'll feel—if I know my mother and father—like punishment."

Girl understands her blood, he thought, have to grant her that. "And the other half?"

Corella shook her head, a little flinch of outrage. "It goes to the nurse."

Raymont put down his drink. "The *bouncer*?"

"'For services rendered charitably, patiently, and generously.'"

Corella seemed about to cry by there was ice in her voice too. "I get nothing."

"You got a half-sister floating around somewhere, too, am I right?"

He might as well have slapped her. "She doesn't deserve anything! Where has she been? What has she done?"

"Easy. Easy. I just—"

"The nurse is bad enough. I'm the one in the family who's been there. Every day, *every day*—"

"Fine. Agreed. Fair enough."

Raymont juiced up his drink with a little more cognac. The girl was getting on his nerves and he needed to think. His mind boiled.

"I'm gonna hire me a lawyer," he said. "A real junkyard dog. You best find yourself one too, girl, before this all gets finalized."

Corella stood up from the table. "You're missing the point."

Lorene left the hotel where she was hiding and arrived in Hunter's Point shortly after dinner to visit with Pilgrim. Robert let her in and said, "Mr. Baxter said you and him would be wanting some private time." She opened her purse, figuring they were back on the old payment schedule, but Robert said, "No need for that, m'am." He grabbed his hat, glanced at his watch and said, "I'll come back in an hour."

She inferred from his cheerfulness that Pilgrim had informed him of his good fortune. Once Pilgrim executed his documents, the former wrestler and part-time bouncer would stand to inherit a princely sum.

Pausing at the window, she watched him flounce out to his beat-up car. He'll buy himself a new one first thing, she thought, something everyone will stare at. New car, new clothes, flash and trash, waste it all. But who's the bigger fool for that—him or Pilgrim?

She went into the bedroom and stood beside the bed. Pilgrim gazed up at her. "You look tired," he said.

She smiled grimly, thinking: You have no idea. Tired of pretending I feel for you. Tired of keeping up that charade just so I can have the one thing I want, my home and the things in it, a safe place as I grow old. Tired of watching you hang on to your miserable life with all its petty jealousy and resentment and hate. Tired of trying to convince myself I can do what you want. You think you can control my life and who I love, now and forever, even from beyond the grave. So yes. I'm tired.

It's always the devil, she thought, who shows us who we really are. She knew Raymont was evil, but so? Love is not a choice and who would want it if it was? He'd taught her things. Fortune favors the bold. No risk, no reward. She did not intend to waste that lesson. And there were hatreds and resentments of her own to abide.

"Come here," Pilgrim whispered. "Visit with me."

She stepped out of her shoes, lowered the bed, climbed on and straddled him, edging forward on her knees. Maybe you'll forgive me, she thought. Maybe not.

"Let me move this," she said, wrestling the pillow from beneath his head.

"Lorene, damn, careful—"

She clamped the pillow across his face and pressed down hard. The plump soft weight muffled his cries. Two minutes, she thought. That's how long they say it takes for old folks in nursing homes and Pilgrim lacked even that much strength.

The killing would leave tiny red dots in his eyes but she would call her own doctor, not his, say he'd just stopped breathing. Her doctor would take her word, sign the death certificate before anyone was the wiser.

And though Robert would be suspicious when he got back—Christ Almighty, he'd be out a quarter of a million dollars—he'd be in no position to make trouble. The police would see right through him. Besides, she made out no better than he did with Pilgrim dead and no documents signed—why would she kill him?

Her heart pounded and she was drenched with sweat by the time it was over. She couldn't bear to lift the pillow, see his face. She just leaned down, listened for sounds of breathing. Nothing.

From behind: "You just do what I think?"

Lorene spun around on the bed. Raymont stood in the door-way. Stranger still, Corella peeked out from behind him.

"We knew you'd be here," Raymont said. "We saw the nurse leave. Corella has a key."

Lorene held out her hand. "Help me down."

Raymont approached her like he thought she might turn into a bat but helped her as she climbed off Pilgrim's body. He caught her when she nearly fell. Her knees felt rubbery. She almost fainted.

"I couldn't go through with it," she said.

Puzzled, Raymont lifted the pillow. "You already did."

"No, I mean go through with what he wanted me to do. Turn against you." A shudder went through her and she began to weep softly. "I'm so sorry."

"It's all right, baby, stop." He stroked her face. "Don't fret. We got it all figured out."

"We?" She wiped her face.

"Corella and me. She's the one stands to inherit, she's the next of kin."

"But Cynthia—"

"To hell with Cynthia." It was Corella, holding herself so tight it looked like she might explode if she let go.

Raymont, more gently, said, "Anybody heard from this Cynthia? Anybody even know where she is?"

"St. Louis. Somewhere near—"

"No, Lorene." He grabbed her by the shoulders, shook her. "No. Listen to me. Corella and me, we've come to an understanding."

He looked at Pilgrim's body, the face exposed now. Vacant. Still.

"Corella's gonna file the probate. She'll say she heard some talk about another daughter, tried hard to find her, couldn't. We ransack this place, destroy any letters or anything else that might give us away, lead somebody to where she is. Hell, why can't we pretend she doesn't even exist?"

"What about the lawyer? The one he's been talking to. What if he's told her—"

"Why should she care? You pay her whatever she's owed, she'll go away, trust me. One thing I know, it's lawyers."

The next impulse took Lorene by surprise. She reached for Raymont's face, clamped her eyes shut and pressed her mouth so hungrily against his she thought, again, she might faint. A cold pulse ran through her, it felt like laughter. *He's dead*, she thought. *He's dead and I'm free and God help me but I have lived for this moment.*

Watching her mother grab the bogus preacher within inches of her father's corpse, Corella suffered a moment of clarity so searing she nearly got sick. Nothing would change, she realized. She'd be used. These two revolting people would get what they wanted then toss her aside. She was a tool. She was baggage.

Raymont had brought a gun in case Robert had to be dealt with. Corella crept up behind him, reached inside his coat pocket.

Raymont tried to catch her by the arm, missed. "What you playin' at?"

Corella gripped the weapon with both hands, waving it back and forth, at Raymont, at Lorene, at Raymont. She was crying.

Raymont held out his hand. "Put that down." Then: "This was your idea, girl."

Corella fired.

Lorene screamed as the bullet hit Raymont in the shoulder. He howled in pain, cursed, reached for the wound, said, "I'll kill you," through clenched teeth but then she fired again, this time aiming for his face.

The round went through his eye. Lorene's screams grew piercing. Raymont tottered, reached for something that wasn't there, and slowly collapsed to the floor.

"My God, Corella, why, Lord, what—"

Corella raised the barrel till it pointed at her mother. "Quiet," she said, barely above a whisper, then fired. The bullet ripped through Lorene's throat. The second went straight through her heart.

Robert came back from the Philly cheese steak shop on Oakdale, the one he liked, chewing gum to counter the smell of the greasy cheese and grilled onions on his breath.

He found the door unlocked. Odd, he thought. Careless of me. Smokehounds could just waltz in.

He went straight for the bedroom, make sure all was well, and stopped in his tracks.

A man he didn't recognize sat slumped against the wall, a bloody hole where one eye had been, another in his shoulder.

Lorene lay in a heap beside the bed, ugly wounds on her chest and neck.

Mr. Baxter lay in his bed, motionless as a hunk of wood, eyes and mouth gaping.

Corella sat on the floor against the wall, clutching a pillow, staring at nothing. A pistol rested on the floor, not far from her feet.

"They killed him," she whispered. "I came in . . ." Her voice trailed away. She glanced up at Robert.

Robert's eyes bounced back and forth, the gun, Corella. "You?"

"They killed him," she said again. Practicing.

Robert studied her, then said, "It's all right. I understand."

He went to the bedside, checked to make sure Pilgrim was dead, then checked the other two as well. From a box beside the bed he withdrew a vinyl glove, slipped it on his hand.

"You hurt?" he asked Corella, walking over to the gun, picking it up.

She shook her head. Then, looking up into his face, she said, "He never signed those documents, you know. You get nothing."

Robert crouched down in front of her. "Sometimes it's not about the money." With one hand he forced her mouth open, with the other he worked the barrel in. "Sometimes it's just the right thing to do."

Two days after the funerals, Marguerite Johnstone sat in her office, meeting with Pilgrim's surviving daughter, Cynthia. She'd traveled from Hannibal, Missouri, for the services. Her mother had stayed behind.

"Your father had me draft two estate plans," Marguerite explained, "one he executed the last time I met with him, the other he was saving."

Cynthia tilted her head quizzically. "Saving?"

She was quite different from Corella, Marguerite thought. She had Midwestern manners, played the cello, wore Chanel. More to the point, she was Korean. Or half Korean, anyway.

"He wanted to see how his ex-wife followed through on certain promises. Obviously, that's all moot now."

Cynthia shuddered. "It sounds so terrible."

The night of the murders, the police received reports of gunfire in the neighborhood but that was like saying it was dark at the time. No one could pinpoint where the shots came from till Robert called 9-1-1.

The detectives working the case had their doubts about his story but he'd held up under questioning and passed his gunshot residue test. Besides, the new mayor was lighting bonfires up their buttholes—their phrase—because of their pitiful clear rate on the dozens of drive-bys and gang hits in that neighborhood. Last thing they wanted to do was waste time on a domestic. As it sat, the case had a family angle and a murder-suicide tidiness to it and that permitted them to close it out with a clear conscience. If justice got served in the bargain, fabulous.

"The documents your father actually executed leave everything to you. The Excelsior house has so little equity and is so heavily leveraged I'd consider just walking away. Let the lenders fight over it. The Hunter's Point lot—forget the house—might bring fifty thousand. That's a guess, we'll have it appraised. That leaves the cash payout from the annuity."

Cynthia looked up. "And that would be?"

"In the ballpark of half a million."

The girl's eyes ballooned. "I had no idea. I mean, my father and I, we weren't in touch. My mother, she's become more and more . . . traditional. She felt ashamed. She and my father weren't married and they—" Her cheeks colored. She wrung her handkerchief in her lap. "I wrote from time to time but never visited. Not even after his accident. Corella was the one—"

"It wasn't Corella's decision to make. It was your father's property. That's the way it works."

"But—"

"From the way he talked about it, I gathered it was precisely the fact you didn't hang around, waiting for him to die, that made him feel benevolent toward you."

Cynthia pondered that, then shrugged. "It still feels a little like stealing, to be honest."

"You can't steal a gift, not under the law anyway." Marguerite glanced at the clock, reminding herself: billable hours. "Are there any questions you'd like to ask?"

Cynthia put her chin in her hand and tapped her cheek with her forefinger. Too cute, Marguerite thought. The innocence was beginning to grate.

"I hope this doesn't sound crass," Cynthia said finally, "But when will I get my check?"

Marguerite bit her lip to keep from grinning. Families, death, and money, she thought. Didn't matter your race or creed—or how far away you lived—the poison always bubbles up from somewhere, often long before the dear departed's body grows cold.

"That depends on the insurance company administering the annuity. Why?"

Cynthia shrugged. "Nothing. I was thinking about maybe traveling." She blushed again. "It's my boyfriend's idea, actually."

Interesting, Marguerite thought. "'Travel is a privilege of the young.' I read that somewhere. Why didn't your boyfriend come with you?"

"He lives here. We just met." The color in her cheeks deepened. "It's sudden, I realize, and he's really not my type but I've felt lonely here and he's very kind. He introduced himself at the church service. You may know him, actually, he took care of my father."

UNTAMED ANIMAL

Andrew never strayed this deep into the Tenderloin except for a bowl of *pho* at Dat Thanh. He'd ordered brisket today and sat chafing his chopsticks, eyeing the garnish plate with its Thai basil and sawtooth herb, when someone passing his table abruptly stopped.

"Andy Paysinger?"

Andrew glanced up into a face he could neither clearly remember nor convince himself he might have forgotten. "Do we know each other?"

Without waiting, the man pulled back the opposite chair. "Mind?" He wore a navy blue gabardine blazer, white oxford shirt, utterly unassuming, and that was the problem—the clothing jarred dramatically with the face, or the memory trying to rise up and claim the face.

"Don't tell me you don't remember."

The hair was short and rough, nutmeg brown, tapering into a widow's peak that gave his harshly angled face a wolfish cast. Classic jaw, like a movie star's—action genre, not romance. Andrew, often accused of being unobservant, at least when it came to people, feared he was staring.

"I'm sorry to draw a blank . . ."

He let the sentence fade away suggestively, invitingly, but the stranger refused the bait. An odd, doggish sort of merriment livened his eyes.

"No need to apologize," the man said. "It's been almost fifteen years."

Andrew reversed into that era of his recall—grad school? Or shortly thereafter.

"Richard Pascoe. You knew me as Richie. Had a shotgun flat on Russian Hill. Eva introduced us." The smile darkened almost imperceptibly. "Eva Saccurato."

The name sailed across the table like a dart. Andrew set down his chopsticks.

"Yes," he said. "You're right. That's quite a long time ago."

He struggled with a shameful sense of reckoning. Inadvertently, his eyes dropped to his bowl. The cooling broth had acquired an oily sheen.

"Long time, you're right," Richie said. "Almost feels like it happened on the moon."

The waiter appeared, bearing a tea-stained menu. Richie lifted his hand. "I'm only staying a minute, catching up with an old friend." The waiter bowed, retrieved the menu, and fled. Richie, turning back to Andrew: "Ironic I'd find you here of all places. Quite a hole-in-the-wall, and not the smartest part of town. Then again, you always were—what's the word . . ."

"I discovered this restaurant a few—"

"Thrifty," Richie said. "That's the word I was after. You were always . . . thrifty."

Andrew clenched his hand to conceal its trembling. "I never would have recognized you."

"I'll bet. Thirty pounds heavier now, and I'm still underweight. Trimmed away the rat's nest upstairs. So long, Richie the Freak. Whereas you," he gestured as though putting the final touches to a display, "you've hardly changed at all. Little bulkier up front, little grayer on the side panels. Same face, though. You've aged well, Andy. Life must suit you."

"Listen, I don't mean to be—"

"Don't worry. I'm not here to dredge up old scores." Richie sat back, folded his hands. He couldn't have looked more comfortable. "Though it's sad how well things turned out for you and me, how bad for Eva."

Once again, Andrew glanced down into his soup. The coiled white noodles made him think of intestines. "I'm not sure I know what you mean."

"I assumed you knew. Eva's dead."

For the merest instant, Andrew caught the scent of charred onion and ginger in his broth.

"Happened about a year after I was arrested. I thought, since you two were close—"

"We were never close." Andrew's voice quavered. "We saw each other."

"Outside looking in?" Richie reached across the table, helping himself to Andrew's glass of water. "You two were quite an item."

"An item," Andrew said. "That covers a bit of ground."

Richie put the water glass aside so he could lean forward, lower his voice. "How about I put it this way. You met Eva when she was working. Working for me. That's what she did. Troll downtown for guys like you. Guys alone at the bar, guys throwing money at the cocktail waitresses so they'd talk to you. She readjusted your focus. Made you feel special. Laughed at your jokes, touched your arm, maybe your face. Looked at you like you were worth looking at. And that got you ready to throttle up and go all night. Only one thing lacking. That's why she'd ask if you could make a little detour, this friend she knew, Richie on Russian Hill. And you didn't mind, no one ever did. Goin' to a party, gotta powder your nose."

Andrew glanced around, checking for eavesdroppers. "I wasn't disputing any of that. I was objecting to your insinuation—I'm sorry, your inference—"

"You remember what you said to me? And fuck you by the way, 'insinuation,' what the hell is that? But you remember what you said? You were coming by three times a week by then, stoking up for another shot at the wonder girl. Seriously, regardless of how it started, you two hit it off."

"We had an arrangement."

"Yeah, you arranged to buy the coke and she arranged to drain your dick. And when you stopped by to honor your half of the bargain, you always wanted to share a toot, remember? Like we were the blow brothers. I figured, Christ, what the hell. Customer's always right. It's a service industry. But one time, when it was just you and me there, *mano a mano*, you said—about Eva—you said,

'She's got the body of an untamed animal. Unfortunately, she's got the mind of one too.'"

"I wasn't being pejorative."

"Whatever the hell *that* means." Richie took another swig from the water glass, ending with a shake of the ice. "Know what else you said? Remember like it was goddamn yesterday—always such a chatterbox, Andy, but then the smart ones always are. 'Sex on cocaine,' if I may quote, 'is like coming with God. Only thing better? Fucking a beautiful woman you absolutely, utterly cannot stand. And she not only gets that, she hates you right back.'"

"I believe I was talking figuratively."

"You were talking about working the kinks out."

"That is totally untrue."

"Suit yourself."

"If that were true, why wasn't I interviewed when she was killed?"

Richie broke into a thin-lipped smile. "How do you know she was killed?"

"You told me—"

"I said she was dead. I never mentioned how."

Andrew felt a sudden pressure behind his eyes, like something was trying to push its way out of his skull. "And I never said I was unaware of her death. Or its circumstances. I said I didn't know exactly what you meant by—"

"Oh come on, Andy, you can't just sit there—"

"I think this little visit, as pleasant as it's been, has pretty much run its course, don't you?"

"Let you in on a secret, Andy. I always thought she was the one who rolled. Made the call, handed me up so she could walk. She was a mess by then. I'd kicked her to the curb, utterly unreliable, dangerous really, and that turned out to be, like, too true. Of course, you'd also stopped coming around by then."

"I went through a rough period."

"Rough—that what it was?"

"I straightened my life out."

"Well, good for you. I was trying to do the same thing, just wasn't as focused I guess. Any event, one day, knock knock, there they are. 'Here's your copy of the warrant, Mister Pascoe, please have a seat.' No forewarning. Had the stuff out, for fuck's sake— powder, scales, Levamisole, the whole bit. Sloppy. And the cops, they're happy as cupcakes, bunch of goddamn comedians, cracking jokes like we're all on Leno."

"I'm sorry you went through that."

"Shut the fuck up and listen." The lines fanning out from his eyes compressed. "Anyway, it's a year later, and I hear from my handler—"

"Your handler." Andrew glanced around the room. They were the only two roundeyes there. Not that that settled anything. "You were an informant?"

"I'll get to that. But yeah, I'm talking with my handler and he lets me know Eva's body showed up around the warehouses near Bluxome and Fourth. Guy walking his dog discovered her under a car, like she'd dragged herself there, trying to find someplace safe, or just someplace to die. Cut to ribbons with a razor. Never did find the guy. Never found her shoes for that matter—body was barefoot when they found her."

He looked off for a second, through the steamy window into the street.

"Eva and her goddamn shoes. Anyway, my handler, he tells me this and I'm still pissed at her, I guess, suspicious to boot, and I pop off. 'Well, you know what they say. Karma's a bitch.' He gets where I'm heading with this, and he doesn't want to work a snitch with a body on his back. So he fronts me up, asks me point blank: Where was I, who can verify it, the whole bit. I tell him: Look, I'm torqued that she dimed me out but I didn't waste the bitch. He looks at me like I've got gravy coming out my nose. Know what he told me? Sentimore, guy's name was, SFPD, inspector in Narcotics. But you know that."

"Yes." Andrew's stomach was churning like a kettle now. "I know that."

"He's the one told me—Eva had nothing to do with handing me up. They popped you on a fix-it ticket, that's how lame this whole thing is. Pulled you over for a goddamn taillight. Guess you were coming from my place and they caught you cresting the hill and hit the lights, pulled you over—sitting there behind the wheel, buzzing like a chainsaw, pupils the size of Michelins. Good boy that you are, you defer to authority. 'May we search your car, Andrew?' 'Why yes, officer.' Two hours later you're blubbering about how you can't afford to have this on your record. Got a degree in math from Michigan, masters from Chicago, you just wrapped up a second masters in accounting—"

"Actuarial science," Andy said.

Richie looked like he'd been poked with a fork. "What?"

"My graduate degree from Stanford is in actuarial science."

Richie cocked his head, like a terrier. "Well, actuarial, I don't care. You whined about how you were too damn important to take the fall, you'd just scored a new job at big-time money from some four-barrel insurance firm here in town. That all disappears if there's so much as a sniff of this arrest. You've got a future. Can't let that vanish. And so they introduce you to Inspector Danny Sentimore. And he lays it out—tit for tat, you scratch my back. You knew just which name to use. Useful for them, forgettable to you. Six weeks later, I'm sitting in the very same chair."

"And apparently," Andrew said, "making much the same choice."

"I'm no dumber than you are. My suppliers were these two Salvadoran brothers, Hector and Leopoldo Duque. Daddy funded death squads, so they liked to say, but here they were just a couple chuckleheads."

"Look, Richard, I'm sure it's cathartic to get all of this out—"

"Andy, I won't say this again, you shut . . . the fuck . . . up."

Using two fingers, he fished some ice cubes from the water glass, popped them in his mouth like lozenges.

"Two years of my life I spent setting up the Duque brothers. Part of that I was working with a task force. DEA agent, guy named Refice, he liked my mustard, bumped me up to federal. So after the Duque trial I'm working Vegas and Phoenix and L.A. Somehow the next six years stream by and if I'd been smart I woulda done what all snitches do, run my own game on the side, used my juice, built a nest egg. Know what stopped me? The thought of Eva under that car."

His eyes locked on Andrew but his focus seemed elsewhere. After a second, he broke the spell with a shrug.

"Put me undercover, I could finesse a crocodile. If it was an act, I was stellar. But for real, I was done. I got scared. And when Refice retired, I thought: What now? Tried to go back to Sentimore but he'd transferred into Robbery, had as much use for me as a third tit. So I took off, traveled a couple years, Asia mostly, Philippines in particular. Very generous people, Filipinos, once you get to know them. But, you know, all good things come to an end. Am I right? Except for you. For you, the hits just keep rolling."

He took a folded set of papers from the inside pocket of his sport jacket, opened them to read.

"Took a look at your resume—gotta love the Internet. Christ, got more letters after your name than a junkie's got excuses. Testified before Congress on commodity hedge funds and derivative risk. Guest faculty at Yale and Dartmouth, guest lecturer at Cambridge and Trinity College."

He clucked his tongue softly, folded the pages over again and nudged them back into his pocket.

"You were right, Andy. You did have a future. Bet you still do. View looks pretty good from where you sit. I wouldn't know, of course. But I wouldn't mind finding out."

"I wondered when you'd come around to it."

Richie, leaning forward now, elbows on the table, hands folded, a shrug. "It is what it is."

"How tautological of you."

"Totally logical, that's me."

"Yes, well." Andrew eased forward as well, in order to lower his voice. "It is what it is indeed. And here, Richard, is what it is: Nothing. If you think I'm scared of you, you've misjudged me."

"You're the one who said it, Andrew, not me. How much fun it is to screw somebody you absolutely cannot stand."

"A great deal has changed since all that happened. People change, Richard. Some do, anyway. They grow up. They wise up. Or they get stuck."

"You never got married, Andrew. I find that interesting. All that money, no one to share it with. Still thrifty, I guess."

"The only power you have over me is hearsay from a police inspector who, I'd guess, would never divulge the name of an informant for anything but official purposes. And shaking me down, no matter how much 'fun' you'd have, isn't an official purpose."

"Know what I think? What happened to Eva eats at you as much as it eats at me. I don't care how much you hated her or she hated you back. She was a skank, a liar, a coke whore, a thief. But you can't get her outta your head any more than I can. We're not as different as you pretend. You're stuck too."

Andrew stood, threw a twenty onto the table, almost twice his tab. "You're wrong, Richard, but I'll grant you one thing. Yes, I have a future. So do you. Neither of us knows what it is—that's why it's called 'the future.' But I can tell you one thing it's not, and never will be. Me, paying you money, for anything whatsoever."

He collected his suit jacket from the back of his chair and shouldered into it. "I'm leaving now. This is the last time you and I will talk. Ever."

He turned and marched toward the restaurant's glass door. From behind, Richie called out, "You're not who you pretend you are."

Andrew walked two blocks before hailing a cab, feeling like a boy, one who'd just survived a fight. Once back at the office, he did his best to act as though nothing had happened—counseling an associate on Tobit modeling for annuity lapse rates, reviewing with a fellow partner linear regression channels in commodity pricing—but he could feel the feathery rush of his pulse, his breath unusually shallow, his sweat heavy and rank.

At 6:30, he headed out, pausing in the lobby to look out through the two-story wall of glass and scan the street—not just for Richie Pascoe but anyone lingering, watching, waiting. When a cab appeared, dropping a couple off, he hurried out, claimed it, and told the driver his address, glancing over his shoulder more than once as they headed toward Rincon Hill.

Once they neared his building he had the driver circle the

block, the better to scour the sidewalks and doorways. Satisfied the coast was clear, he had the cabbie stop, tipped him generously, and hurried to the door where Rudolfo, the night guard, buzzed him in.

Apparently, his apprehension showed. Rudolfo, in his chirping Nicaraguan accent: "Some trouble, Mister Paísinger?"

Andrew, suddenly realizing how much he was sweating, took out a handkerchief to mop his face and neck. "As a matter of fact," he said sheepishly, "we did have a bit of bother at the office this afternoon. Disgruntled client, lost millions in the meltdown, blames everyone but himself, of course. In the heat of the moment, some threats were made. I'm sure it's all hot air, but one can never be too careful."

Rudolfo produced a pen. "What is the name of this person?"

"Richard," Andrew began, then checked himself. "You know, that's not so important. As long as the usual procedure's in place." He smiled weakly, wondering if a gratuity under these circumstances would seem appreciative or insulting. Don't second-guess yourself, he thought, removing a hundred from his billfold. Third extravagant tip of the day, he thought, thrifty my ass.

"Call before letting anyone up," he said, "anyone at all." Pressing the bill into Rudolfo's hand, he added, "My apologies for being a bother."

In the elevator, he at last began to breathe more easily. Rudolfo had worked the front desk for a decade, and the security team was painstakingly vetted, the men compensated handsomely enough that no bribe, regardless how lavish, would reasonably tempt them. And Andrew doubted that Richie's resources, given his tale of woe, would qualify as adequate, let alone lavish.

Even so, letting himself into his apartment, he took a second to listen before turning on the lights. How does one judge a silence? The same way, he supposed, one weighs the future.

He dropped his briefcase onto the dining room table, made the rounds of the penthouse rooms, checking to be sure he was, in fact, alone. Kicking off his shoes, stripping off his tie, he went to the closet and crouched, working the combination on his safe.

Tugging open the thick metal door, he first took out the weapon, a 9mm Sig Sauer, then checked to be sure the magazine was fully loaded, a round in the chamber.

Finally, he reached beyond his disaster cash and passport toward the back, found the large velvet bag, and took it out.

Sitting on the bed, he undid the satin ties and opened the soft dark sack, removing from inside first one pump, then the other—Franco Sarto, a style called Cicero, blackberry suede, both freckled with blood. As always, he told himself that this was the last night he could keep them. And for the first time, he knew this was true.

WHAT THE CREATURE HATH BUILT

He wasn't sure how long he'd driven or exactly why he'd stopped. The sign read *Scully's*: wood-shake roof and faux-stone cladding, glass brick windows, almost more a bunker than a bar. Even here, the smell of cinders.

He'd slalomed down the hills in a fury—curving parkways with overgrown medians: sawgrass, wooly sage, towering eucalyptus—glancing again and again at his rearview, watching the sky turn a plummy shade of brown. He'd finally hit traffic near the bottom, joining the stop-and-go, others fleeing. Act normal, he'd told himself, and carried that thought with him now as he pulled on the heavy studded door.

The deep room blurred. Hazy late-day sun behind, murk and glow within.

Finally his eyes adjusted and he spotted two men at the bar. They turned toward the doorway and stared. Beyond them, a TV flickered high in the corner, sound muted, the channel set to news of the fire.

"In or out, cap'n," one of them said.

The thick door whispered shut behind him.

A chaos of filthy, half-filled glasses cluttered the length of the bar, each one bearing the filmy remains of some concoction, grown watery from melting ice. A party, Bernardo thought, or its aftermath, wondering if it was just the pair of them here now, left behind.

The nearer of the two had bristly, straw-colored hair and a hefty build, with a sunburn that stopped midway up his face like a soot line. The eyes were small and lifeless, despite the welcoming smile. He wore painter pants and a white *guayabera* with embroidered tracery down the front.

The other was knobby and tall with a backdraft of nutmeg hair curling away from his brow. He too wore a billowing shirt, adorned with hula girls and pineapples.

Taken together they looked like refugees from a redneck cruise. That or a Baja wedding.

"Bartender around?" Bernardo pulled back a stool, tried to arrange himself on it with conviction.

"You mean Henry," the thin one said. A smoker's voice, like a wasp in a jar.

"I suppose I do." Despite himself, Bernardo glanced up at the TV. An aerial shot, houses engulfed in flame. Boiling smoke. "Or Scully. Whoever."

"Scully's just the name on the sign." Sunburn offered that same blank smile. "Place been through a couple hands since Scully left the scene. New owner tends bar himself sometimes, name is Henry."

Bernardo surveyed the derelict glassware. "Whoever he is, looks like he's been busy."

"Hell, Henry's got nothing to do with this. Had to run, square away the homefront, told us to help ourselves. We took him kinda literal. You heard about the fires."

"Yeah." Bernardo was trembling. The surface of the bar felt gritty. "Sure."

"In Henry's regrettable absence, Eddie here's pouring." Sunburn clapped his hands. "Eduardo, where's your manners?"

The rangy one jumped up and bit back a grin as he scuttled around to the other side of the bar. The state of things back there was worse yet—ravaged lemons, eggshells cradling unused yolks, maraschino cherries bleeding into the sink. Bernardo guessed the two characters had been here alone for a while.

"Name's Glendon." The sunburned one stuck out his hand.

Bernardo took it, felt the intimate leathery callouses. "Jason."

Glendon, still in Bernardo's grip, thumbed his lighter's flint wheel with the other hand, caught a flame, lit his cigarette. Taking a deep drag, he smiled through his exhale. "Welcome to Scully's, Jason."

"Name your poison." Eddie leaned forward, fingering a cigarette from Glendon's pack. Smoking prohibitions clearly had no truck here. "Happy hour's never been happier."

The two men laughed. Bernardo could not remember ever feeling so tired.

Glendon added, "Least not since we got rid of Bitchy Miss High Hat."

Eddie chuckled, lit up. "Tell him the story."

"Oh, he don't want to hear—"

"C'mon, tell him the damn story."

Glendon tapped some ash onto the floor. "About fifteen minutes before you got here, Jason, there was this woman sitting right where you are. Kinda full of herself, if you know what I mean. Had an attitude."

"Thought she was tits and turmoil," Eddie said.

"We're all just sitting here watching the news," Glendon continued, "and there was talk about this and that and finally some damn thing about *trauma*—you know, the people who stand to lose everything up there, oh boo hoo. Anyways, this woman, she apparently thinks 'trauma' is some kinda cue. Like we'd just been sitting around waiting to hear all about her sad and screwed-up life."

"Says, 'Oh, I know about that,'" Eddie chimed in. "'I know about trauma,' like it's someplace with a tour. Graceland. The Alamo."

"Anyway, off she goes. Tells us some guy busted into her house one night, held her at knifepoint for two hours—so she said, God only knows if it's true—but giving her the benefit of the goddamn doubt and assuming, yes, some nitwit snuck into her house, put a blade to her throat, she just—now these is her words, not mine— 'did what she always does.'"

"Always," Eddie noted, "meaning with damn near every man she meets."

"That was kinda the gist," Glendon agreed. "Like the guy's having a knife wasn't the issue. The fact he was male and standing there was the damn issue."

"Not the most charming woman on the planet," Eddie said. "Butt ugly to boot."

"Be that as it may," Glendon said, "the story goes on and the meaning of 'what she always does' becomes a little clearer. She didn't fight. She didn't just lie there and let him get it over with. She whined and wheedled and basically just nagged the poor bastard out of the house."

"Got so sick of the sound of her voice," Eddie said, "he just turned around and left."

"And Eddie and me, we're sitting here listening to this, wondering why the hell any sane woman would admit to such, at which point suave Eduardo here—"

Eddie grinned. "Sometimes I don't know when to bite my tongue."

"He looks this ogress dead in the eye and says, 'You mean to tell me, the point of the goddamn story is not even a rapist would fuck ya?'"

They broke into a helpless spate of laughter, Glendon slapping the bar and spewing smoke, Eddie shivering with the giggles. Bernardo worked up a go-along smile.

Glendon wiped away a tear. "Where's our manners? Seriously, Jason, have a drink. Eddie here's quite the mixologist. Tequila gimlet, rum alexander, sloe gin rickey—if he don't know how to slap it together, he'll look it up in the Mr. Boston. Or just improvise." Another laugh, low and chesty. "He does like to improvise."

Bernardo surveyed the glowing shelves behind the bar, noticed the conspicuous absences—Courvoisier, Bushmills, Boodles, Pernod—the distinctive bottles plucked from their spots and abandoned elsewhere. The gaps in the backlit array conjured a strange feeling of lonesomeness, like he was looking at the future.

He spotted his brand finally. "Crown Royal," he said, "double, neat. Water back. If you don't mind."

A kind of nervous attention rose in Glendon's face, like a blush beneath the sunburn, stopping at the eyes. "Mind? Eddie, you mind?"

Eddie stared. "I can mix you a first-rate cocktail." The scratchy voice low, not inviting. "Don't mind the glassware, plenty more in back. Nothing *but* fucking glasses in back."

They both eyed Bernardo. He was spoiling the party. The hair on his neck bristled, he knew what came next—a flinch, a reckless grin, a swing. Leave, he thought, too weary to move. "Sure. Sorry." He glanced back and forth, one man, the other. "How about an old-fashioned."

Like that, Eddie clicked back to affable. "Now you're talking." He rapped the top of the bar. "Crown Royal your brand, I take it. Top-shelf Canadian, nice rye. Should work well."

Drunks and their mood swings, Bernardo thought. He felt like he was looking up from underwater. "If you would."

Eddie chafed his hands and went to it. Bernardo glanced up at the TV again. Same image, different angle, the view from a hovering chopper. Flame and smoke and devastation.

"So what line of work you in, Jason?" Glendon lifted a nearby glass, thought better of it, nudged it aside and chose another.

Bernardo lowered his gaze from the TV. "Real estate," he said, the lie bubbling up from nowhere he could name. He almost laughed, the irony.

Eddie and Glendon exchanged another glance.

"Huh," Glendon said. "Seriously."

"Yeah. Seriously. That a problem?"

Glendon studied him, as though taking his measure. "I dunno, Jason. Build like yours?" He gestured to suggest the arms, the chest. "I woulda figured you for a cop. Firefighter maybe."

Eddie mulled an orange slice and cherry in the bottom of a glass, tossed in a sugar cube, dashed in bitters. "But if he was a firefighter, Glendon, he'd be up there on the hill, you know, fighting the god damn fire. Cops no doubt are all up there too."

The ensuing silence lingered. Glendon lifted the plastic sword from his nameless cocktail, plucked the cherry off it with his teeth. "Touché, Eddie. Looks can deceive. Am I right, Jason?"

Six months earlier, Leeanne had buzzed his cell mid-shift at the station house, telling him they had to meet. "Rickshaw, booth near the back. I'm here now. Please."

Eight years they'd been married, he'd never heard that voice.

He begged off a civilian volunteer seminar on triage and hoofed over to the restaurant in his blues, six blocks away. Sinewy and freckled, cornsilk blond, Leeanne was already working on her third Tanq & T as he sat down. "Hey," she whispered, finger-brushing her bangs.

The tiny smiling waitress appeared. Her nameplate read May but Bernardo, a regular, knew her as Meifeng. Beautiful wind. She took his order—coffee, black, two sugars—then scooted out of earshot.

"You may want something stiffer," Leeanne said.

She was the scrappiest, sunniest woman he knew, poster girl for the ongoing experiment known to the world as California, but in that moment he saw thunderheads behind her eyes.

"What's this about?"

Things had taken a turn between them a little over two years before, when she teamed up with Coughlin and his mortgage operation. She began having grand ideas, all anchored to money. Bernardo felt all but certain she and Coughlin were catting around, the only thing keeping her in the marriage being a half million in shared equity on the house in Montclair and his healthcare package through the IAFF. But that was okay; he was hardly a saint himself.

"How much cash," she said, "can you put your hands on right now?"

"You call that an answer?"

The coffee arrived. They smiled grimly and asked for more time with the menus. Beautiful Wind rushed away.

"You know those properties I told you about up in Black Diamond?"

What he'd known, up to that moment, was that she and Coughlin had "invested" in a half dozen languishing McMini-Mansions on a cul-de-sac in the toniest new enclave up near the Mt. Diablo foothills. Called Black Diamond Estates, the development sat backed up against a protected wilderness, which, to men of his profession, meant fire country. She'd promised him they'd insured wisely.

But what he learned that day, his stomach shrinking to peach-pit dimension as she explained, was that they'd used straw buyers on title—creative paperwork, fake occupations and incomes plucked from thin air—no money down, teaser-rate monthlies. She said everyone had done it, only a fool wouldn't. Join the stampede or get trampled. "Besides," she said, "high-end demand is inelastic." Geniuses do love their jargon.

The goal was to let the straw buyers enjoy the extravagant houses, pay the monthlies on the underlying notes as rent, while Leeanne and Coughlin worked to flip the properties before the balloon payments hit. Once the houses rolled over, everyone would earn points on the windfall.

That all seemed a cruel joke now. The economy hadn't just hit a ditch, it was cratering. Four of the six bogus owners were jobless or chasing ghost commissions. They couldn't make the monthly nut and were threatening mutiny.

"I don't get it," he said. "They've got no stake. Why not just walk away, hand the damn things back to the bank?"

"It'll tank their credit. Seven years in financial purgatory's a lot to ask."

"Work a short sale."

"Same deal, Jason. You think we haven't thought this through?"

"Honestly?"

"State passed a new law this year—bank agrees to a short sale, they can't go after the difference between the sale price and the amount of the note. That's frozen things up. Lenders are hanging tough."

"Then I'm unclear on what 'mutiny' means."

She downed the rest of her gin and tonic, shook the ice, went after the dregs. "Ever hear of the Financial Fraud Enforcement Task Force?"

Bernardo took a quick glance outside the booth, make sure no one was listening in. "That's FBI. You mean these *prestanombres* of yours would rather wear a snitch jacket than botch their credit? Where did you find these toads?"

"Coughlin's golfing buddies. One sells Chris Craft. Another,

I dunno, has a car lot out in Turlock I think. The others are in the biz."

"You got played by your own kind."

"Don't start, Jason, okay? Besides, you're kinda in the biz yourself, yeah?"

One of the perks about life as a firefighter, especially in Contra Costa, was the time and means it gave you to pursue a second career. Given his rank and seniority, Bernardo's salary topped two hundred grand, at a job that amounted to working out, eating well, and tagging along on the pumper truck to watch paramedics deal with accident victims. House fires were almost history; if they fought a blaze, it was almost always in the grassy hills out in the tractless boonies.

He worked on the side renovating fixer-uppers, and thus had the same flip mentality she did, except he aimed somewhat lower: neglected Craftsman bungalows in west county, Martinez and San Pablo and Richmond. He liked the work, the physicality of it, the demands it placed on your concentration—tearing out the old knob-and-tube, running new wire through the walls, stripping the roof, taking a crowbar and hammer to the ancient cabinets, slamming in new sinks and shower stalls, bolting the foundation, sanding, caulking, painting. End of the day, you felt like something had happened.

"How much are we talking?"

She was staring at her placemat, the Chinese zodiac. Year of the Rabbit, a time for peace and prosperity. "One point two-five."

A needle-like numbness tinged his skin. "A hundred twenty-five grand?" He did a quick mental tally, working it out. Six loans, all top of market. "That per month or . . ."

She fiddled with her glass then leaned out of the booth, scoured the room for May the waitress, gestured for a refill.

"Leeanne—"

She looked ready to get hit. He felt ready to oblige her.

"One point two-five mil."

The floor buckled. "How many fucking months—"

"Don't be an ass, Jason. Keep it down."

"How stupid could you two—"

"The loan desks are crazy, all the repos and walkbacks and REOs, we figured we had time."

"No way I can put my hands—"

"I'm not asking for it all, just—"

"Even if I did, you'd just be caught up. What about next month, the month after—"

"Don't lecture me."

"Don't come begging."

He got up to leave. She latched onto his wrist. "Jason, don't. You can't." She swallowed hard. "One of the houses is in my name."

He cocked his head, wondering if he'd heard right. She just stared, her eyes locked on his, and for some reason he flashed on the last time they'd gone at it, down in the den, watching *The Naked Kiss* on IFC, a mid-flick urge, both of them half in the bag, pink sweats yanked down from her hips, one knee on the sofa, one foot on the floor, him pounding away from behind as she glanced over her shoulder, tucking her hair behind her ear, waiting for him to finish. For better or for worse, till death.

The waitress delivered the Tanq & T, took the empty away, no pretense of ordering lunch anymore.

"You were gonna tell me this when?" California was a community property state. He was on the hook right with her.

She shrugged, scraped at her bangs, drank.

"We'll call a lawyer."

"There's no bankruptcy protection for fraud, Jason."

Now he really, truly wanted to pop her.

"I'm not gonna waste time saying I'm sorry, because time's what we haven't got. But money buys time. I mean it, I don't need the whole amount. But I need something. We do."

Nice touch, he thought, hating her. "No way I can pony up even a fraction of that kinda money."

She studied her glass, like the gin might speak. "Then I need to hear some ideas, hon. Like, now."

"What's this?"

The cocktail was in a bucket glass, bits of savaged orange and cherry floating in shaved ice. Smell of whiskey but something else, something medicinal.

Eddie beamed, leaning forward. "I call it a Dirty Rotten Secret."

He looked like the kid at the birthday party everybody's scared of.

"I thought you were making a Crown Royal old-fashioned."

"I did. More or less. Just added a Benedictine floater, plus some of this stuff." He held up a bottle of something called Fernet.

Glendon wagged a finger. "I told you he liked to improvise."

"Made from a blend of rhubarb, chamomile, ginseng," Eddie recited, reading from the label, "and a secret combination of herbs."

Bernardo stirred the cocktail so the weird liqueurs blended a bit better with the whiskey. He needed something, his nerves were a mess. If this was it, bottom's up. "Thanks," he said, and drank. It tasted like something worked up by his little league buddies after a raid of the parental liquor cabinet. He tried not to wince.

"I'm still working on the right proportions," Eddie admitted.

"It's fine." Bernardo resisted an urge to spit. "Might think about easing back a touch on the rhubarb."

"Work in progress," Eddie said.

"Isn't everything."

Looking back, he would wonder at how even bad love reasserts itself, insinuates itself into the gentler regions of memory, sweet-talks your conscience, reminding two people that despite all the resentment, the unanswered want, the squandered hope, they're still bound together. All it takes is a threat from outside—the messy, cruel, indifferent world—to re-knot the ropes, lash you together tighter than ever. No love was perfect, nor needed to be. What family he had was her. You could talk it through with any-one you wanted—lawyer, shrink, priest, the ER nurse you met at a fundraiser who dragged you back to her place—it was all just that, talk. Better to stand pat with the unhappy past then stagger blind into the shapeless future.

And once he agreed to help, Leeanne did soften a bit.

He was assistant treasurer for his local, and as such, served as the hands-on man. They were gearing up for elections across the county—mayor and council races in five key cities, all trying to arm-twist concessions in pensions, benefits, wages, staffing—and the war chests were flush. They had five PACs, two held jointly with the police union, one with the IBEW, and were constantly shuffling money around to fund this candidate or that, and make the money trail hard to figure. The state lacked the manpower to audit, and the self-reporting was farcical. Thousands routinely tumbled out of one fund, suddenly materialized in another, the amounts rarely if ever matching up. If that ever became a problem, they'd hang their heads and admit to being sloppy—hey, they were heroes, not abacus jockeys.

But the PAC accounts afforded seventy grand at best, and that had to be plucked from several different places after a lot of sleight-of-hand, phantom transfers of varying amounts, a head-scratching smokescreen. If he pilfered any more than that, it'd stand out as a fistful of missing change even to a bunch of lunks.

That meant he had to turn to the operating accounts—non-interest bearing money funds for day-to-day operations held by various local banks. He mocked up work orders for station-house repairs and renovations, shoved them in a file he buried in a cabinet, buying in to Leeanne's theory that all they needed was time.

The thing about thievery, he discovered, is that once you make a few moves and don't get caught, you get a bit more bold, which is to say clever, otherwise known as reckless. He managed to scratch up just shy of three-hundred-fifty grand, more than he'd ever thought he could realistically bring to the table. Leeanne seemed pleased, and showed it with a bit more wag in her tail, as it were.

But if the money bought them time, that was all it bought. A developer Coughlin knew supposedly hoped to muscle the lenders into a package deal for a majority share of the enclave, but if such a maneuver was ever real it quickly turned to myth. After that, isolated buyers appeared and vanished like trick-or-treaters, and what money they offered was always a joke. Not even the hard money boys were stepping up; they knew all they had to do was wait.

Meanwhile, a citizens group was crowing for accountability in the union PAC funds. Then, out of the blue, the assistant chief wanted a work-up on a new roof for Station House 5, including funds on hand. And the FBI, of course, lurked in the wings.

I need to hear some ideas. Which was how Jason the Firefighter came up with Plan B.

"Real estate," Glendon said, like it was the name of a despised aunt. He sat with his arms twined across his paunch. "Not to beat a dead horse, Jason, but I gotta tell ya, you just don't fit my picture."

Bernardo took another sip of Eddie's concoction. *God help me,* he thought, *getting used to the taste.* "Not sure I can do much about that, Glendon." Sensing that this might seem snide, he added, "I like to work out."

"Real estate mucks I know," Glendon said, "how should I put this. Fat boys and fairies."

Eddie, looking up at the TV, nodded. "Pussies, not to put too fine a point on it."

The crawl at the bottom of the screen reported that the entire Black Diamond enclave had been evacuated. Every property on the perimeter was now involved, total losses. Bernardo knew he should feel relieved, but instead the weariness just burrowed deeper.

"A cleansing fire." It was Glendon, arms still wrapped across his belly, eyes glued to the TV screen.

Eddie said, "That'd be the bible, right?"

"The bible, or something like it." Glendon tapped out another cigarette, lipped it, struck a flame from his lighter. "And God shall come as a cleansing fire, not to consume the creature, but what the creature hath built—of wood, of hay and chaff."

"Damn straight." Eddie set his chin on his arms, still peering at the screen.

"Everything you need to know about property," Glendon said, pointing at the TV with his cigarette, "you can learn from watching that right there."

Bernardo reached for his cocktail but couldn't quite bring himself to drink.

"And the people who work in real estate," Glendon went on, "they don't make nothing, they don't fix nothing, they just keep selling the same chunk of dirt and wood over and over so they can take a bigger cut. They don't add value, just add cost. And who ends up having to pay for that? Not them. Never them. Biggest racket there is. People need a place to live, a home for themselves and their families, but what they get, day after day after god damn day, is cheated."

"Brought down the whole damn economy," Eddie said, "bankers and real estate people. Politicians in their pocket."

Bernardo, now regretting his lie, considered telling them what he really did for the bulk of his money, but he wasn't sure at this point what difference it would make. He felt like he'd walked in on an argument that had started long before he'd arrived, and would continue long after he'd left, if he was given that chance. A quick glance for weapons discovered only the paring knife behind the bar—no truncheon near the cash register, no pistol or shotgun that he could see. He told himself to relax.

"Like I say, don't mean nothing personal, Jason. But people are angry. Right, left, middle, they're pissed. They know the treasure is gone. And they know who took it."

Bernardo realized silence was no longer an option, but neither was ass-kissing agreement. "Look," he began, "the economy's not simple. It's like the weather. More factors than you can think of, so many unknowns. The tiniest thing can have the strangest consequences." He felt his heart ticking inside his chest, his hands felt hot. "Know how many supercomputers the National Weather Service uses? Any idea how massive the system of differential equations is they need to predict whether it's sunshine tomorrow or rain? The answer they come up with, it's just an approximation, it's guesswork. But that doesn't make it random. Any more than the wind is random. There's answers, is what I mean, even if we don't always like what they are."

Stop talking, he told himself. Say thanks for the drink, put down some money if they ask for it, get up and walk out. Something inside him, though, cautioned that a little more defraying of the tension might be wise before he made a move for the door.

The two men studied him, their faces blank. Smoke from Glendon's cigarette curled upward.

"You guys ever hear of the Diablo winds?"

He'd explained it to Coughlin and Leeanne, when it became clear only a disaster could save them. The Diablos, northern California cousins of the Santa Anas, came every spring and fall, the latter season particularly dangerous because of so much buildup through the drought months of fire-ready vegetation—flashy fuel, it was called. The winds developed from high pressure systems to the east, off the sunbaked Great Basin, the air squashed by storms over Nevada and Idaho, with low pressure systems squatting off the coast, pulling like gravity, like an atmospheric sump, dragging the winds west through the Sierra canyons, down the arid foothills and across the scalding central valley—perfect fire weather. Case in point: the Oakland hills disaster.

And the Black Diamond layout was particularly ripe: high parched grass in steep ravines just beyond the enclave, with dense pockets of non-native eucalyptus, ornamental clumps of wooly sage, sawgrass. The place was landscaped in tinder.

They met to talk through the final details at Leeanne's property, a sprawling four-thousand-foot monument to misbegotten greed: long granite counters and towering cherry cabinets, beveled glasswork and Florizel parquetry with its churchy accents and eerie 3D feel. More to the point, it sat in precisely the right place, at the cul-de-sac's tip, right at the mouth of a deep arroyo winnowing east. Stand out there on the patio, the furnace-like wind almost knocked you down.

Coughlin looked like he'd stepped off the back nine, moussed and tan, with hints of work around the eyes, that sandblasted squint. Leeanne wore white—sundress and sandals, a billowing hat—an outfit Bernardo remembered from a garden party at a Livermore vineyard years before. Despite the incongruity, she looked good. She looked happy.

"I've been tracking the weather service," he said. "It's this week or never. Today's likely best."

"Unless I'm missing something," Coughlin said, a voice honed on cold calls, "you're leaving a lot up to random chance."

"Wind's not random," Bernardo said, "neither are fires. I don't believe in luck. There's planning, and then there's ignorance and miscalculation. Been plenty of that already, by my reckoning."

Coughlin started to fire back but Leeanne cut him short with a look. They'd already decided it was Bernardo's show, no point sniping. He needed to slip money back into the operating fund and PAC accounts, and fast. Leeanne and Coughlin needed to be able to walk away with everyone's credit intact and nothing to trigger audits on the underlying loans. The houses were insured at replacement value, including contents, and they'd mocked up invoices for furnishings far in excess of what was there. That would be their cushion, their walkaway money. And that meant whatever happened, it had to be a total loss—no salvage, no rebuilding, no sifting through the wreckage by bean counters, arson wonks. It had to be a holocaust. Leeanne and her seven dwarves would slip away, collect a measly couple hundred grand for some made-up finery while the banks and insurance companies squared off over the big money. Let the lawyers hammer away. Can't foreclose on an ash heap.

Because arson was easier to allege than prove, Bernardo felt certain he could rig things—not perfectly, no such thing—but create enough of a nightmare any foot-dragging would look cruel and venal, justifying a claim of bad faith. The insurers would waive off the bother. To get there he needed to create both interior and exterior points of origin without making it look too obvious what had happened. An accident triggered by a catastrophe—who couldn't comprehend that? Coughlin assured him the rest of the dunces had signed on. But Bernardo also knew, if things went south, he'd be the one left to hang.

The solution, he decided, was linseed oil, mixed with nitrocellulose, the touchy stuff film stock used to be made of, back in the days of projector room fires. The oil and oxidizer combined to make an unparalleled varnish, but the mix was also insidiously flammable. The One Meridian Plaza fire, caused by spontaneous

combustion of rags left piled at the worksite, killed three Philadel-
phia firefighters. And that risk of fatality, given how hot and fast
the fire would spread, would push the engine crews toward containment—they'd let the houses already involved burn out.

"You can't have the fire start inside the house, not with the loan
in arrears the way it is. But if the fire starts outside, moves close,
and triggers secondary combustion in here—that's the way to go."
Bernardo fingered the smooth, elaborate carvings in the cabinetry,
an interlocking design with deep relief, a pattern called Portland
Scroll—nothing like what he was used to in the houses he rebuilt.
"Bad enough we haven't got time to strip every house, just this one.
But if it burns the way it should, the rest are close enough along
the cul-de-sac, all nestled in this little pocket, they all should go
up pretty quick."

They got to work, donning coveralls, sanding off the old finish
in three of the rooms, not worrying about completion, just making
it look like they'd made a good start. Now and then they practiced
aloud the story they'd tell the insurers: Leeanne had decided to
upgrade, hoping the improvements would help move the property
quicker—high-end demand being, after all, inelastic. When she
saw the grass fires barreling toward her from the hills, she'd had no
time to store the rags properly, needing to get out while she could.
Keep it simple, Bernardo told her. A mistake, especially in the face
of danger, doesn't equal motive. Hold that thought.

Three hours passed. Coughlin was the first to bag. "I'll leave it
to you two to wrap this up." He combed his hair in the doorway,
and Bernardo doubted he'd ever hated anyone more.

Leeanne stepped out of her coveralls as Bernardo arranged
the rags. This part was critical—piled too close, they'd lack the
air needed to ignite, too loose and they wouldn't generate suffi-
cient heat. He dragged the containers with the rest of the mixture
near, so once the flames hit there'd be no doubt the stuff would
catch. The fire outside would follow its natural path, the ravine
like a funnel of boiling wind, plus all the sun-shriveled grass and
bark and leafage. Once flame reached the house, with the pile of
oil-soaked rags inside, it would go up quick, take the neighboring

houses with it, and after them, the rest of the cul-de-sac. As for all the other houses up here—well, that was up to the wind. The wind and the fact that, strapped for funds, the county had closed the two nearest firehouses.

He was still in his coveralls finishing up when he felt Leeanne's hand settle gently on his arm. "Jason, I know I've been short in the sorry department, but that's not because I'm ungrateful." She straightened the sundress, shouldered her handbag. The broad-rimmed hat rested like a giant lily on a nearby table. "I know this is all on me. Without your help, we'd be screwed. I don't know how to thank you."

She eased up on tiptoe, left hand on his shoulder, lips pursed. Despite the stinging oily scent of the varnish, the worry knotted up in his midriff, he readied himself for her kiss. They'd regained a little juice the past few weeks, the old slap and tickle. And yet something felt off. Maybe it was the fact her eyes stayed open, maybe it was the fact she'd only balanced herself with the left hand, the right hand free, but when the knife came out of her purse, Bernardo had her wrist locked tight almost instantly. He twisted outward, her face contorted in pain. The knife dropped.

She grimaced. "You're hurting me."

He let her go, leaned down to pick up the knife, and she was on him with a fury he'd never seen. Hammering with her fists, raging against the sheer injustice of her lousy life. Of course he had to die—the weak link, last man in, the one who didn't understand that the point was to be free and that meant money. Jason the Firefighter, Mister Fixer-Upper. The fists turned to fingernails, she clawed at his eyes, a mewling growl in her throat that came from some part of her he didn't know and at last he felt afraid.

The knife went in easily, and he wasn't even sure at first where his hand was or what he'd done. But she winced as though from a punch, buckled, backed away, holding her side. The blood came quick, bubbling between her fingers—he'd cut an artery—a giant smear on the sundress where she pressed her hand.

He remembered that very first night: dinner at Enoteca, champagne with appetizers, a velvety Barolo with the entrées, Armagnac with espresso and dessert, then speeding in her Miata ragtop to the condo in Lafayette, her unbuckling and unzipping him, stroking him, gripping him, that distinctly feminine brand of ownership, then almost stumbling up the walkway to her door, his pants slipping to mid-hip, a couple teenagers whisper-giggling around the pool—he pressed her against the door as she worked the key, then the two of them tumbled inside, he lifted her off her feet in the entry, her legs locked tight around his waist as he entered her, a good hard hello, a shot across the bow of love, pushing, pushing as she whispered—*yeah, come on, yeah, Jay, yeah, give it to me*—and he exploded within her then as the knife did now, for he'd stepped in close to stab, stab again.

She did not fight or even cry out. Call it what remained of their marriage, he supposed, that silence. The blame was hers, after all. Except, of course, it wasn't. Not hers alone. She'd made sure of that.

She clutched his arm as she fell, no strength in the grip, dropping raggedly to the floor. She bled out—legs tangled, breaths quick and shallow, mouth open, eyes like glass. His rage dissolved, leaving behind a regret he felt in his body like a need to lie down. And from somewhere in the back of his mind, a flicker of dread, like lightning spotted through trees.

After a moment, he sensed it, someone there, and glanced up. Coughlin stood in the coved entrance to the room, staring. At her. His protégé, his accomplice, his squeeze. He too held a knife, had come back as part of the plan, finish it, except he'd come too late— cowardice or second thoughts or who knew what? Finally his gaze rose, their eyes met, and he dropped the knife, got halfway to the door. Bernardo would feel a little embarrassed by how hard and deep he ripped the blade across the man's throat, damn near severing his head. And as Bernardo crouched against the wall, eyeing what he'd done, his mind clicked like a machine, trying to remember what fire would destroy and what it wouldn't.

"Glendon, fetch me some ice from the walk-in, will ya?"

The larger man belched, glanced at the welter of glassware atop the bar, and slid off his stool. "Make me something normal while

I'm gone, Eduardo. Early Times, rocks, with a splash. See if that's artistic enough for your newfound sensibilities."

Once Glendon was gone, Eddie leaned forward, rested his elbows on the bar. "Don't make nothing out of all his guff about real estate," Eddie said quietly. "He's just kinda bitter."

Bernardo, from manners as much as thirst, sipped his drink. The flavor was evolving. "About what?"

Eddie had gone off somewhere in his mind. He looked like he was struggling with a calculation—carry the seven, divide by five. Snapping back: "Excuse me?"

"Bitter about what?"

"Oh, him and me, we used to work at the shipyard over in Richmond. Pipefitters, the both of us. Good work, union wage, but that's all gone. This country ain't got use for the workingman no more. Not 'less he's Mexican. Anyhoot, we been scraping by, doing a little this, a little that, and we stumbled on this thing called Cash for Keys—you heard about this?"

Now it was Bernardo's turn to wander off. He was back up the hill, outside the house, following through on the plan, figuring even with two bodies to incinerate the surest path to a big mistake would be to change things up. Reaching into a bag of M-80s and cherry bombs, he waded into the knee-high grass, dry as straw, covering the hills rising up behind the property and rippling in the westerly wind keening through the ravine, blasting hot and dry against his skin. He glanced around, here and there a scrub oak but mostly eucalyptus, God's gift to fire.

"It's this program through the banks," Eddie said, "Cash for Keys, all these empty houses, the foreclosure mess. Well, you leave them untended, you're just asking for trouble. Damn gangs move in, set up grow houses or meth labs, jerry rig the electric—I seen jumper cables trailing down from a high-tension wire and hooked up to a junction box, I'm not making that up. Juice for all the lights you need, grow marijuana." He pronounced it *merrywanna*. "But there's some folks, they just need a place to stay, you know? Glendon and me, we had some rough luck lately, we're just looking for a roof over our heads as we settle up accounts, you know, ride out this damn economy. And once we got good and comfortable in this one place—"

"Squatters," Bernardo said, regretting it instantly.

Eddie shot him an acid look. "That's a damn unpleasant word."

"Sorry, I didn't mean it that way. I just . . ." He shrugged, lifted his cocktail, Dirty Rotten Secret, rattled the ice in appreciation. "I'm sorry."

He knew the problem too well. You bought a house on spec, property underwater, previous owners walked away, and you're hoping for an easy rehab and then a quick flip. But you head on over to the address and find there's someone living there, people no one's ever talked to or heard of. Whole clans—kids, cousins, grandparents, goats.

"We weren't taking advantage. We kept the place up—repaired the plumbing in the kitchen, the brass pipes were all corroded. Rewired the living room, there was an outlet that'd shorted out, faceplate all black. Picked the apples off the ground so they don't attract rats, put out poison for the snails, must've killed a zillion spiders. Bagged up the garbage, touch of paint here and there. Bank saw what we were doing, they were grateful. Woman comes over, VP of something, got her card in my wallet, introduces herself, says we keep the place up the way we're doing, we'll get a thousand crisp ones a month."

Hidden in a stand of eucalyptus, he began lighting cherry-bomb fuses—major cause of wildfires, fireworks set off in tinder-dry conditions. Sure enough—*boom*—and a patch of grass caught, the flames licked up the nearest tree, the ratty bark glowing into ember then a pop, a spark, ignition. He tossed the remaining fire-crackers around and headed back, hearing the staccato explosions behind him like gunfire as he ran.

"And okay," Eddie continued, "so we saw an opportunity, put down roots in more than one house. What's the crime in that? We was looking after each place, we deserved every goddamn check. Oh but the neighbors, they start bitching about property values. They start moaning about strangers with no investment in the community and how we're, like, scamming the system. And they get this local real estate agent, Mister Plumpfuck from Pussyville, got several houses up for sale in that neighborhood, and he decides he's gonna ride to the rescue—gathers signatures on a petition, goes on TV, identifies the houses and the banks, figuring, 'Hey, this here's cheap publicity for me, I'll score big with the locals, get me a dozen new clients.' Next thing you know, me and Glendon, we get the heave. Sheriff telling us we got thirty minutes to quit the premises, camera crews on hand, details at eleven. So there we are, on the street, no roof over our heads, nothing."

Back inside the house, he tried not to look at Leeanne or Coughlin as he peeled off the coveralls and set them beside the stack of rags, soaked in linseed oil. The rags were already beginning to smolder, a thin acrid plume of smoke rising from the pile. Looking out the patio door, he saw the hillside flames gaining ground, the rapid combustion creating its own weather—fire whirls, hairpin vortices, forward bursts—gathering speed, moving close, windswept cinders or whole tree branches blazing away, exploding, rocketing into the parched yard, onto the roof, hurled by the fire's own force. Given the contour of the hillside, the strength and direction of the wind channeling through the arroyo, its dryness and heat, the pressure differential between inland hills and coastal plain, the tonnage of fuel load provided by the eucalyptus and scrub oak, the sawgrass and wooly sage, the ratio of surface area to volume for every desiccated twig, the flash point of all that withered vegetation—flashy fuel—in conjunction with the blistering heat, the severity of the drought conditions and the rate of acceleration for the downhill flames, the topography of the rags, the chemistry of the oil and nitrocellulose, its auto-ignition temperature, the abundance of interior wood, the precise moment of the first 9-1-1 call, the response time required for an engine crew to make it up the switchback parkways from a firehouse thirty-five miles away, the tactical on-scene decisions made, primacy of evacuation, containment versus combat, what structures if any to save, which to surrender. It wasn't luck, it wasn't random. It was the inscrutable calculus of complexity, a world beyond our knowing. It was the wind.

"So that's why Glendon's got a hair up his hind parts about real estate agents. Me too, truth be told. But like he said, don't take it personal. We're not on some kinda rampage."

Good for you, Bernardo thought, remembering the arrangement of the bodies as he'd placed one knife near Leeanne, the other near Coughlin, making it look like they'd gone at each other. He stepped toward the entrance and opened the door, creating a cross-draft of oven-like air. The rags ignited, a sudden bright flash filling the room like a vengeful djinn. And he'd felt tired. A weariness like poison in his blood. It hadn't lifted.

"Hey Eddie, Jason!" It was Glendon, bellowing from the walk-in. "Come on back here, will ya? You're not gonna believe this."

Eddie shot Bernardo a glance and a shrug, then the two of them filed back through the storage room, past shelving piled high with glassware, napkins, swizzle sticks, olives and cherries, sour mix, Snap-E-Tom, heading toward the open door of the cavernous fridge.

Glendon stood inside, near the back. The overhead light was off, burned out maybe. On second glance, though, Bernardo realized the bulb was shattered. Glass shards littered two lumpy forms heaped beneath a tarp on the cold damp floor. Amid the frigid mildewy odor of the space, a faint scent like firecrackers—or was he imagining that?

Glendon raised his voice to be heard over the condenser's rattle and hum. "Guess me and Eddie here got a confession to make, Jason." All things considered, he sounded contrite. His breath formed a misty cloud. He gestured to the motionless forms on the floor.

"This here's Henry. And the woman we told you about, Ol' Tits and Turmoil, never did get her name. But Henry, he owns this bar, owns a couple others in Oakley and Clayton, even a strip mall, if you can call it that, out on Bethel Island. But given your professional inclinations, you may also know him as Henry Ireton, Ireton Realty, LLC."

So that's what this is about, Bernardo thought. "I lied," he said, realizing it was too late for the truth. "I should've told you earlier. You were right, I'm no realtor. I'm a firefighter."

Glendon and Eddie looked at each other, like that was just the damnedest thing.

"Don't quite know what to make of that information, Jason."

"If you're a fireman," Eddie said, "how come . . ."

The rest of the question drifted off, which apparently was answer enough. Bernardo couldn't take his eyes off the bodies. The biting cold of the walk-in created a burning sensation on his skin, a kind of hallucinatory recompense for the scalding, charring heat inflicted on the other two bodies he'd left behind, one of them his bride. He felt an eerie sense of déjà vu, as though the bodies had somehow followed him here.

"All we was after," Eddie said, "was a place to stay. This damn economy. But Henry here, he couldn't have that. He had to play hero, kick us out."

"Some have, some don't," Glendon said. "And those that have, more times than not, they got more than their honest share. No logic to it. Just luck."

"Like you walking in here when you did," Eddie said. "Lousy god damn luck. Sorry."

Bernardo felt the tip of the gun barrel pressed against the base of his skull, Eddie behind him with the weapon. I don't believe in luck, he wanted to say, wondering if he'd already mentioned that.

A BOY AND A GIRL

What Jimmy wanted? Be just a little bit smarter. But smart's a lot like tall. Comes a point, it just stops.

She's working swing at the Peppermill when he first lays eyes on her. Name tag reads: Renda Rader—Tonopah NV.

He comes in every night for two weeks, orders 7-and-7s and works them slow, making them last, just for the opportunity, looking at her. Kind of body you don't really see much anymore. Women, Jesus, they're hippos or piccolos these days, nothing in between.

The uniform: black tux jacket with a burgundy leotard underneath, all bunched in the bosom like an invisible hand's grabbing hold. Great legs, seamed stockings. Gotta love that. Jimmy sure does.

Mostly, though, it's the face. Light makeup, dusty freckles. Reminds him of a young Donna Reed, vintage *It's a Wonderful Life*, that sheen in her hair, the wavy bounce. The innocence.

But Christ, what to say? Lousy at small talk, dipshit smiles and moron nods, pretending to watch TV or playing video poker at the bar. Loses his fucking shirt. Not like he's got one to lose. But that's love, right?

Every time she passes by, he catches a whiff of her perfume, his dick like an antenna for the stuff. One night he overhears her tell another waitress the name—The Malignant Dreams of Choo-Choo in Love, something like that, "It has accents of chocolate and seaweed," she says, adding, "Smells better than I'm making it sound"—and he writes the name down on a napkin, tells himself, I'll buy her a bottle.

Try that for an icebreaker. Hey, from me. Happy malignant dreams.

Then comes one night, end of shift, she high-heels over, drops off one last drink. On the house, meaning her.

"You come here a lot," she says.

He's tongue-tied. Flustered. Busted. "Yeah?"

"You're a good tipper."

"Thank you."

She looks at his eyes like she's reading tiny print. His instructions.

"You look like you can handle yourself."

This one really throws him, but before he can get his head around an answer, she adds, "My ex wants to meet you."

That right there, you know?

But Jimmy, it's like pussy's a zombie and it's eaten his brain. He hears: Ex? He's thinking: Hey, she's available.

He follows her out to the edge of Sparks, the house not much to look at. Coupe de Ville in the driveway, mid-nineties model, not old enough to be vintage. Besides, there was rust, little scallops of it bubbling up beneath the chrome.

Turns out the guy's not at all what Jimmy expects.

Edwin, the guy's name. Picture a bow tie, then take it away, leave the rest. That's him. First impression, anyway.

"Have a seat." He nods to a spot beside him on the leather sofa. Man cave, high-def TV, surround sound. Movie posters on the wall, nothing with Donna Reed. "Watch the rest of this goddamn train wreck."

Game Seven, National League Championship, Giants up on the Cards nine-zip in the eighth. Rain's coming down so hard it looks like sheets of tinsel but the umps won't call it, they want the thing over. Crowd too, they're going nuts. Probably even the Cards just want to pack up their gear, go home. Jimmy gets that. He truly does.

Edwin sits there with a ball bat between his knees, resting his chin on the knob.

"St. Louis was three-to-one, win the World Series," he says. "Goddamn Giants, what were they? Eleven-to-fucking-four."

Jimmy thinks about it a second, figures there's no right thing to say. No wrong thing, either. "Yeah, but the books had the Tigers and Yankees even, look what happened. Yankees tank, Detroit takes a four-game sweep. No rhyme, no reason. Been a crazy year."

"That it has." Edwin picks his drink up from the coffee table, something dark and herbal from the smell, Benedictine maybe, on the rocks. Sips. Puts his chin back on the bat. "I'm losing twenty large on this game."

Jimmy tries to do the math, gets lost. Looks around. They're alone. "Renda not into baseball?"

"Not into watching me lose. Did enough of that when we were hooked up."

Jimmy feels this faint wave of relief. He'd been worrying she was changing out of her work outfit in the bedroom, which meant she kept clothes here, maybe still lived here, or at least stayed over some nights. That'd make things complicated. As it was, they were just uncomfortable.

Edwin asks, "How long since you been inside?"

Jimmy likes to think it's not obvious. When he came back from the 'Stan, couldn't find work to save his soul, fucking Obamaconomy. Taking day-labor gigs unloading UP freight cars at Parr Yard and living in his Le Mans, taking splash baths in men's rooms. Half step from homeless.

Tried to win a little back at the tables but it's like a smell you can't get out of your clothes, bad luck.

One day, he indulges a few too many 7-and-7s, eyeballs a tourist in the Circus Circus parking tower. Asian guy, blue suit, almost giddy from winning. Jimmy waltzes up, coldcocks him, grabs the cash, walks away like it's nothing. A conversation. He'd stripped Taliban towelheads of their *pesh-kabz* daggers, searched their rank, scrawny, leathery torsos for boom girdles. Rolling a flush gook? Party time.

Didn't figure on the cameras.

He gets double charged, assault and robbery, works a plea deal

and catches a light one, two years—judge is a vet, semper fi—
serves eighteen in Lovelock, early parole.

Sure he looks rough but not tatted up as bad as some, and he
tries to dress nice, sport coat over the yoked shirt, decent jeans.
Mostly, it's the eyes—"Seen more depth in a windshield," one chick
told him—but he blames that on Kandahar, not prison. Lovelock
was a nap.

"Got my release in July," he says finally.

Edwin nods. "How's it feel?"

Better than losing twenty large, Jimmy wants to say, but bites
that one back. Shrugs. "One more jump on the trampoline."

Edwin nods like he knows what that means—that makes one
of us, Jimmy's thinking, wondering where the hell it came from—
then the guy stands, eyes still lasering the TV screen, like that
might reverse the score. "Tell you what. I'll change my shirt, then
we'll go."

On his feet, he seems less of a priss. Lanky build, topping six
foot. Still, the glasses, the curly hair. Kinda like a tall Elvis Costello,
if he was actually Italian.

Jimmy says, "We're heading someplace?"

Edwin rests the bat against the sofa. "Be right back."

This point, Jimmy thinks: Time to log in with Renda. Ask:
What the fuck? Politely.

Checks out the kitchen, the living room, looks for a door to a
basement. Nothing. Not so much as a whiff of seaweed or chocolate. No choo-choo in love.

Pulling back a curtain at the living room picture window, he
checks the street. Her Camaro's still there. Where did she go—the
neighbors? There an attic?

Edwin reappears, buttoning the cuffs of a leather car coat.
Black. Same as the silk shirt, the pleated slacks, the natty loafers.
Didn't just change his shirt. He did the whole funeral.

"We'll take your car," he says.

"Renda head off someplace?"

"Renda," he says, heading for the door. "This isn't her thing."

Out at the car, he waits for Jimmy to unlock the doors, like he's the boss. Or they're on a blind date. Jimmy takes out his keys.

"Look, no offense but, you know, would it be too much . . ." A little in-place shuffle, dance of doubt. A shrug. "Kinda in the dark here."

"It's simple," Edwin says. "You'll see when we get there."

This is where Jimmy really needed to be smarter. Instead, he says, "And my end?"

Edwin lifts his arms and rests them on top of the car. Easy. Breezy. "You like Renda."

Jimmy waits.

"She wants you should do me this favor."

"How come she doesn't ask me herself?"

"Renda? She ain't here."

"Her car's right there."

"I didn't say she went anyplace. I said she's not here." Edwin gestures with his finger back and forth. "As in you and me."

"I'd like to hear about this favor from her."

"Yeah, well, she asked me to pass it along."

"I don't get this."

"I'll explain on the way."

"You got her tied up in there or something?"

"No, Jimmy. That's your department."

Jimmy's confused. It comes out like a dig, but it's kind of a compliment, too. Like yeah, you've got a shot, you play it right. Still, the guy's right, she's not here. And she's what he came for.

"I'm gonna take a pass." He slips his key into the door lock.

"How much you want?"

Jimmy stares across the top of the car. Unsettling, the stones on the guy, given the way he looks. Ichabod Macho.

"How much of what?"

Edwin stuffs his hands in his pockets, rocks on his heels. "How *much*," he says, "do you *want*?"

"I need to know what you're talking about."

"No you don't." The guy's laughing. "How much are you worth?"

"It depends."

"No it doesn't. Come on. You *know*. Pick a number. How much are you worth?"

Jimmy tries to think it through, see the angle, but instead he keeps coming around to Renda with her merry cocktail tray, her spiffy tuxedo jacket and burgundy leotard, her knockout hose and come-hither freckles and exotic perfume. That smile, the eyes, the hair—young Donna Reed, vintage *The Human Comedy* and *Faithful in My Fashion* and *They Were Expendable*.

He thinks of what it'll feel like, showing up at the Peppermill, nothing to show for himself, nothing to answer if she asks: So how'd it go? That look she'll give him. *Then what are you worth?*

"Five grand," Jimmy says, thinking a quarter of the hole the guy's in.

Edwin and his catbird smile. "I'll give you two."

"Five or I walk."

Edwin waits. Thinks. "I can't guarantee five. I can guarantee two."

Fucker, Jimmy thinks, unlocks his door. "Get in."

The place is only like five blocks away. Suburban tract house, mountains for a backdrop, quiet neighborhood, couple houses clearly empty. Lot of foreclosures that neck of the woods.

Jimmy's not out of the car two seconds before he smells it. The curb like an ashtray, maybe a hundred crushed butts. The faint stench of cat urine, sweetened by ether.

Jimmy heads for the porch but Edwin points down the driveway, waves him along. "In back."

A dim lamp glows in one window of the house—seahorse pattern on the curtains—otherwise the place is dark.

They turn the corner at the back and a pit bull goes nuts, crashing against the chain-link fence of its pen, all fangs and slobber, barking like a crosscut saw. Edwin acts like it's nothing.

"His name's Cochise," he says over his shoulder. Way he pronounces it, rhymes with: Coat, please.

Garage has a window but there's a black plastic bag tacked up across the inside.

Edwin knuckles the glass. From inside, a grimy set of fingers appears, nudging the edge aside. Feverish eyes, rat-like and red, the face lean and stubbled. The man nods, lets the edge of the black bag go.

Shortly the clatter of locks, the door to the garage opens, the man steps out. Raggy clothes. Jumpy as a cricket. Drag a man two hundred yards across gravel, Jimmy thinks, he'd end up looking better than this.

Edwin says, "Meet Wilton."

Jimmy's not sure of the protocol. Nod? Shake hands?

Guy looks at Edwin, checks out Jimmy, back at Edwin. "Wasn't s'pecting you."

"Didn't think you were."

Wilton snatches a cigarette pack from his back pocket, taps out a smoke, lips it, lights up with a Bic. So bone thin he makes Edwin look husky.

In a raspy whisper: "Got nothing for you just yet. Middle of a batch right now."

"I can tell."

Wilton draws on his cigarette, eying Jimmy. "Who's your friend?"

Edwin looks around, as though to make sure no neighbors can see. Not a window in sight isn't dark. "I need to collect on my investment."

Wilton's eyes narrow. He picks tobacco off his tongue. "Not sure I know what you mean."

"My investment," Edwin says. "I need to collect."

"I didn't ask you to shuffle the words around. I asked what you meant."

Edwin takes a step back, eyes to the ground, like he's sorry. To Jimmy, he says, "Take care of it."

Jimmy and Wilton stare at each other like they've been asked the same question in different languages.

From somewhere in Jimmy's gear-locked mind, the words come. "Give the man what he came for."

"Are you both fucking deaf? I got no damn idea what you're talking about."

"I think you do." Jimmy playing tough, a part. No idea why, where it's going.

"I don't know what this faggot told you." The man points the red tip of his smoke toward Edwin. "But there ain't no *investment* in nothing. Now he wants some takeaway, he's gotta wait. Like I said, I'm in the middle—"

"I want my money," Edwin says, stepping closer. Bold, with Jimmy there.

Sucking on his cigarette, hollow-cheeked, Wilton: "For the last fucking time—"

"You've got it here, stop dicking me around, open the fucking safe or wherever the hell you've got it stashed and give me my goddamn money."

The guy's eyes flicker back and forth, Jimmy, Edwin, then he seems to shrink an inch, fold in on himself. Softly, a confession: "Sure. Okay. Wait here."

He turns and shuffles back toward the garage and Edwin catches Jimmy's eye, gestures for him to hurry up, follow along.

Jimmy takes a step and sees Wilton's spun around, trying to slam shut the door. Jimmy lunges, gets his boot in, feels it crushed as the guy uses his shoulder, the pit bull launching off again, Jimmy buckling from the pain but shouldering back on the door.

Almost unfair, given his strength and how scrawny Wilton is. But that's why Edwin brought him along. Fuck fair.

Jimmy forces the door back, catches the overpowering stench of the cook, feeling it burn his eyes as he reaches around for something to grab. Wilton thrashes around, trying to get his hand on an aerosol can of Jump Start sitting on his work bench, singling it out among the clutter of paint thinner, toluene, glassware, tubing. Jimmy wraps one hand around Wilton's wrist, the other around his throat, ducking a blast of noxious spray and lifting the man up the bare-stud wall, pinning him off the ground. He lifts a knee and lodges it deep into Wilton's scrote.

"Drop it. Drop the fucking can or so help me God."

It's when he hears the can hit the floor and his eye follows the sound that he spots the girl.

She's maybe six, peeking from behind a wood box filled with charred beakers and blistered tubing and other gunked-up trash. Ashen and thin with a junkfood pot belly, blotchy skin, eyes watery and pale. Wearing a cotton onesie, pink with seahorses. Clutching a naked Barbie.

"Hey," Jimmy says, can't help himself. Still got his chokehold on Wilton.

And for the merest instant, he sees the dusty street and the crowd spreading back on all sides, taking cover in market stalls or just crouching behind tables, leaving the boy alone in the street, just one more scrawny kid in a *salwar kameez* and a *kufi*, no different than the others selling scarves and bracelets on the edge of the bazaar, except this one's got his fist clenched, thumbing the trigger to a bomb vest.

Jimmy's platoon had set up a checkpoint on the market's south side, blocked off the street with the Humvee and wire and maybe ten minutes later the boy drifts up like a ghost, something in his face bothering the unit's terp.

Laiq, the interpreter's name is. It means "deserving," but the marines call him Extra Serving. Plump, a jokester, can't get enough of the pot roast MREs. Born and raised in Kandahar, the rest of the planet mere rumor. Bobby Steeplehorn shows him a Playboy centerfold one day and Laiq doesn't just stare. He licks the page.

Now he's telling the marines to stand back, walking up all alone, arms held out—*stay calm*—talking to the boy like an uncle.

Jimmy can't understand a word but he'll learn later from one of the merchants that Laiq just keeps telling the boy, You don't have to do this.

And the boy answers back: They told me I'd be safe. If the Americans fire, they cannot hit me.

What's your name, Laiq asks, and after the third time, the boy answers: Azizullah. And how old are you, Azizullah? Ten, the boy says.

Well, Azizullah, ten is a marvelous age, a perfect age. You're a good boy and a brave boy but this is not necessary. I promise the marines will not hurt you. Please.

Laiq inches closer—the boy is crying, ashamed to fail, ashamed to succeed—the interpreter close enough to touch the kid finally, gently stroke his arms and let him know he's safe, it's okay, hand me the trigger, and the boy, Azizullah, in the saddest, sorriest voice Jimmy's ever heard, like some poor dog crushed beneath the wheel of a car, cries out *Inshallah!*

Allah be willing.

Turns out, Allah's plenty willing.

Light rips through the stifling air with a jarring pulse of heat. An instant later, the windstorm hits, spraying dust and blood and bits of cloth and jagged little missiles of bone.

The memory slips by in a second, trailing like an afterburn: *What are you worth?*

Jimmy drops his hold on Wilton, heads over to the girl, tries to scoop her up but she shrinks away. Her face looks feral. Jimmy can barely stand to look.

"It's okay. I don't want to hurt you."

There's a stillness to her, not like calm. Like the silence inside a cave.

Behind her, beyond a sheet of plastic, maybe a dozen coffee-makers bubble with reddish orange liquor, the hot plates covering two folding tables. A mad science of tubing, power cords coiling toward surge protectors. The stench overpowering here. Nothing but a sheet of plastic, he thinks. Jesus.

"What's your name," he asks. "How old are you?"

The girl just stares. Seen more depth in a windshield, Jimmy thinks.

"You like seahorses," he says. "You know seahorses are monogamous? They mate for life. Boy seahorse, girl seahorse, they get together and stay together. Forever."

"Leave her be," Wilton says. He's crouched on the floor where Jimmy let him drop, head buried in his arms as though fearing a deathblow. "She's had her fill of strangers."

Jimmy feels it in his chest, like a tripped switch. He stumbles past Wilton, out to where the pit bull's going crazy, lunging against the shivering wall of its pen.

The air feels like dust, but cold.

Edwin looks put out. "Well?"

Jimmy grabs his face as though for a kiss, twists once hard, snapping his neck.

Back at the house, her car's gone, the place locked up tight, no lights. Renda, Jimmy thinks, please. You got me into this. Okay, not this exactly.

Or maybe this exactly. Something close enough.

Faithful in her fashion. They were expendable.

Forty-five minutes later, he sits in his usual spot at the Peppermill, feeding a sloppy thirst. Seems like every time he checks his watch, the bartender's looking. Yeah, Jimmy thinks, I'm waiting for somebody. And if I'm guessing right, in a mere twelve hours, she'll show up for her shift.

Then again, I could be wrong. I'm not really all that smart.

ARE YOU WITH ME, DOCTOR WU?

Shocker Tumbrel first encountered the loving Buddha inside a padded holding cell at San Francisco County Jail.

Twelve hours earlier, a SWAT team had dragged him out of a shooting gallery two blocks from the Bottom of the Hill, the club where his band had joined a handful of other outfits in a benefit to save the venue, one of the few left in town to offer live music, now targeted for condo gentrification at the hands of the usual cabal of City Hall sellouts and bagman developers.

The night had ended with a beautiful mosh-pit frenzy unlike anything the locals had seen in years: multiple swan dives off the stage monitors from dervish girls and acrobat boys, not just fans but band members too. Pinball aggression. Brothers and sisters united in pain.

At night's end, stoked from adrenaline, Shocker stowed his gear in the van and headed off to mellow the edges with his best friend and band mate, Mousy Tongue.

The two had met through sheer dumb luck in middle school, all but inseparable since: skateboarding, tagging, paint sniffing, runaway odysseys to Portland and Vegas and Burning Man, multiple stints in juvie detention, moving up the buzz ladder to reefer and meth and smack as they formed and dissolved a slew of bands—Molotov Snot, Flaming Citadel, Deathwagon Ponies— culminating finally in the latest, the truest, the fiercest, the best: Acid Prancer.

Shocker writing the songs and playing bass, Mousy up front on guitar and vocals, Clint Barber on drums—they remained true to the poverty-fueled rage, the misfit love, the howling anarchy of punk. They promised themselves they'd never succumb to the soul-sucking über-capitalist fame machine, never cave to money. They started their sets screaming, "This ain't no fucking White Stripes," then kicked into their signature cut, "Shopping Mall Shootout."

Seriously, when 5 Seconds of Summer, an Aussie boy-band rehash of One Direction pop schmaltz bullshit gets crowned as the latest messiahs of hardcore, what could you do but drop trou, moon the power, and hit the spike?

Which was exactly what he and Mousy did after the gig, trundling over to a long-familiar nod pad, scoring from an obese albino named Jelly Stone and heading upstairs to the playroom. The shit Jelly sold them was powdery and fine, a fresh batch of china white, he said, new to the street. Mousy fired up first, passed the gear, and Shocker tied himself off, slapped up a vein. He eased back on his first hit, figuring he could bump it up if need be. Hearing a deep, chesty sigh beside him, he figured Mousy had slipped into the haze, and settled in to do likewise.

By the time it dawned on him Mousy hadn't spoken or even stirred in far too long, no amount of shouting or shaking could bring him back. Neither one of them had brought along naloxone, the thinking man's OD antidote, because, well, they hadn't been thinking. Jelly hadn't offered any, either—I'm your connection, he'd say, not your mother. The Free Clinic and the needle exchanges handed out injectable vials to any dope fiend who bothered to ask—Christ, they practically forced it on you.

But that argument was over. Mousy had wandered across that invisible line where your lungs forget to breathe. All things considered, a gentle death.

Born Robert Sean McFadden, Hayward, California. Twenty-three years old.

Shocker didn't exactly remember stacking the moldy couch and two broken chairs in front of the door, or screaming at anyone standing outside that he had a gun and would shoot to kill any motherfucker dumb enough to try to force his way in.

The clearest thing he recalled was dragging Mousy into the

corner, sitting there curled up with him, the lifeless head in his lap, that handsome, waxy face staring emptily up into his own as the SFPD busted their way in—battering ram, follow-up kicks, a final shoulder or two—suited and booted in storm-trooper black, aiming their AR-15s in his face and screaming like Warg riders: "On the floor! Show your hands, asshole! Do it! Now!"

Time swirled in and out—he sat cocooned in a straitjacket, entombed in his quilted cell—until finally the lock clattered open, the door swung back.

Even if given a thousand lifetimes of lovely dreams, he could never have imagined the person who entered, sat beside him, and said gently, "Would you rather I call you Shocker, or Lonnie?"

It wasn't how she looked that made her sitting there astonishing—just another tall, slender, California blonde: center part on the pulled-back hair, fat brown eyes but prim lips, a dusting of mustard-brown freckles. Her voice had a clipped warm twang—Midwestern vowels wrapped in tortilla consonants—but that, too, seemed irrelevant. She wore an ID card on a lanyard that read simply "Visitor." Given his savage state of mind, though, where the edge of the universe felt intimately close, he misread the word as "Visitation." And that seemed perfectly right. She wasn't just someone from beyond the locked door. She'd been transported here from a totally different plane of existence.

"How did you know that name?"

"You mean Lonnie?"

He nodded, thinking: I probably look like a missile went off inside my head. Nerve endings were crackling back to life. His blood had started to itch.

"It's on your booking sheet. They printed you on intake, remember?"

He didn't. Suffering a sudden wave of shame that quickly metastasized into utter self-loathing, he dropped his eyes, studied the straitjacket's crisscrossed sleeves, the security loop pinning them to his chest. He caught a whiff of bleach off the white cotton canvas.

"My name is Katy," she said, leaning a bit closer. "I'm a counselor here at the jail. I've come to help you feel better."

Good luck with that, he thought, even as, from somewhere beyond the oily skid at the bottom of his mind, he sensed a feeble hope that it just might be true.

She sat back, folded her hands in her lap, and crossed her ankles, as though in sympathy with his bound arms.

"I'm going to guide you in some breathing exercises, very simple stuff. It's the principle aspect of Buddhist meditation. I think it might help calm you."

He considered spitting back: *What fucking makes you fucking think I'm not fucking calm?* His skin felt like a carpet of chiggers, the air in his lungs had been set on boil. And there's this guy they found with me, he thought, fella named Mousy, sweet skinny fuckup with a chain-lightning mind—we grew up in the same stinking shithole—maybe you've heard of him?

"Close your eyes," she said, "not completely, you don't want to fall asleep."

By way of demonstration, she dropped her eyelids to half-mast, while Shocker flashed on trying to bitch slap his only real friend back to life. Yeah, he felt pretty sure he didn't want to fall asleep.

"Be present," she said, "but focus on nothing except your breath. Inhale . . . Let the air fill your lungs, drop your diaphragm. Gently, gently. Then just let it go, exhale . . ."

She did it herself a few times, as though to show him how, and he figured, why not? What other miraculous plan is in the works?

"If thoughts enter your mind, don't dwell on them. Let them go. Return to your breath. Focus on that. There's nothing so important it can't wait."

He couldn't imagine such a thing could be true. My brother-from-another-mother died a few feet away and I was too loaded to save him. There was a thought to latch on to, cling to, like an anchor dragging him down to the bottom where he belonged.

Except maybe he didn't. Maybe, just maybe, he belonged here, with this woman named Katy, nothing to do but breathe in . . . breathe out . . . breathe in . . .

He wasn't sure how much time passed, but the freedom to let go, the simplicity of nothing in the world to do but breathe, felt strangely forgiving. He imagined her hand on his chest, just above the solar plexus, creating a kind of radiance, a warm rush not unlike heroin, and all the nagging, bitchy questions of his life seemed answered, or answerable.

He opened his eyes a little and looked at her, wondering if it could be true. This stranger, this visitor—could she possibly be the person who might save him?

He whispered, "I don't want to die."

She glanced up—no expression at first, like she was waking from a dreamless sleep—then offered a smile.

"We all want to live and keep living," she said. "Unfortunately, that's not a viable long-term option."

After that, he let her call him Lonnie, a name he'd long associated with a mother drowning in self-pity, a father too focused on being pissed off to make a living, a ratty house in a crap town. But Shocker would no longer do. Shocker died with his unlucky friend.

From an investigator at the public defender's office, he learned that the stuff he and Mousy booted that night wasn't heroin at all, but fentanyl, and there'd been a flood of overdoses all across town. Useless knowledge in retrospect. Meanwhile, Jelly Stone had disappeared, haunted by hindsight or just run out of Dodge by an angry mob of fist-shaking junkies. That won't last long, he thought. The strung-out are notoriously indulgent.

Katy's visits continued. His parents had split up and moved to their separate redneck havens far away and out of the picture—happy chance, to his mind—and no one from the scene, not even Clint, bothered to come by, no doubt meaning they all blamed Guess Who for Mousy's death. Get in line, he thought. Regardless, for all intents and purposes, Katy became his world.

She and the center she worked for helped liaison with the public defender handling his case, offering to provide housing, oversee and monitor his diversion to rehab. He took heart in that show of confidence. Besides, he felt no inclination to backslide. The very idea, in fact, came to terrify him.

But being an addict by nature, and having discovered something that made him feel good, he couldn't help but want to do it relentlessly. So within the confines of his cell, he dove into not just meditation but the dharma, memorizing the Four Noble Truths and the Eightfold Path, devouring every text Katy provided: the Mahayana sutras, the *Dhammapada* (Treasury of Truth), the *Visuddhimagga* (Path of Purification).

By the time he walked out of the detention facility into the foggy burn-off of a mid-winter morning, carrying his shoebox of books and dressed in the spanking-new jeans and sweatshirt Katy had brought him (the better to obscure the freakish ink scrolled across his skin from knuckle to neck and down to his skinny flat butt), he felt reasonably ready to confront the monster he'd always pretended didn't exist: the future.

She drove him to a quiet street on the edge of the Presidio and parked outside a sprawling three-story Shingle Victorian with a brick façade—an anomaly in a town known for its earthquakes. It seemed to suggest either reckless optimism or uncanny luck, and that struck him as only too apt for a rehab center.

Banyan trees shaded the pebbled walkway, and Lonnie half expected to spot a smiling monk perched beneath one of them plucking an angular banjo. Similarly, he wondered what kind of wistful muzak might be playing inside the house, and whether, with its flutes and singsong chants, it would conjure a spa or a noodle house.

Neither, as it turned out. As Katy led him through the thick front door, nothing but silence greeted them.

The place resembled a professor's home, or what he imagined one might look like from movies and TV. Katy introduced him briefly to a couple other residents shelving dishes in the kitchen—both twenty-something, strangely scrubbed and ruddy for recovering addicts, no piercings, no tats, no scarification—then led him up two flights of stairs to an office at the back of the house.

A black-haired man in a cardigan and slacks sat at a desk with his back to the door. Through the giant windows along the north wall, Lonnie spotted, beyond the tops of the eucalyptus trees in the near distance, the Golden Gate, the Marin Headlands.

Katy knocked gently. The man did not move.

She didn't speak or knock again, just patiently waited. Finally the man removed his glasses and set down the book he'd been reading, rose from his chair, turned and approached the door. He was Asian, trim with an athletic gait, handsome if a bit sharp-featured, the angles of his face accentuated by the impeccably combed-back hair. Scholarly eyes, a careful smile. Two red discs on the bridge of his nose marked where his glasses had rested.

"Welcome to Metta House." Hint of an accent. He extended his hand. "I am Doctor Wu."

The ensuing handshake was clumsily formal and gratefully brief.

As though sensing the awkwardness, Katy interjected, "*Metta* means loving-kindness. It comes from the Pali word *mitta*, which usually translates as 'friend.'"

Doctor Wu nodded. "More accurately," he said, "'the true friend in need.'"

Lonnie shrank a little, feeling their eyes on him.

As though reading his mind, Doctor Wu said, "Your friend, the one who died, I believe he called himself Mousy Tongue?"

Lonnie swallowed what felt like a burr. The floor seemed to buckle. It wasn't meant as an insult, he thought, to Mao or you or anyone else. The kind of thing white people always say.

Finally, he managed to whisper, "Yeah."

Doctor Wu clasped his hands behind his back and stared a hole through Lonnie's skull. Then, ever so gradually: a mischievous smile.

"That's rather clever."

The following day, Lonnie commenced his daily routine, which involved the usual recovery *diktat*—making a fearless inventory of people he had injured, preparing to make amends—though without the self-flogging he'd expected.

Instead, the practice focused on cultivating *bodhicitta*, the arousal of the compassionate heart, and each day ended not with groveling prayers of contrition but a vow of empowerment—to live as a *bodhisattva*, dedicating this life and all subsequent lives to help alleviate the suffering of others.

Every morning, Doctor Wu led the residents in an hour of sitting meditation, followed by a session of *tai chi chuan*, another of *qigong*, moving meditations that gave Lonnie a sense of his physical presence he'd never before known. He'd previously thought of his body as nothing more than a machine of meat, an animated coffin waiting for its corpse. Now he came to recognize the flesh and the spirit as mirror images, deepening his resolve to stay clean.

His energy normalized, without the crazed swings between mania and lethargy. The monkey in his head began to settle quietly in the branches of his mind.

Where he'd once flaunted his tattoos, they came to embarrass him as hopelessly crass, but that too evolved into humble acceptance: they were him. In fact, as his skin and muscle tone improved, the ink seemed to flare more vividly, like the plumage of a wild parrot.

Afternoons were spent in more meditation, some with chanting of mantras focused on healing or transformation, then study and discussion of Buddhist texts and concepts. He came to learn that Doctor Wu had once been a prominent biochemist, whose work—to the extent Lonnie understood it—concerned revealing how both classical Newtonian mechanics and quantum physics were necessary to explain the workings of a living cell. But then some kind of scarring inside his retina began to cloud his vision, making it all but impossible to read the small print in most scientific journals, and two operations only made it worse. So he elected for disability retirement and, needing to redirect his life, chose to dedicate himself to teaching Americans the benefits of Eastern traditions.

Not just any Americans. He found he had a special calling, a particular aptitude for helping those whose talent had only created chaos. The gifted but broken, the brilliant but lost.

That explained, Lonnie realized, the peculiar breed of cat inhabiting Metta House. Unlike the losers, skeeves, and derelicts he'd only recently considered his tribe—and whom he'd reasonably imagined would reappear in rehab—everyone here had been successful, some insanely so.

Victor Mazur had been a hired gun in Silicon Valley specializing in network penetration, exploitation, and defense. Eleanor Tosh had been the assistant director of research for the Pacific Stock Exchange. Jonathan Adler had taught both political philosophy and economics at Stanford. Even Katy had a hotshot resumé—she'd been the youngest faculty member ever at the San Francisco Academy of Ballet.

Sure, they'd all had their problems, cocaine mostly, pharmaceutical uppers, nothing so white-trash as crank. To ease the inevitable crash or just mellow their buzz they'd used Nembutal, Seconal, good old reliable booze. A few had toyed with pharmaceutical opiates, Oxy and Percocet mostly, the occasional flirty snort of heroin. None had mainlined like Lonnie, or sniffed paint from a paper bag or raided a neighbor's medicine cabinet and swallowed literally everything he'd found. None of them had gone on a week-long meth binge only to wake up in a truck-stop toilet in Cheyenne, swatting at invisible bats, no idea how he'd gotten there. Their addictions hadn't been a lifestyle choice so much as self-medication, stress management, the dark underbelly of American mojo.

Leaving Lonnie with the nagging question: What in the name of God-and-weasels am I doing here?

That became clearer as he got better acquainted, not just in class but performing the daily chores. And the answer, again, surprised.

Household duties were performed communally, shoulder-to-shoulder, care of the house and garden, preparation of meals. Only illness excused you. And as he joined in with everyone else to rake leaves and weed flowerbeds and trim back trees, empty the trash and wash the dishes and sweep the floors, change beds and, yes, scrub out shower stalls and toilets, he learned that he wasn't alone in feeling a profound disaffection with the Land of the Free.

The others may have avoided the bitter grind of growing up working class—coming from presentable families, enjoying an actual shot at prestige and money—but they'd come to see the trap in that. Each of them shared Lonnie's utter contempt for the capitalist shell game, the perpetual hustle of working people, the naked rape of the poor. And they'd earned that disaffection not from the outside like him, but from deep within the system. They could genuinely claim the mantle of traitor, to their kind if not their country. Lonnie admired that.

One night, as they sat around shooting the breeze over white tea and sesame brittle, he got a deeper sense of what *bodhicitta* and the vow of empowerment meant among these people.

In contrast to the usual silence that characterized the house, a CD of classic chants crooned softly in the background, performed by Shi Changsheng, the former pop star turned Buddhist nun.

"This may not be your kind of thing," Katy had said with a shrug when she'd slipped in the disc, "but I find it kind of soothing." Lonnie took note of the title, "Mantras for the Masses," wondering why dancers so often had such sentimental taste in music, then tried to ignore the syrupy, over-sincere production, focusing instead on the weightless melodies.

Meanwhile, the conversation ambled from this to that, until Victor, the former cyber-warrior, casually kicked it into a different gear.

"You hear all this stuff about Chinese hackers." He was burly, stern, wild-haired, clean-shaven. "How on a daily basis they're raiding not just military and intelligence databases but corporate ones, even hitting small businesses. They're probing utility networks to fine-tune a potential crash of the power grid, stealing patent applications, pirating software."

"Planting rootkits and Trojans in stock market computers," Eleanor, the finance maven, added. A comfortably plump woman, disheveled in earth tones, sensible shoes.

"Don't forget the Sony hack." Jonathan, the philosopher, finger-tapped his mug of tea like an ocarina—cowboy handsome but eerily tall, slouching in his armchair, stretched out like a ladder. "Seventy percent of the company's hard drives trashed, handiwork of the scurrilously named Dark Seoul."

Eleanor shook her head. "All for a Seth Rogan movie. Bad? Meet worse."

"What they never tell you?" Victor again, leaning into his message. "We're doing the same damn thing, only ten times worse."

"God forbid," Jonathan said, "the rest of the world defend itself."

"We're the good guys." Eleanor bit off a morsel of sesame brittle. "You know, because we're us."

"Beware the inscrutable Asian." Jonathan glanced inside his mug as though distressed by its emptiness. "Yellow Peril 2.0."

Finally Katy spoke, directing her words to Victor, nodding toward Lonnie. "Tell him about Site M."

"Site M?" Eleanor chuckled acidly. "Christ, tell him about MonsterMind, Treasure Map."

Victor smiled and edged a little closer to the others, like Uncle Buddy preparing to tell the kids their favorite story, but he focused his gaze on Lonnie. In the background, Shi Changsheng sang in prayerful monotony: "*Om mani padme hum . . . Om mani padme hum . . .*"

"There's a wastewater pump station that just got built deep in the woods along the Little Patuxent River outside Fort Meade, Maryland. County officials told reporters that the National Security Agency made anyone working on the project sign a piece of paper agreeing that if they ever talked about the job to anyone, in any way, they'd go to prison for life."

"*Amerika über alles,*" Jonathan said.

Lonnie glanced back and forth between them. "I don't get it. Wastewater—like what, a sewage treatment plant?"

"The pump station," Victor continued, "will provide around two million gallons of water a day to this huge, top secret lair codenamed Site M. Located right next to NSA headquarters. Guess why."

"Here's a hint." Eleanor waggled her fingers. "It's not for flushing toilets."

"Site M," Victor said, "is the $900 million center that houses the US Cyber Command."

"More specifically," Jonathan said, "High Performance Computing Center-2, which all would agree sounds far less ominous."

"Think of it as a missile silo," Victor said, "only there's a computer inside, not an ICBM."

"Not just any computer," Jonathan said. "A gargantuan cyber-brain that consumes 600,000 square feet."

"That's about ten football fields," Eleanor said, "assuming you share the average American's fondness for sports analogies."

"A computer that large," Victor said, "needs perpetual cooling, which means it has an insatiable thirst for water. That's why the NSA spent $40 million on a nearby pump station that no one who helped build it can talk about."

"Unless they want to disappear," Eleanor said.

Jonathan added, "Which segues nicely to TreasureMap, no?"

Victor tented his fingers thoughtfully. "The purpose of this massive computer is essentially to track every single person on the planet connected to the web—mainframes, laptops, tablets, phones—an almost real-time map of every Internet user in the world."

"Not just to know where they are," Eleanor said. "You know, send a friendly email, cute little emoji—Hey, just checking in, hope everything's lovely."

"We'll be able not just to access, but to attack. An operation code-named Turbine will allow us to infiltrate any device in the world with malware."

Katy made a face. "I'm not entirely comfortable with the word 'we.'"

"It's our tax money," Eleanor said. "Over which we have zip control."

"Ah yes," Victor said. "Lack of control. Which brings us at last to MonsterMind."

He turned once again solely toward Lonnie, the focus of his gaze even more severe. Shi Changsheng and her mantras for the masses seemed to fade further into the background.

"This cyber-center will not only be tracking incoming attacks, singling out suspicious algorithms as they flash through communications links. There's going to be an automated strike-back capacity, where the computer, with no human input, can, in a microsecond, launch a counterstrike at the source of the intrusion."

"Too bad if the source computer's a proxy," Eleanor said. "Or a zombie."

Jonathan: "Some kid in Slovenia hijacking an Iranian computer."

"And Obama has refused to rule out nuclear retaliation for a massive cyber-attack," Victor said. "We're talking the reincarnation of Mutually Assured Destruction. With robotic computers in charge of the nukes."

"The infamous Doomsday Machine." Eleanor tilted her head toward Lonnie and smiled: "I'm assuming you've seen *Dr. Strangelove*?"

Jonathan raised a cautionary hand. "But we all agree the problem isn't technological. It goes a great deal deeper than that. It goes to the self-destructive nature of what the West considers freedom."

"The freedom to be miserable," Eleanor said. "The freedom to ruin your life."

"To be greedy and cruel and self-idolizing," Katy said.

An addict, Lonnie thought.

"When most Americans think of freedom," Jonathan said, "what they mean is power."

"I don't entirely agree," Victor said. "Yes, I get what you mean. But some just want to be left alone."

"In a trailer somewhere in Idaho." Eleanor struggled forward in her chair to set her empty cup down on the coffee table. "Head off with the guns and dogs, get away from the niggers and spics and Chinks."

Lonnie thought: my parents.

"Money is power," Jonathan said. "Money is liberty. This is America."

"I am free to ride the dragons of want," Katy said, paraphrasing one of the sutras. "Free to chase my illusions."

From which Lonnie inferred *the dharma is freedom*, feeling too timid to say it out loud.

Jonathan rose to stretch his spidery limbs, his fingers almost reaching the ceiling. "The world isn't a mess because we're denied opportunities to discover the truth. We already know the truth. It lies in virtually every spiritual and philosophical system in the world. Abandon the ego. Still the mind, calm the passions, look within. Do unto others as you'd like to get done."

"Simple to state, hard to live by," Eleanor said. "Much easier to be free, which is to say lazy and frightened and restless."

"Speaking of rest," Katy said, "perhaps it's time to turn in."

After turning off the music and joining hands for the vow of empowerment, dedicating themselves to the end of suffering for all living things, they headed up to their separate rooms.

Katy, touching Lonnie's arm, suggested they linger downstairs for a moment.

"Doctor Wu wanted me to let you know he'd like to speak with you tomorrow after morning practice." A puckish smile. She took his hand. "Don't worry. It's a good thing."

Almost instantly upon rising at 5 A.M., Lonnie became plagued by a state of doubt so fierce it swelled to the level of panic as he pulled on his square-necked tunic, tied the drawstring on his loose-fitting pants, stepped into his rubber-soled slippers.

Throughout the hour of sitting meditation his mind hissed with negativity and self-doubt. During *tai chi* his attempts to perform even the simplest movements of the *kata*—Cloud Hands, Parting the Wild Horse's Mane, Grasping the Sparrow's Tail—created such uncontrollable trembling he all but lost his balance, and he actually fell attempting Snake Creeps Down. As for *qigong*, the Five Animals never frolicked more miserably.

He wasn't surprised when Doctor Wu, at the conclusion of the morning's final session, all but fled the garden patio without so much as a glance back. The ensuing sense of foolishness tinged with devastation only broke when a hand settled gently on his arm.

"You look like you could use something cold to drink," Katy said.

Until that moment, he'd barely noticed the sheen of sweat covering his skin, soaking his armpits and the back of his tunic.

In the kitchen, she withdrew a pitcher of water from the fridge, filled a tumbler, and passed it to him. Parched by a thirst that felt greedy and small, he downed the entire glass in one go, only realizing at the end what she'd so clearly intended. Words from the *Tao*:

> *True goodness*
> *is like water . . .*
> *It goes right*
> *to the low, loathsome places*
> *and so finds the way.*

Taking the glass from his hand, she said, "Doctor Wu is waiting in his office."

Lonnie climbed the steps to the third floor with the deliberation of someone unsure whether he was ascending an altar or the gallows. Wondering as well: did it matter?

The office door stood open. Doctor Wu, smiling, gestured him inside. "Have a seat," he said in a voice both calm and pleasant, then closed the door for privacy. Lonnie doubted he had ever felt more scared.

He chose a rocker near the bookshelf, thinking movement might ease his jitters, while Doctor Wu wheeled his desk chair over, like a physician preparing for a consult—eyes with their usual imperturbable focus, now graced with something not unlike warmth.

"I must admit," he began, "I did not know much about your world until Katy recommended you join us."

"My world," Lonnie said. He was gripping the rocker's arms like the railing on a boat about to capsize.

"The music business," Doctor Wu explained. "Specifically, the form I believe you refer to as as 'punk.'"

The word had never sounded so cheesy, so petulant.

"I believe there is a recording company," he continued, "that takes a particularly spiritual perspective on the form."

Lonnie bit back a chuckle. *The form.* Like concertos, the minuet.

"Equal Vision," he said, thinking: lightweight boojie pseudo-angst. Not quite as lame as Christian metal, but who wants nihilism with a melody, let alone a message. "I know about them, yeah. Based in New York?"

"I was wondering if you would be interested in developing something of that sort out here on the West Coast."

Lonnie, unaware up to that point that he'd indeed been rocking, stopped.

Doctor Wu leaned a bit closer, grazing one hand pensively across the other. "Much of Buddhism focuses on the wisdom of emptiness, the perfection of silence. But the arts, when practiced with right intention, can be useful as teaching tools. Stories excel at demonstrating moral truths. Are you aware of the *Shasekishū,* the Collection of Stone and Sand?"

"Not . . ." The rest of whatever his mind had hoped to say abandoned him. He shook his head, swallowed. "No."

"It's a collection of Zen stories from the thirteenth century, written by a master named Mujū." He glanced around the room. "I'm sure I have a copy somewhere, I can loan it to you."

"Okay."

"It's a wonderful example of how stories can enlighten and guide."

Almost imperceptibly, Lonnie resumed rocking.

"As for music, nothing so touches the heart, ennobles the mind."

Yeah, Lonnie thought. Same thing occurred to me last time I slam-danced.

"The popularization of the traditional chants, such as I heard all of you playing downstairs last night, is one such example. Though I must admit, to my taste, Shi Changsheng, for all her good intentions, is a bit . . ."

Slick, Lonnie thought. Cloying. Sanitized.

Doctor Wu reached out, set his hand on Lonnie's knee. A gaze to cut glass. "I realize that what I'm saying may seem outlandish in the context of . . . 'punk.' But as you've already admitted, there is a spiritual side, and certainly a political side, to the music as well. It is not all swagger and attitude."

"No," Lonnie said. "It's not."

Doctor Wu withdrew his hand and sat back. "I've read the lyrics to some of your songs."

Lonnie crossed his legs, feeling a sudden, overpowering need to urinate. "How—"

"Katy sought them out, found them online, your musical troupe's website. They are very powerful, very true to the spirit of anti-materialism, the quest for truth."

"Thank you . . ."

"Most of what one hears and sees in this culture is commercialist propaganda. Advertising for excess and vanity. An ironic pose masquerading as wisdom. I gather you agree."

"I . . ." Lonnie felt a sudden mysterious weightlessness—and feared he might pass out. *Breathe, fool.* "Yeah. Sure."

"So." Doctor Wu laced his fingers together. Two hands joined as one. "Do you know of anyone to whom we might turn to help us with our enterprise?"

Two hours later, dressed in a crewneck sweater and jeans, a simple blue windbreaker, Lonnie found himself, courtesy of several bus transfers, seven miles south of downtown outside a ramshackle row house along the Islais Creek Channel, the borderland between Hunters Point and Dogpatch.

He knocked on the door. Middle of the afternoon, he thought, hard to know if anybody'd be up yet.

No answer, he knocked again—not louder, though. Why be a dick?

Finally, muffled footsteps thumped down an inner hallway. The door swung open. An immediate waft of tobacco, reefer, and something sweet, Jack & Coke maybe.

"Hey, Clint."

He hadn't been sure what to expect. What he got was a stunned, brutal stare, eyes blasted—Clint shirtless, shoeless, just a pair of black leathers worn low on his hips, boxer mushroom at the waist. Pipe-thin torso, ropey arms, every inch blazing with tats. Barbell studs in the nose and lip. His hair, as always, shaved away on the sides, madly disheveled up top.

Lonnie said. "Been a while."

Clint crossed his arms, leaned against the doorframe, glanced quickly up and down the street, like Lonnie might conjure a posse of narcs.

"Just me," he said. "Sorry I've been out of touch. Been stuck way across town."

Silence.

"I've gotten clean, been—"

"The fuck you want?"

So this is how it'll go, Lonnie thought. I'm the stooge. The one to blame.

"I just wanted to see you. Thought we might talk."

"About?"

"What happened." Lonnie swallowed. "What's going on. I dunno . . ."

Clint's eyes tightened, like he was trying to get Lonnie a bit more in focus. "I got something going on right now."

"Sure, I understand."

"No you don't. That's not the point. I'm tied up the next hour. Come back then, we'll sit and . . . you know." He nudged off the doorframe, stood upright. "That work for you?"

"Yeah," Lonnie said. "I'll come back."

He turned to go. Clint called him back with, "Hey, Shocker."

It took a second for Lonnie to remember: That's me. Over his shoulder: "Yeah?"

That tight-eyed stare again, like there was just too much to take in. "You look good."

Lonnie found a sandwich shop, feeling too shaky even to risk a café on the off chance they'd have beer and wine on hand. He couldn't risk a relapse. Cardinal rule of rehab: avoid all triggers, like former friends.

He ordered a Snapple and took a seat by the window. A processed, instrumental version of "The Ballad of John and Yoko" simpered through an overhead speaker, as though to remind him that nothing is sacred.

Focus, he told himself. Three months you've been at Metta House, a devoted student, steady and strong. Worthy of trust. Why else would the man in charge send you on this mission?

And yet, having now seen Clint eye-to-eye, he felt groundless. Maybe this is what they mean, he thought, when they talk about No Self. An anxiety-tinged emptiness.

It was way too soon to bring up starting a production studio, no matter how he pitched it. Sure, he could make the case that they'd weed out the listless cutesy poseurs so typical of the scene now: Doom Dirge, Bitch Pop, Sad Core, Lo-Fi Bedroom Grunge. He had no intention of selling out, going mainstream, becoming the Shi Changsheng of punk. They'd restart true hardcore, give a voice to the angry young and poor, speak the ugly fucking truth to power.

Clint would laugh in his face. How many times had he said it? *The minute you think you have something to say, you're on the path to asshole.* Kind of thing you expect from a drummer.

But jacking the system was righteous—what did punk mean if not that? And what better way to answer back to the sniveling greedy horseshit than selflessness? Not groovy peacenik sniveling, that's not what I mean—I'm talking defiance of the emperor, like the venerable Tano and his warrior monks of Shaolin.

Buddha is true revolution. Buddha is the real Mao Tse Tung.

Which brought him back around to the real problem. They had to talk that out, Mousy's death. He had to own the rage, the spite. Cop to the guilt. All grand plans for anything else lay on the far side of that. Regardless, this was the place to start, for a thousand and one reasons.

Clint met him at the door, now wearing an Evil Conduct t-shirt—admittedly not a positive sign—and gestured him toward the back of the flat. "We'll talk in the kitchen."

From somewhere on the second floor, a stereo blasted "Slave State," one of Acid Prancer's signature numbers. Lonnie stopped in his tracks and glanced up the smoke-hazed stairwell. Mousy's vocals stitched through the air:

A sweat-soaked bed
Then daylight and dread
Stuff whatever you're dreaming
Back inside your head

How many lifetimes ago, he thought, did I write those words? How many eternities have come and gone since I showed them to Mousy, watched him make that wicked, lopsided grin. "Let's work up a tune, Shocker McRocker." So full of faith. So present.

Clint, standing halfway down the hall, snapped his fingers. "You coming?"

"Yeah." Lonnie shook off the moment. "Sorry."

It wasn't till he passed the first doorway that he sensed the other presence in the house. Two presences, actually.

One had a ball bat, but by the time Lonnie noticed the thing coming at him all he could make out was a blur. The wood shaft crashed across his temple and ear, knocking him down like a bag of cement. Instantly all but deaf. Blinded by pain. Wetting himself.

The three of them kept him down with kicks to the kidneys, the groin, the head. He curled up like he had with his father so many times, making out little by little that the other two were Mousy's sister, Jordan, and her old man, Gearhead Greg, who continued chipping in with the bat.

A voice for the angry young. Speaking the ugly truth.

About the time he was choking on blood and his right knee felt on fire, Greg and Clint got down on the floor to hold him down, one pinning his legs, the other his shoulders, while Jordan knelt beside him, leaning close to be heard over the music from upstairs, everything swathed in hiss.

"You remember what you said, cocksucker?" Her breath smelled rank from cigarettes, Southern Comfort & Coke—the sweet smell he couldn't quite make out earlier. "I'm outside the room, pounding on the door, trying to get inside—see my brother, see if he's okay, see if he's fucking alive—you remember that?" She grabbed his chin, squeezed like she wanted to rip it off. "Remember what you fucking said? 'He don't want to know you, you smokehound cunt.' But those weren't his words. That was you. My beautiful little brother was already dead."

Even with it pressed so close, he could barely make out her face, his vision fragmented from the pounding, blood streaming into his eyes. But despite the angry buzz inside his brain and the thundering music upstairs, he could suddenly make out nearby sounds with eerie clarity. What he heard was a match scrape a friction strip, the whisper of the flame, the singed tobacco of the cigarette. And he could smell: not just her breath but the billowing exhale smothering his face. Just beyond the smoke, in the haze, the red tip of ash glowed like the eye of an angry angel.

Two strong hands gripped his head and Jordan's thumb pushed back his eyelid. Even then, he couldn't see, but that was the least of his problems just then.

She said, "He didn't belong to you, asshole. He was mine, too. He was everybody's."

He wasn't sure whether he merely thought the words or screamed them—*he died quiet, he died peaceful . . . if you wanted in so bad why didn't you force the door, why leave it to the cops*—but he also realized none of that mattered. This was the price of finding his way. This was the low, loathsome place.

He shuffled up Third Street toward Mission Bay, bent over like he'd been gut-shot and dragging one leg. A bus was out of the question: one, Gearhead Greg had taken his money. Two, the driver would no doubt call the law. And that just wouldn't do. They could have killed him, that would've been just and fair, but they hadn't.

So, as best he could, he walked.

The dragged knee buckled every time he tried applying weight, the joint a grinding, boiling knot of gristle. Given the stab in every breath, at least one broken rib seemed likely. As for the eye, an oyster couldn't clench shut tighter, and the scalding pain sent sickly orange flashes throughout his body, crackling and sparking along every nerve.

He crossed Lefty O'Doul Bridge where China Basin narrows into Mission Creek and kept trudging up Third, ballpark looming to the right, downtown a mile ahead. Avoiding eye contact as pedestrian traffic intensified, he continued across Market with its trolleys and traffic and crowds, aiming almost unaware toward Chinatown, sensing somehow he could find a place there to sit, rest. No one would trouble over him. For all intents and purposes, he'd be invisible.

He passed through the pagoda-style gate on Grant Avenue and dragged himself up the steep hill, maintaining his balance any way he could, bracing himself on cars or delivery vans along the curb, latching onto parking meters, grabbing lampposts entwined with dragons, trying not to tumble into the vendor tables mounted outside every storefront.

Somehow he managed the two long blocks to California Street and planted himself breathlessly on a wooden bench in the shaded square across from Old St. Mary's. Rest here, he thought, not long. Once you've got your strength back and can talk without choking, maybe ask a lady with a kind face if you can use her cell, call Katy at the center. Say you were mugged, which is true after all.

Wiping tears from his good eye, he glanced up at the cathedral's bell tower and felt a sudden, powerful sense of release. He'd reached a place of reckoning, acceptance, and felt ready to surrender. If he could only decide: to whom?

In time, he spotted a familiar figure at the corner, waiting for the light. A slender man in a sport coat, a scarf knotted at his neck. His appearance seemed incongruous, even impossible, and yet not. Excluding Metta House, where else but here to encounter Doctor Wu?

Lonnie scrambled from the bench and headed toward the corner. He didn't make it in time for the light, and he lacked the strength to call out, but he watched Doctor Wu continue down Grant, deeper into old Chinatown.

Traffic was light so Lonnie crossed against the red, shambling as quickly as he could. He spotted Doctor Wu turning into an alley and hurried to catch up, forgetting his pain, his weakness, his savaged eye and ribs and knee. When he reached the corner where Doctor Wu had turned he found himself facing a narrow cul-de-sac cluttered with nondescript shops and restaurants at street level, tenements overhead, towering above the damp pavement.

He went storefront to storefront, glancing through steam-fogged windows. At last he spotted the telltale sport coat vanishing up a stairwell inside a crowded dim sum tearoom. Totally Asian clientele, not a round eye in the place—it worked to his advantage. Nothing but stunned glances tried to stop him as he plowed through the dining room to the doorway that led upstairs.

His good fortune ended at the top. A wide, thick-necked, short-haired guard in a black suit manned the door at the hallway's end, the one just now closing. He stood with his open left hand covering his right fist, as though ready for a *Bao Quan* bow.

"I need to speak with Doctor Wu."

It came out slurred—the damage to his face, the stabbing lack of breath from his stairway climb. Bracing himself with one hand against the wall, he shoved off with each step, pushing himself along. The guard simply stood there, eyes front, the empty gaze of a temple dragon.

"I *need* to *speak* with Doctor Wu!" Bellowing now, as best he could.

That brought the door guard forward, ready to wrap Lonnie up, pitch him back down the stairs into the clamor of voices and hissing oil, clanging pots. Lonnie slammed his palm against the wall, pounding against the ancient plaster as he continued shouting, "I need to speak to Doctor Wu! It's me, Doctor Wu, Lonnie, I need to speak with you, please! Please come out, talk to me, please!"

He was thrashing in the guard's vise-like arms when the door opened. Doctor Wu stood there, ashen but otherwise expressionless. Beyond him, inside the room, a number of stern-faced men in suits, white shirts open at the neck, no ties, sat around a conference table in utter silence.

Doctor Wu whispered something harshly over his shoulder to someone inside the room, then entered the hallway, closing the door behind him. He said something in Chinese to the guard who, after a long moment, released his hold.

Lonnie collapsed to the floor. Doctor Wu bent over him,

checking the various wounds, specifically trying to look at the shuttered eye.

"You need medical attention," he said.

A short time later, Katy arrived and, with the help of the thickset guard, managed to get Lonnie down to her car. Doctor Wu had long since vanished back inside the room with the other men.

She turned up California, heading west. Lonnie said, "Don't take me to a hospital."

She didn't respond—just kept driving, eyes straight ahead, hands at ten-and-two.

"If I wanted to go to a hospital I could've stopped at SF Gen."

"Lonnie—"

"It was on the way. Kinda. Given where I was coming from. Where I . . . ended up."

She stopped at a crosswalk and they watched a gaggle of Asian school kids troop merrily corner to corner, the sound of their laughter dulled by the windshield.

"Why didn't you?" She looked both ways, then accelerated from her stop. "Go to the hospital, I mean."

He sank a little deeper into the car seat. In a whisper: "I don't know . . ."

They continued on in silence for several blocks. "Well, never mind. Doctor Wu feels terrible about what happened—he assumes it had to do with the errand he gave you—and he's already called his personal physician. He's waiting for us at Metta House."

How responsive, Lonnie thought. How discreet.

"Those guys back there at the tea house," he said, "the ones Doctor Wu was meeting. Who are they?"

Katy shrugged. "I'm not sure. Businessmen, I suppose."

Lonnie managed a small laugh. "Think I don't know a gangster when I see one?"

"Lonnie, please." Like she was talking to a feverish child. "You've been beaten nearly to death, who knows what kind of damage you've suffered, shock alone, but that's no reason—"

"The Triads are in bed with the Chinese military."

"According to who—the US press?"

"He's a spy, isn't he—Doctor Wu, I mean."

Katy put her hand to her head. "Lonnie, for God's sake—"

"Christ, for all I know, you're all spies. Mazur for sure. Jonathan?"

"Yes, yes. You've found us out. We're all . . . spies! What better way to end the infinite afflictions of all living beings. You know what *bodhisattva* really means, right?"

"Secret agent?" He'd never seen her angry before. She looked on the verge of tears. "Have to admit, it's a perfect front. Put a little 'boo' back in Buddha."

She shook her head. A small, miserable laugh. "You ungrateful prick."

"Who says I'm ungrateful?"

"Please, just be quiet." She redoubled her focus on the street ahead. "At least until we get home."

So that's what we're calling it now, he thought. Not the center, not Metta House. Home.

Except for the doctor, the place was empty when they arrived. Not uncommon, most of the others still worked. Katy helped Lonnie to the sofa nearest the fireplace and the physician, an affable, melon-faced Asian perhaps ten years younger than Doctor Wu, commenced with the expected Q&A—*what happened, where does it hurt, are you experiencing flashes of light or a buzzing in your ears*—his voice calm and caring and precise.

Rummaging in his pebbled black bag, he said, "I understand you are a recovering addict. I therefore need to ask your informed consent before administering a painkiller. But I would like to get a better look at that eye. The knee as well, of course, but that may require a specialist."

A painkiller, Lonnie thought. Probably an opiate. Fentanyl, maybe.

He nodded. "Sure. Why not?"

The doctor took out a sterilized needle and a vial, the print too small and faraway for Lonnie to read. As the syringe's cylinder filled, Katy came closer, crouched beside the sofa, and took Lonnie's hand. Her grip felt reassuringly cool and dry.

The doctor came close. "I'm going to lift your eyelid, which may be very tender and painful. But I need to anesthetize the area, and the best spot for that is the eye itself."

Lonnie decided not to tell him he'd shot up in his eye before.

"From the needle itself, you'll only feel a pinprick, nothing more. Okay?"

Lonnie nodded again and braced himself and, all things considered, it went quick. He lay back and closed both eyes and waited for the effect to hit, only realizing once the numbing warmth began to spread throughout his body that the doctor had emptied the entire syringe. And, from what he shortly gathered, it wasn't just an opiate. It was a paralytic—at least, he couldn't move. And yet, with Katy's fingers still entwined with his, panic seemed a thousand miles away.

If he were to describe the ensuing sensation to someone, he'd say that it was like wandering into a strange, small church, no one there but you, except for an unseen organist playing up in the choir loft, which you can't see no matter where you look. You can hear the music, though: a hymn you think you recognize, the name right there on the tip of your tongue. But then the music falters, the organist loses the tune—stops, goes back, repeats an earlier phrase, but once again turns into a musical cul-de-sac. The organist retreats, revisits another beautiful line, then wanders off, stumbles across another hymn, diddles with that, then strays into odds and ends from other songs: "Fools Rush In," "River Deep, Mountain High," "Mary Had a Little Lamb" . . .

And everywhere that Mary went . . .

Someone should wise up the lamb, he thought, as the cool dry fingers he'd been clutching slipped free. Following Mary is not a viable long-term option.

THE ANT WHO CARRIED STONES

The woman, on her knees, pressed her lips against the man's rough palm. "I swear, all I've told you, every word—"

"Run through it again." He took back his hand. "All of it."

She didn't dare look at his face. "I haven't lied."

"A thief too proud to lie."

"I didn't steal—"

He got up, kicked his chair backwards. It clattered across the bare floor. "I said tell me what happened. Again."

She clenched her hands beneath her chin, steadying them. "My cousin, Marisa—we live in Boca del Monte—she told me all I had to do was carry a suitcase to Panama. I lost my job at the hotel. My daughter, Rosela, she cries herself to sleep—"

"Leave your daughter out of it."

"'People do it every day,' Marisa said. Yes, some get stopped at the airport, the suitcases ripped apart, the money found stitched up inside. But the amounts are legal, just under 78,000 quetzales. No one gets arrested. 'That's why they call us ants, because the amounts are small.'"

"Small to who?"

"Please, I know I made a mistake—"

"A *mistake*?" He snagged the chair, slammed it against the floor. "Talk!"

"Marisa and I delivered our suitcases to a house in Zona 18. They said come back the next day. We did, with maybe twenty others, sitting on the floor in an empty room like this but bigger. Eventually they came and gave us back our suitcases, drove us to the airport. A man named Lorenzo met us there."

"Count yourself lucky you're not him right now."

"It's not his fault."

"You're protecting him?"

"No. I—"

"No means yes. He was in on it."

"There was nothing to be in on, I just . . ."

He snapped his fingers. "Come on."

"We boarded our plane. Despite what Marisa said, despite the amounts, I was terrified. The police are so corrupt, there's no telling—"

"Getting ahead of yourself, no?"

"Once the plane took off, the others relaxed. I couldn't. Marisa tried to calm me, holding my hand, praying with me—"

"You talked about how you'd get away with it."

"No! Listen to me, she had nothing . . . It was my stupidity. Mine alone."

She glanced toward the window. Sunlight flared through slatted blinds.

"You landed at La Aurora."

"Lorenzo told us, stay together. But the terminal's so crowded, like fighting a river swollen from rain."

"Screw the crowd. You snuck off."

"I saw a counter, selling blouses. The embroidery, so beautiful. I thought: Rosela would love something like this. My beautiful girl, she's so brave, I've given her so little—"

"I said leave her out of it."

"I didn't even realize I'd stopped walking."

"You thought, 'Oh, look what I could buy with all this money.'"

"No. It was a blouse, a simple blouse!"

She put her hand to her face and quietly wept. He let her go for a moment, then another finger snap.

"The others—they were where?"

"I looked, but there was just this sea of people." She wiped her face. "Suddenly, these policemen appeared."

"Yes, your corrupt police."

"They said they were with the Policia Nacional and ordered me to give them the suitcase."

"Naturally, you obeyed."

"I told you. I fought. They tried to grab it from me, I held on with both hands. I was afraid to call out. What if I just got the others in trouble as well? Try to imagine what I felt. I've never done this, never done anything like it, I'm a simple, silly woman from a poor town, I've never even been in an airport—"

"Yes, yes. These corrupt cops, phony police, whatever, they went for the suitcase."

"One of them slapped me across the face."

He chuckled. "Surely you've been struck before."

She flushed from shame. "I was stunned. I didn't—"

"And they snatched the money."

"They vanished into the crowd. I tried to get my bearings, running one direction, then back, looking for Lorenzo, Marisa."

He turned his head and spat. "You got in a cab."

"I had only a little money, not enough to get back to Guatemala. I didn't know what else to do."

"Who did you call?"

"No one. Who could I—"

"You knew the name of the hotel where the others went."

"I didn't have my suitcase! I was so scared. I needed time to think."

He dug something from his pocket. She dared a glance. The hand she'd kissed now held a pistol.

"Perhaps there's some truth in your story. The river makes noise because it carries stones. But you lost a lot of money."

"Marisa will tell you—"

"She washes her hands of you. Called you a scared, stupid fool."

"Lorenzo—"

"He thinks you went running to the first cop you saw."

"That's a lie! I was confused, scared, I swear—"

"It doesn't matter now." He thumbed back the hammer. "What matters is the money. And the money is gone."

Feeling the gun barrel nestle in her hair, she shut her eyes tight, praying: Lamb of God, who takes away . . .

He didn't fire. Her terror broke, like a fever, dissolving into clarity, and she could feel, however slightly, that now he was the one trembling.

"I am not a thief," she said. "You are not a killer. And yet here we are, two stones in the river."

"Stop talking."

"I understand now. Do what you must. I forgive you. Please forgive me."

"Listen to you."

"Whatever happens, you'll go to the airport. You won't be able to help yourself. You'll look for the counter, the one with the blouses. And you'll find it."

"That proves nothing."

"One blouse in particular, with dragonflies and sunflowers and lace. You'll buy it. Tell them to wrap it. Rosela Melendez, Boca del Monte."

"Stop saying her name."

"She's the reason I'm here. Just as you are here because of me."

Finally, she looked up into his face.

THE AXIOM OF CHOICE

As I sat here waiting, wondering how to explain things, I caught myself remembering something often said about set theory.

I teach mathematics at the college, I'm sure you know that already. It's sometimes described—set theory, I mean, excuse me—it's oftentimes described as a field in which nothing is self-evident: True statements are often paradoxical and plausible ones are false. I can imagine you describing your own line of work much the same way. If not, by the time I'm finished here, I suspect you will.

I see by your ring you're married. Perhaps you'll agree with me that marriage, like life itself, is never quite what one expects. I've even heard it said that, sooner or later, one's wife becomes a sister or an enemy. I'm sure for a great many men that's true.

I'd put it differently, however. Again, if I can borrow a phrase from my area of expertise, I suppose I might say of Veronica's essential nature—her soul for lack of a better term—what Descartes said of infinity: It's something I could recognize but not comprehend.

Now, I can imagine you thinking, given what you saw in our bedroom, that such a statement reveals a profound bitterness, even hatred. I assure you that's not the case.

But there's no getting inside another person, no rummaging around inside a wife's or a lover's psyche the way you might dig through a drawer. The gulf between me and my wife, her and Aydin—that's the name of the young man whose body you found beside my wife's: Aydin Donnelly, he was my student—the gulf between any two people may feel negligible at times, intimacy being the intoxicant it is, but the chasm remains unbridgeable.

It has nothing to do with facts—my God, who has a greater accumulation of *facts* than a married couple? No, I'm not speaking out of bitterness. On the contrary, I feel humbled by this observation. What I mean to say is this: If you simply bother to reflect on the matter seriously, or just open your eyes, absolutely everything, even oneself—and especially one's wife—remains mysterious.

Veronica and I met at university—which school isn't important, one of those giant Midwestern diploma mills attended by middle-class *untermenschen* on the cusp of discovering their utter ordinariness. I was finishing my doctoral studies in math, she was pursuing music.

Veronica's instrument was the viola. There's a joke about violists, perhaps you know it. *What is the difference between a coffin and a viola? With a coffin, the corpse is on the inside.* Tasteless, I know, considering the circumstances. What I mean is that Veronica, for most of her life, lacked the expressiveness, the passion, to be anything but merely functional as a performer.

She had an excellent memory and commendable dexterity, she fooled a great many people. But there was a wooden, colorless quality to her playing that no amount of practice could transform. She realized early on that she would be a teacher, like me—and yes, when I spoke of utter ordinariness, you didn't think I was excluding myself, did you?

We met the way most graduate students do—in the library. I wonder how many campus marriages find their beginnings in the stacks. Such a strangely erotic locale—the order, the stillness, it cries out for something heated and spontaneous, something messy. But we did not desecrate the library. Not Veronica's style.

By that point she was already recognizing her limitations. The company of other music majors only hammered that home, so she steered clear of the music building, holidayed over to the main library to study, and one day by chance took up position across the table from me. Luck is the heart of romance, they say, not fate. I cannot dispute that.

I was torturing myself in preparation for my orals. Almost

every great mind in mathematics did his most creative work by the age of eighteen. I was twenty-five at that point—a confirmed mediocrity, struggling with all my might not to become a joke.

Veronica plopped herself down not three feet away, spread out her sheet music for compositional analysis—it was Bach, of course. Musicians uncertain of their talent always gravitate toward the Baroque: so dense, so artificial. Music to hide behind.

I know I sound callous but that's not at all my intent. The state in which you found Veronica is hideous. Perhaps you took the time to look at some of the pictures around the house. If so, you saw that she was quite lovely in her way, bigger than is considered fashionable, I suppose, but when has fashion ever understood women? I found her softness beguiling. I'm hardly svelte, obviously, but it's different with men.

Such a shy, defenseless smile—that's what I noticed when I glanced up that first time and saw her across the table. Of course, like everyone else in that library she was frightened, overwhelmed, miserable with doubt, but she looked at me so sweetly. I wasn't one to believe love could solve my life but I was overdue for a little kindness.

We popped out for coffee, the ritual chat, feeling each other out, where we came from, where we hoped to go. The kindness, I learned, was genuine. Soon enough, we were inseparable.

It's hard to describe to people who've never known it, the pressure, the grinding isolation of graduate school. A great many campus marriages are formed from the simple need for companionship and commiseration. Ours was. We were lonely, we tended not to get on each other's nerves, we respected each other's privacy. The next thing we knew, five years had gone by. I received my position here at the college, she found herself a chair in the local chamber orchestra.

Eventually, as all couples do, we had our problems. Veronica was too self-conscious to genuinely enjoy sex—that may seem overly personal, what my students refer to as Too Much Information, but I'd be surprised if you hadn't been waiting for me to bring it up.

What I mean is, abandon was not a quality she possessed or aspired to possess—that too showed in her playing. I won't psychoanalyze her for you, drag out all the family trash, but shame factored heavily in her upbringing. She could pet and kiss and cuddle, I never felt a lack of affection, but—excuse me, again, if this sounds coarse—good old-fashioned fucking was simply too intrusive.

To her credit she didn't find my appetites perverse or unwholesome. She did not love me less because of what I wanted.

So—a sister or an enemy. I suppose one could say Veronica became my sister, though that's both too cynical and too superficial a way to put it. It was decided I would have my affairs, as long as they remained dalliances and not devotions. She would keep her home, which she suffered over as only a woman can. The marriage would remain intact.

You may think me a monster at this point. But reflect on what I just said: We reached an understanding—how many couples fail or refuse to do that? Part of that understanding was that I would stay. I did. Right up until the end.

You're probably asking yourself: How did this man ever get anyone but his wife to so much as look at him? Trust me, I'm not unaware of my homeliness. I used to wear a beard as a sort of disguise, it gave me a bearish, rakehell appeal, or so I liked to think. But I'm not blind to what an unlikely Lothario I make.

I've even talked about it with some of the woman I've been with, a few of whom were by any objective standard completely out of my league. And I've heard this response often enough now to consider it more than likely to be true: A great many men simply don't like sex. They either find it a messy obligation involving smells and feelings they abhor, or a kind of athletic event at which their prowess must never be questioned.

Well, I don't share such inhibitions, and I'm not shy about my pleasures. It's amazing how appealing that can be to a woman. Especially a woman who, like me, is cheating on her spouse.

Now, I can imagine what you're thinking. Anyone who walks

away from the scene you discovered in my house, then talks about his sex life, his lack of inhibition, his pleasures—not to mention set theory and Descartes, for God's sake—you have to wonder: Is he demented? Is he a sociopath? Or, on a far more rudimentary level: Is he lying?

I assure you, I am not deranged, nor do I lack a conscience. As for lying—well, that's always an interesting question, isn't it?

I'm sure you're aware of the Liar's Paradox. Consider the statement, "I am lying." If the statement is true, it means I'm not lying when I say I'm lying, which is nonsense. Contrarily, if the statement is false, it means I'm lying when I say I'm lying and thus I'm telling the truth. Again, ridiculous. I can only imagine every cop in the world knows that one, not to mention the average nine-year-old.

You may not know this, but paradoxes like that were the bane of mathematics at the turn of the last century. Damn near brought the whole field to a screaming halt. And paradoxes—or antimonies, as they're now called—are always the sort of thing that most fascinate my students, which brings us at last to Aydin.

The name's Turkish. Curiously enough, it means "enlightened." I told you his surname: Donnelly. A particularly intriguing American mutt—workaholic father of famine Irish stock, Turkish-German scold for a mother. All that unruly black hair, those Levantine eyes, the bucket-shaped head and nail-driver hands. Even his slump was oddly beguiling—he looked burdened.

Aydin attended my course on the history of mathematics—an easy "A" for those in the humanities needing a science credit. I don't fool myself regarding my function on campus. It's a small liberal arts college of no particular reputation, a dumping ground basically for those with little promise beyond money. My job is to help them toward a degree so they don't further embarrass their families. A little calculus, maybe an intro to stat, remedial trig for most of them—all topped off with a course on the *history* of mathematics, the *philosophy* of science. It's about as much rigor as the poor darlings can stand.

Aydin stood out to the extent he actually made an effort to pay attention. Believe me, that's enough to endear a student to a teacher these days. I looked forward to his visits to my office. His conversation, if not exactly profound, at least displayed some fire.

He developed a fascination with what is known as the Axiom of Choice—I assure you this is relevant. It's a fundamental principle that states we can create a new set by choosing one item from each of an infinite number of other sets.

There, simple to state, but the idea is implicitly fantastical: Who would do the choosing? When would he finish? Never, of course, by definition the task is infinite. The physical universe would come to an end before the selection process was complete.

But by assuming that the task can be accomplished, by acting as though we can step outside time and treat infinities like common objects, we find ourselves capable of constructing the lion's share of modern mathematics. Deny ourselves this trick, we close the door to much of what we have accomplished for the past century—and these achievements are astonishing, not just in abstract mathematics but the applied sciences.

All those little geniuses out on the quad, listening to their iPods or thumbing away on their ubiquitous phones—not even gizmos of that order would be possible without the Axiom of Choice, let alone recent progress in advanced circuitry and theoretical physics.

It's one of the great ironies of modernity. By turning a blind eye to an intellectual sleight of hand, we have created some of the greatest tools for understanding the physical world in human history.

All of this fascinated Aydin, but he was inclined to fuzzy thinking—one of those easily distracted, poetic souls who get snarled in a confusion and think they've beheld the profound.

For him the Axiom of Choice got all mixed up with other things, like the notion that real world success necessarily results from self-delusion. That appealed to him in a fundamental way, something to do with his father I think. The man's a securities lawyer in Chicago, very connected, impressively rich. To Aydin, he was a pompous phony.

My point, though, is that the young man obsessed over the ways we fool ourselves, and so the Axiom of Choice became a kind of a symbol for our inescapable self-deceit. We trick ourselves into believing in freedom, for example, when in truth everything's pre-ordained. We're hormonal robots, he said, prisoners of biology. All of which is just warmed-over Platonism. And as Plato himself so deftly pointed out, the inescapable implication is that we're all just shadows.

But Aydin took it a step further. If choice is an illusion, then there's also no responsibility. If you had him here in this chair, not me, that's what he'd tell you. Even murder is nothing more than the turning of a page in some inscrutable book.

And there's the greatest paradox of all, he'd say: We convince ourselves we're free in order to escape the terror of realizing it doesn't matter. The game's been over from the start.

This sort of thinking is very common among the young. They worry themselves sick about authenticity because they sense themselves to be, at root, fundamentally artificial. For Christ's sake, they haven't lived yet, what is there to be authentic about? I try to tell them that. In particular, I tried to tell Aydin. But he was obsessively earnest the way only a twenty-year-old of middling intelligence can be, which is why he appealed so much to Veronica.

Veronica felt a special devotion to wanderers. If you were lost, she found you. And Aydin was desperately, irretrievably lost. You could see from the scars on his wrists he'd made a hash of at least one suicide attempt. That too seems to be required for modern adolescence, like computers and tattoos. But it only stirred Veronica's pity.

They met when she stopped by my office late one day, picking me up for some dinner engagement with the director of the chamber orchestra—God, there's something I won't miss. She paid poor Aydin little mind, being preoccupied, but there was no mistaking *his* reaction. He stared at her as though she were literally incandescent.

Here again, you may think me a monster, but I found Aydin's

infatuation the perfect solution to a problem. He could be the pet Veronica craved, a way to nourish her insatiable need to be *involved*. God knows Aydin was in desperate want of a woman's *involvement*. Maybe I felt guilty—I was having a particularly heated liaison at the time, a woman in Veronica's string section no less.

How did I hatch my plan? I invited Aydin over to dinner—there, simple, like sin itself. And all I had to do was wait for him to reach for something, expose those tortured wrists—Veronica's eyes popped like flashbulbs.

After we cleared plates and put on the kettle for tea I feigned a need for some air to give them the necessary privacy. I knew Aydin would take care of the rest. He'd say it was predetermined.

You'll find this absurd but I honestly did not foresee their becoming sexual. Oh, I didn't doubt they might come to exchange some tenderness, and I could well imagine poor sad Aydin planting his face between Veronica's ample tits to weep. But sex?

As I said, I recognized my wife but did not comprehend her. The shame surrounding her body, her uneasiness with anything untidy—well, apparently that had far more to do with me specifically than either of us realized.

That wasn't all I didn't see coming. Veronica lost weight. Her playing improved dramatically—she gave a solo recital of the Sonata Pastorale and seemed a different person during the performance. She blossomed, became the woman she'd secretly wanted to be all along. And she had Aydin, not me, to thank for that. She calmed him down. He made her feel needed.

Now, if I were you, I'd hear all this and be thinking: Here's a man who thought he had life figured out, an understanding wife, a slice on the side—do people still say it that way?—every need gratified. Then he discovers that in fact he had it all wrong. Not just that, but his wife's aversion to good old-fashioned fucking, as he put it, was really just revulsion for him. How humiliating. Must've royally pissed him off.

I wouldn't fault you for jumping to such a conclusion. But you'd be wrong.

I loved my wife. I was happy for her. I was pleased she'd solved the riddle of her sexual indifference, even if it was less than flattering to me. As I said, I knew how to find gratification elsewhere. We should all be happy, the world being what it is.

And no, this isn't where my wife stopped being a sister and began life as my enemy. That would be ironic, yes, but what actually occurred was even more ridiculous: I lost all interest in other women. As a kind of penance, a way to own my faithlessness, I shaved off my beard. All of which, of course, was secretly a way to prepare myself for returning to Veronica's affections.

Like some character in a farce I began to long for her in a way I never knew I could. But she would not entertain my interests there—who could blame her?

Even so, I wanted to be worthy of her when her liaison with Aydin finally ran its course. And yes, I believed that was inevitable. Veronica and I would rediscover each other. I knew that as certainly as I knew anything. What I didn't anticipate was how it would occur, but I'm getting ahead of myself.

We actually managed to live agreeably, the three of us, for nearly a year. I grew into my newfound humility, even as Aydin became prone to fits of indignation—he had rights, don't you know. Talk about smug.

Thank God Veronica put him straight on such nonsense. This is how it is, she said, you can behave or be alone. After a day or two of miserable fuming he'd come around. But honestly, episodes like that were quite rare. He wasn't a bad young man. He was just so damn sentimental.

Then Veronica began having these odd pains in her joints. She wondered if it weren't some kind of arthritis, every musician's nightmare.

Soon her breathing became labored. The nurse at our doctor's office referred her for a sonogram. The results indicated she had what was euphemistically described as a "complex mass" in her pancreas. A few tests later, and she was diagnosed with Stage IV pancreatic carcinoma. She already had tumors in her liver and lungs as well, and they were spreading to the lymph nodes and beyond.

If you doubt my love for my wife, ask the doctors and nurses at the cancer clinic what sort of husband I was once Veronica fell sick. I'm not bragging—I can think of nothing more hideous than taking pride in being a commendable Joe when one's wife is dying—but I need to make sure you don't misunderstand the true nature of what happened. That's very important to me. And my behavior stood in stark contrast to Aydin's.

Just when he could have done us all a favor and grown up, he reverted to the most grotesque childishness. Suddenly only he understood what Veronica needed. I was complicating her relationship with the nurses at the clinic. I was confusing her, confusing the doctors, all out of some perverse narcissism. I've no doubt he blamed the cancer itself on me, my neglect of her sexually all those years.

Meanwhile, things at home grew increasingly hard. Veronica's hair began falling out with the chemo and she decided to have it all shaved off. That, combined with the dark patches under her eyes, the grayish tint of her skin—I removed as many mirrors as I could. Then pile on the mental confusion, the lack of balance, the nausea, the pain—such a miserable, pitiless, degrading way to die.

As for music, she wanted nothing to do with it, threw a fit if the radio was on. It reminded her of everything that would never be.

Don't get me wrong, there were also days when Veronica was incredibly heroic. She could be so outgoing, especially to other patients at the clinic. But yes, she could also be petty and bitter and scared. She was human, for Christ's sake.

Meanwhile, Aydin seemed to think the tragedy was his. I couldn't keep him away from the house. Trying to explain that she needed rest only degenerated into screaming matches, so I invariably relented.

Veronica, true to her nature, couldn't refuse him. She was the one dying but he was the one who needed care. He'd finally become authentic.

I will admit, yes, that infuriated me. But what came next cannot be laid solely at the door of my rage.

Last night, about nine or so, Veronica started screaming suddenly from the bedroom. She'd been asleep and a nightmare woke her—she dreamed she was drowning from the fluid building up in her lungs. She was terrified: Don't let me die like that, she begged.

I called the on-duty nurse, asked her to talk Veronica down, explain to her what was happening. The nurse told her that no, she wouldn't drown, most likely she'd die as her organs shut down one by one. It wasn't a painful way to go, she said.

Veronica snapped back: And how could you possibly know that? By this point, after all the chirpy prognoses followed by one round of bad news after the next, she was convinced absolutely everyone was lying.

She asked me to get my gun and shoot her. She couldn't take it anymore, she wanted to put an end to it all, stop dragging it out: Kill me, she said. Please. If you love me, you'll do that for me.

I told her I couldn't. We needed to see the current chemotherapy regimen through to the end to learn if there was any progress. If not, there were other regimens and even clinical trials, experimental treatments. It was far too soon to give up, I said. But we both knew I was being dishonest. Worse, selfish.

The thing neither of us dared to say? She was going to die and I was not. She'd run out of luck. If I did as she asked, killed her, I'd be surrendering my luck as well.

Perhaps she needed to know I understood what she was going through, what it felt like. Perhaps she wanted vengeance on the thousands of humiliations I'd inflicted on her during our marriage. Perhaps both. Regardless, I saw the demand as unfair. I felt sorry for her. But I refused to give up the rest of my life for her.

What a miserable night. Sleep was out of the question—we talked, we argued, we wept. She remained afraid and ready to die. I remained unwilling to oblige her. All the while, we both danced around the real issue lying there between us.

But something else happened too. I've already said I recognized Veronica but did not comprehend her—and once her connection with Aydin took hold I didn't entirely recognize her either.

Well, that night, as I faced her hour after hour, trying to reason with her, trying not to get swallowed up by the despair that was dragging her under, my lack of recognition became complete. The chafing voice, the vacant eyes. The hollowed-out ruin her face had become. I no longer saw her there. I saw someone else. I saw myself.

Come morning, Aydin appeared. The night had taken its toll, I'm sure it showed. He asked what was wrong and I simply lacked the wherewithal to make up a lie.

He was horrified—not at Veronica's wanting to die but my refusal to do what she wanted. He called me a weakling, a coward. How could I let her continue to suffer?

Of course, the real question was: How could I continue to let *him* suffer? He couldn't bear the sight of her misery anymore. He wanted it over with. Christ, who didn't?

I wouldn't let him in. He flew into a rage right there on the porch—neighbors peeked out past their curtains at us—but this time I refused to bend.

He wasn't used to being denied. Incensed, he said that before she'd fallen ill, Veronica confessed that she intended to leave me, divorce me, rid herself of me once and for all. She'd come to despise me, then he rattled off all the things she loathed about me, how cold, how resentful, how selfish, how predictable I am. How ugly in every conceivable way.

To have this shouted in my face, by a boy, after the night I'd just spent—especially while harboring the ridiculous illusion that, had Victoria's luck been different, she would have returned to me—I will admit, I did not respond wisely. I'm sure you know this, sure the neighbors told you. I shouted right back that, if he didn't leave, I'd kill him.

He shambled off, seething. An hour or so later I had to step out. Veronica was short of Fentanyl patches, I needed to run to the pharmacy.

It's hard to describe the level of distraction I've been operating under, one minute panicked into focus, the next I'm standing somewhere, at the sink or in a parking lot, completely oblivious to how much time has passed. And today, as I wandered around the drugstore, God only knows how long, I got lost in my own self-pity, wondering how I could have been such a fool not to grasp Veronica's true feelings. I miss things, is what I mean to say, things I should have noticed. Like the fact that, when I drove away from the house, Aydin was nearby, watching me leave, probably hiding in the park down the block.

When I got back home from the pharmacy I could feel it, the stillness. I called out. The house swallowed up the sound.

Perhaps Veronica let him in, perhaps I forgot to lock the door, like I said I've been strangely abstracted of late. I climbed the stairs, went to the bedroom, found them. I guess it was his turn to calm her down, her turn to make him feel needed.

She must have told him where I kept my gun—I didn't see any signs he went scavenging for it himself. Of course, he botched it, like he had before, only now he'd included Veronica. He'd fired one round into her skull, but couldn't bother to see if she was actually dead before turning the gun on himself. That would have sullied the drama. He was very sentimental, like I said, yes, which is just another way of saying he was incompetent. But what's the point of competence if you're never responsible?

I'm sorry. I sound angry. Bitter, yes. I suppose I am. But not at Aydin. Not at Veronica. Not anymore.

I stood there wondering: What to do? I could leave, pretend I'd never come home, let a few hours pass so they could lie there like that until they finally got what they'd wanted—would that be denying them anything?

Or I could call 9-1-1, have the paramedics rush over, fuss over them, dash them off to emergency, maybe even save them. For what—so Veronica could suffer even worse than before, only to die in a few weeks regardless? And Aydin—say he lived, what would he wake up to? Imagine it. Imagine discovering yourself in a hospital bed, instead of hell where you belonged.

I understood that. I understood because I realized that's how I'd spent every day of my life, finding myself unjustifiably alive, furtively killing everything around me.

I'm a coward, yes. They were right: I'm selfish and shallow and vain and weak. And yet oddly enough—here's one more paradox for you—it was Aydin, the one who believed in fate, the one who believed that nothing changes, we are who we are, for better, for worse, forever: He was the one who gave me one last chance. The chance to redefine myself.

He'd done what I couldn't bring myself to do—he failed at it, but why punish him for that? Why punish either of them? I tugged the gun from his hand, then took a moment. I had to collect myself, wait until it wasn't revenge or disgust or rage in my heart. Maybe it was just one more trick of the mind, the self-delusion that makes the rest possible, but I told myself: Remember, you know what it means to be overdue for a little kindness.

PRETTY LITTLE PARASITE

One hand on her hip, the other lofting her cocktail tray, Sam Pitney scanned the gaming floor from the Roundup's mezzanine, dressed in her cowgirl outfit and fresh from a bracing toot in the ladies.

Stream-of-nothingness mode, mid-shift, slow night, only the blow keeping her vertical—with this odd craving for some stir-fry—she stared out at the flagging crowd and manically finger-brushed the outcrop of blond bangs showing beneath her tipped-back hat.

Maybe it was seeing her own reflection fragmented in dozens of angled mirrors to the left and right and even overhead, or the sight of the usual trudge of losers wandering the noisy maze-like neon, clutching change buckets, chip trays, chain-smoking (still legal, this was the `80s), hoping for one good score to recoup a little dignity—whatever the reason, she found herself revisiting a TV program from a few nights back, about Auschwitz, Dachau, one of those places. Men and women and children and even poor helpless babies cradled by their mothers, stripped naked then marched into giant shower rooms, only to notice too late—doors slamming, bolts thrown, gas soon hissing from the showerheads: a smell like almonds, the voice on the program said.

Sam found herself wondering—no particular reason—what it would be like if the doors to the casino suddenly rumbled shut, trapping everybody inside.

For a moment or two, she supposed, no one would even notice, gamblers being what they are. But soon enough word would ripple through the crowd, especially when the fire sprinklers in the ceiling started to mist. Even then, people would be puzzled and vaguely put out but not frightened, not until somebody nearby started gagging, buckled over, a barking cough, the scalding phlegm, a slime of blood in the palm.

Then panic, the rush for the doors. Screaming. Animal terror.

Sam wondered where she'd get found when they finally reopened the doors to deal with the dead.

Would she be one of those with bloody nails or, worse, fingers worn down to gory bone, having tried to claw her way past so many others to sniff at an air vent, a door crack, ready to kill for just one more breath?

Or would she be one of the others, one of those they found alone, having caught on quick and then surrendered, figuring she was screwed, knowing it in the pit of her soul, curled up on the floor, waiting for God or Mommy or Satan or who-the-fuck-ever to put an end to the tedious phony bullshit, the nerves and the worry and the always being tired, the lonely winner-takes-all, the grand American nothing . . .

"Could I possibly have another whiskey and ginger, luv?"

Sam snapped toward the voice—the accent crisply British once, now blurred by years among the Vegas gypsies. It came from a face of singular unlucky pallor: high brow with a froth of chestnut hair, flat bloodless lips, no chin to speak of.

The Roundup sat just east of Las Vegas Boulevard on Fremont, closer to the LVPD Metro tower than the tonier downtown houses—the Four Queens, the Golden Nugget—catering to whoever showed up first and stayed longest, cheap tourists mostly, dopes who'd just stumbled out of the drunk tank and felt lucky (figure that one out)—or, most inexplicably, locals, the transplant kind especially, the ones who went on and on about old Las Vegas, which meant goofs like this bird.

What was his name? Harvey, Harold, something with an H. He taught at UNLV if she remembered right, came here three nights a week at least, often more, said it was for the nostalgia . . .

"You are on the clock, my dear, am I right?"

She gazed into his soupy green eyes. Centuries of inbreeding. Hail, Brittania.

"I'm pregnant," she said.

Come midnight she began looking for Rick, and found him off by himself in the dollar slots, an odd little nook where there were fewer mirrors, and the eye in the sky had a less than perfect angle (he thought of these things). He wore white linen slacks, a pastel tee, the sleeves of his sport jacket rolled up. All Sonny Crockett, the dick.

"Hey," she said, coming up.

He shot her a vaguely proprietary smile. His eyes looked wrecked but his hair was flawless. He said, "The usual?"

"No, weekend coming up. Make it two."

The smile thawed, till it seemed almost friendly. "Double your pleasure."

She clipped off to the bar, ordered a Stoli rocks twist, discreetly assembling the twelve twenties on her tray in a tight thin stack. The casino's monotonous racket jangled all around, same at midnight as happy hour—the eternal now, she thought, Vegas time.

Returning to where he sat, she bowed at the waist, so he could reach the tray. He carefully set a five down, under which he'd tucked two wax-paper bindles. Then he collected the twelve twenties off her tray, as though they were his change, and she remembered the last time they were together, in her bed, the faraway look he got afterward, not wanting to be touched, the kind of thing guys did when they'd had enough of you.

"Whoever you get this from," she said, "I want to meet him."

From the look on his face, you would've thought she'd asked for the money back. "Come again?"

"You heard me."

He cocked his head. The hair didn't budge. "I'm not sure I like your attitude."

She broke the news. In the span of only a second or so, his expression went from stunned to deflated to distinctly pissed, then: "You saying it's mine?"

She rolled her eyes. "No. An angel came to me."

"Don't get smart."

"Oh, smart's exactly what I'm going for, believe me."

"Okay then, take care of it."

With those few words, she got a picture of his ideal woman—a collie in heat, basically, but with fewer scruples. Lay out a few lines, bend her over the sofa—then a few weeks later, tell her to *take care of it.*

"Sorry," she said. "Not gonna happen."

He chuckled acidly. "Since when are you maternal?"

"Don't think you know me. We fucked, that's it."

"You're shaking me down."

"I'm filling you in. But yeah, I could make this a problem. Instead, I'm trying to do the right thing. For everybody. But I'm not gonna be able to work here much longer, understand? This ain't about you, it's about money. Introduce me to your guy."

He thought about it, and as he did his lips curled into a grin. The eyes were still scared though. "Who says it's a guy?"

A twinge lit up her lower back. Get used to it, she thought. "Don't push me, Rick. I'm a woman scorned, with a muffin in the oven." She did a quick pivot and headed off. Over her shoulder, she added, "I'm off at two. Set it up."

It didn't happen that night, as it turned out, and that didn't surprise her. What did surprise her was that it happened only two nights later, and she didn't have to hound him half as bad as she'd expected—more surprising still, he hadn't been jiving: It really wasn't a guy.

Her name was Claudia, a Cuban, maybe fifty, could pass for forty, calm dark eyes that waxed and waned between cordial welcome and cold appraisal—a tiny woman, raven-black hair coiled tight into a long braid, body as sleek as a razor, sheathed in a simple black dress. She lived in one of the newer condos at the other end of Fremont, near Sahara, where it turned into Boulder Highway.

Claudia showed them in, dead-bolted the door, offered a cool muscular hand to Sam with a nod, then gestured everyone into the living room: suede furniture, Navajo rugs, ferns. Two fluffed and imperial Persian cats nestled near the window on matching cushions. Across the room, a mobile of tiny tin birds, dozens of them, all painted bright tropical colors, hung from the ceiling. Thing must torment the cats, Sam thought, glancing up as she tucked her skirt against her thighs.

"Like I said before," Rick began, addressing Claudia, "I think this is a bogue idea, but you said okay, so here we are."

Sam resisted an urge to storm over, take two fistfuls of that pampered hair, and rip it out by the roots. She turned to the woman. "Can we talk alone?"

"That doesn't work for me," Rick said.

With the grace of a model, Claudia slowly pivoted toward him. "I think it's for the best." For the sake of his pride, she added, "I'm sure I'll be fine."

That was that. He sulked off to the patio, the two women talked. It didn't take long for Sam to explain her situation, lay out her plan, make it clear she wasn't being flaky or impulsive. She'd thought it through—she didn't want to get even, pick off Rick's customers, nothing like that. "I don't want to hand my baby off to daycare, some stranger. I want to be there. At home."

Claudia eyed her, saying nothing, for what seemed an eternity. Don't look away, Sam told herself. Accept the scrutiny, know your role. But don't act scared.

"There are those," Claudia said finally, "who would find what you just said very peculiar." Her smile seemed a kind of warning, and yet it wasn't without warmth. "I'm sure you realize that."

"I do. But I think you understand."

It turned out she understood only too well—she had a son, Marco, eleven years old, away at boarding school in Seville. "I miss him terribly." She made a sawing motion. "Like someone cut off my arm."

"Why don't you have him here, with you?"

For the first time, Claudia looked away. Her face darkened. "Mothers make sacrifices. It's not all about staying home with the baby."

Sam felt backwards, foolish, hopelessly American. Behold the future, she thought, ten years down the road, doing this, and your kid is where? In the corner of her eye, she saw one of the cats rise sleepily and arch its back. Out on the patio, Rick sat in the moonlight, a sudden red glow as he dragged on his cigarette.

Claudia steered the conversation to terms: Sam would start off buying ounces at two thousand dollars each, which she would divide into grams and eightballs for sale. If things went well, she could move up to a QP—quarter pound—at $7800, build her clientele. She might well plateau at that point, many did. If she was ambitious, though, she could move up to an elbow—for "lb," meaning a pound—with the tacit agreement she would not interfere with Claudia's wholesale trade.

"I want you to look me in the eye, Samantha. Good. Do not confuse my sympathy for weakness. I'm generous by nature. That doesn't mean I'm stupid. I have men who take care of certain matters for me, men not at all like our friend out there." She nodded toward Rick all alone on the moonlit patio. "These men, you will never meet them unless it comes to that. And if it does, the time will have passed for you to say or do anything to help yourself. I trust I'm clear."

The first and oddest thing? She lost five pounds. God, she thought, what have I done? She checked her sheets for blood, then ran to Valley Medical, no appointment, demanded to see her ob-gyn. The receptionist—sagging desert face, kinky gray perm—shot her one of those knowing, gallingly sympathetic looks you never really live down.

"Your body thinks you've got a parasite, dear," the woman said. "Just keep eating."

She did, and she stunned herself, how quickly her habits turned healthy. No more coke, ditto booze—instead a passion for bananas (craving potassium), an obsession with yogurt (good for bone mass, the immune system, the intestinal lining), a sudden interest in whole grains (to keep her regular), citrus (for iron absorption), even liver (prevent anemia). She took to grazing, little meals here and there, to keep the nausea at bay, and when her appetite craved more she turned to her newfound favorite: stir-fry.

She continued working for three months, time enough to groom a clientele—fellow casino rats (her old quitting-time buddies, basically, and their buddies), a few select customers from the Roundup (including, strangely enough, Harry the homely Brit, who came from Manchester, she learned, taught mechanical engineering, vacationed in Cabo most winters, not half the schmuck she'd pegged him for), plus a few locals she decided to trust (the girls at Diva's Hair-and-Nail, the boys at Monte Carlo Tanning Salon, a locksmith named Nick Perino, had a shop just up Fremont Street, total card, used to host a midnight movie show in town)—all of this happening in the shadow of the Metro tower on Stewart Street, all those cops just four blocks away.

Business was brisk. She got current on her bills, socked away a few grand. At sixteen weeks her stomach popped out, like she'd suddenly inflated, and that was the end of cocktail shift. Sam bid it goodbye with no regrets, the red pleated dress, the cowboy hat, the tasseled boots.

From that point forward, she conducted business where she pleased, permitting a trustworthy inner circle to come to her place, the others she met out and about, merrily invisible in her maternity clothes.

The birth was strangely easy, two-hour labor, a snap by most standards, and Sam shed twenty pounds before heading home. The best thing about seeing it go was no longer having to endure strangers—older women especially, riding with her in elevators or standing in line at the store—who would notice the tight globe of her late-term belly and instinctively reach out, stroke the shuddering roundness, cooing in a helpless, mysterious, covetous way that almost rekindled Sam's childhood fear of witches.

As for the last of the weight gain, it all seemed to settle in her chest—first time in her life, she had cleavage. This little girl's been good to you all over, Sam thought—her skin shone, her eyes glowed, she looked happy. Guys seemed to notice, clients especially, but she made sure to keep it all professional: So much as hint at sex with coke in the room, next thing you knew the guy'd be eyeing your muff like it was veal.

Besides, the interest on her end had vanished. Curiously, that didn't faze her. Whatever it was she'd once craved from her lovers she now got from Natalie, feeling it strongest when she nursed, enjoying something she'd secretly thought didn't exist—the kind of fierce unshakeable oneness she'd always thought was just Hollywood. Now she knew better. The crimped pink face, the curled doughy hands, the wispy black strands of impossibly fine hair: "Look at you," she'd whisper, over and over and over.

By the end of two months, she'd pitched all her old clothes, not just the maternity duds. Some old habits got the heave-ho as well: the trashy attitude, slutty speech, negative turns of mind.

Nor would the apartment do anymore—too dark, too small, too blah. The little one deserves better, she told herself, as does her mother. Besides, maybe someone had noticed all the in and out, the visitors night and day. Half paranoia, half healthy faith in who she'd become, she upscaled to a three-bedroom out on Boulder Highway, furnished it in suede, added ferns. She bought two cats.

Nick Perino sat alone in an interview room in the Stewart Street Tower—dull yellow walls, scuffed black linoleum, humming fluorescent light—tapping his thumbs together and cracking his neck as he waited. Finally the door opened, and he tried to muster some advantage, assert control, by challenging the man who entered with, "I don't know you."

The newcomer ignored him, tossing a manila folder onto the table as he drew back his chair to sit. He was in his thirties, shaggy hair, wiry build, dressed in a Runnin' Rebels T-shirt and faded jeans. Something about him said one-time jock. Something else said unmitigated prick.

Looking bored, he opened the file, began leafing through the pages, sipping from a paper cup of steaming black coffee so vile Nick could smell it across the table.

Nick said, "I'm used to dealing with Detective Naughton."

The guy sniffed, chuckling at something he read, suntanned laugh lines fanning out at his eyes. "Yeah, well, he's been rotated out to Traffic. You witness a nasty accident, Chet's your man. But that's not why you're here, is it Mr. Perry?"

"Perino."

The cop glanced up finally. His eyes were scary blue and so bloodshot they looked on fire. Another sniff. "Right. Forgive me."

"Some kind of cold you got there. Must be the air-conditioning."

"It's allergies, actually."

Nick chuckled. Allergic to sleep, maybe. "Speaking of names, you got one?"

"Thornton." He whipped back another page. "Chief calls me James, friends call me Jimmy. You can call me sir."

Nick stood up. He wasn't going to take this, not from some slacker narc half in the bag. "I came here to do you guys a favor."

Still picking through the file, Jimmy Thornton said, "Sit back down, Mr. Perry."

"Don't call me that."

"I said—sit down."

"You think you're talking to some fart-fuck asshole?"

Finally, the cop closed the file. Removing a ballpoint pen from his hip pocket, he began thumbing the plunger manically. "I know who I'm talking to. Chet paints a pretty vivid picture." He nudged the folder across the table. "Want a peek?"

Despite himself, Nick recoiled a little. "Yeah. Maybe I'll do that."

Leaning back in his chair, still clicking the pen, Jimmy Thornton said: "You first blew into town, when was it, '74? Nick Perry, *Chiller Theater*, Saturday midnight. Weasled your way into the job, touting all this 'network experience' back east."

Nick shrugged. "Everybody lies on his resume."

"Not everybody."

"My grandfather came over from Sicily, Perino was the family name. Ellis Island, he changed it to Perry. I just changed it back."

"Yeah, but not till you went to work for Johnny T."

Nick could feel the blood drain from his face. "What are you getting at?"

The cop's smile turned poisonous. "Know what Johnny said about you? You're the only guy in Vegas ever *added* a vowel to the end of his name. Him and his brother, saw you coming at the San Genero Festival, they couldn't run the other way fast enough, even when you worked for them. Worst case of wanna-be-wiseguy they'd ever seen."

Finally, Nick sat back down. "You heard this how? Johnny doesn't, like—"

"Know you were the snitch? Can't answer that. I mean, he probably suspects."

Nick had been a CI in a state case against the Tintoretto brothers for prostitution and drugs, all run through their massage parlor out on Flamingo. Nick remained unidentified during trial, the case made on wiretaps. It seemed a wise play at the time—get down first, tell the story his way, cut a deal, before the roof caved in. He was working as the manager there, only job he could find in town after getting canned at the station—a nigger joke, pussy in the punch line, didn't know he was on the air.

"All the employees got a pass," Nick said, "not just me. Johnny couldn't know for sure unless you guys told him."

"Relax." Another punctuating sniff. "Nobody around here told him squat. We keep our promises, Mr. Perry."

Nick snorted. "Not from where I sit."

"Excuse me?" The guy leaned in. "Chet bent over backwards for you, pal. Set you up, perfect location, right downtown. Felons aren't supposed to be locksmiths."

"Most of that stuff on my sheet was out of state. And it got expunged."

A chuckle: "Now there's a word."

"Vacated, sealed, whatever."

"Because Chet took care of it. And how do you repay him?"

"I don't know what you're talking about."

"Every time business gets slow, you send that fat freak you call a nephew out to the apartments off Maryland Parkway—middle of the night, spray can of Super Glue, gum up a couple hundred

locks. You can bank on at least a third of the calls, given your location—think we don't know this?"

"Who you talking to, Jack Lally over at All-Night Lock'n'Key?
You wanna hammer a crook, there's your guy, not me."

"Doesn't have thirty-two grand in liens from the Tax Commission on his business, though, does he?"

Nick blanched. They already knew. They knew everything. "I
got screwed by my bookkeeper. Look, I came here with information. You wanna hear it or not?"

"In exchange for getting the Tax Commission off your neck."

"Before they shut me down, yeah. That asking so much?"

Jimmy Thornton opened the manila folder to the last page,
clicked his pen one final time, and prepared to write. "That
depends."

Sam sat in the shade at the playground two blocks from her apartment, listening to Nick go on. He'd just put in new locks at her
apartment—she changed them every few weeks now, just being
careful—and, stopping here to drop off the new keys, he'd sat
down on the bench beside her, launching in, some character
named Jimmy.

"He's a stand-up guy," Nick said. "Looker, too. You'll like him."

"You pitching him as a customer, or a date?"

Nick raised his hands, a coy smile, "All things are possible,"
inflecting the words with that *paisano* thing he fell into sometimes.

Natalie slept in her stroller, exhausted from an hour on the
swings, the slide, the merry-go-round. Sam wondered about that,
whether it was really good for kids to indulge that giddy instinct
for dizziness. Where did it lead?

"Tell me again how you met this guy."

"He wanted a wall safe, I installed it for him."

She squinted in the sun, shaded her eyes. "What's he need a
wall safe for?"

"That's not a question I ask. You want, I provide. That's business, as you well know."

She suffered him a thin smile. With the gradual expansion of her clientele—no one but referrals, but even so her base had almost doubled—she'd watched herself pulling back from people, even old friends, a protective, judicious remove. And that was lonely-making.

Worse, she'd gotten used to it, and that seemed a kind of living death. The only grace was Natalie, but even there, the oneness she'd felt those first incredible months, that had changed as well. She still adored the girl, loved her to pieces, that wasn't the issue. Little girls grow up, their mothers get lonely, where's the mystery? She just hadn't expected it to start so soon.

"He's a contractor," Nick went on, "works down in Henderson. I saw the blueprints and, you know, stuff in his place when I was there. Look, you don't need the trade, forget about it. But I thought, I dunno, maybe you'd like the guy."

"I don't need to like him."

"I meant 'like' as in 'do business.'"

Sam checked the stroller. Natalie had her thumb in her mouth, eyes closed, her free hand balled into a fist beneath her chin.

"You know how this works," Sam said. "He causes trouble, anything at all—I mean this, Nick—anything at all comes back at me, it's on you, not just him."

They met at the Elephant Walk, and it turned out Nick was right, the guy turned heads—an easy grace, cowboy shoulders, lady-killer smile. He ordered Johnny Walker Black with a splash, and Sam remembered, from her days working cocktail, judging men by their drinks. He'd ordered wisely.

And yet there were signs—a jitter in the hands, a slight head tic, the red in those killer blue eyes. Then again, if she worried that her customers looked like users, who would she sell to?

"Nick says you're a contractor."

He shook his head. "Project manager."

"There's a difference?"

"Sometimes. Not often enough." He laughed and the laugh was self-effacing, one more winning trait. "I buy materials, hire the subs, make sure the bonds are current and we're all on time. But the contractor's the one with his license on the line."

"Sounds demanding."

"Everything's demanding. If it means anything."

She liked that answer. "And to relax, you . . . ?"

He shrugged. "I've got a bike, a Triumph, old bandit 350, gathering dust in my garage." Another self-effacing smile. "Amazing how boring you can sound when stuff like that comes out."

Not boring, she thought. Just normal. "Ever been married?"

A fierce little jolt shot through him. "Once. Yeah. Highschool sweetheart kind of thing. Didn't work out."

She got the hint, and steered the conversation off in a different direction. They talked about Nick, the stories they'd heard him tell about his TV days, wondering which ones to believe. Sam asked about how the two men had met, got the same story she'd heard from Nick, embellished a little, not too much. Things were, basically, checking out.

Sensing it was time, she signaled the bartender to settle up. "Well, it's been very nice meeting you, Jimmy. I have to get home. The sitter awaits, with the princess."

"Nick told me. Natalie, right? Have any pictures?"

She liked it when men asked to see pictures. It said something. She took out her wallet, opened it to the snapshots.

"How old?"

"Fifteen months. Just."

"She's got her mother's eyes."

"She's got more than that, sadly."

"No. Good for her." He returned her wallet, hand not trembling now. Maybe it was the scotch, maybe the conversation. "She's a beauty. Changed your life, I'll bet."

Yes, Sam thought, that she has. Maybe we'll talk about that sometime. Next time. "Have kids?"

Very subtly, his eyes hazed. "Me? No. Didn't get that far, which is probably for the best. Got some nephews and nieces, that's it for now."

"Uncle Jimmy."

He rattled the ice in his glass, traveled somewhere with his thoughts. "I like kids. Want kids. My turn'll come." Then, brightening suddenly: "I'd be up for a play date some time, with Natalie. I mean, if that doesn't sound too weird."

That's how it started, same playground near the apartment. And he hadn't lied, he hit it off with Natalie at first sight—stunning, really. He was a natural, carrying her on his shoulders to the park, guiding her up the stairs to the slide, taking it easy on the swing. He had Sam cradle her in her lap on the merry-go-round, spun them both around in the sun-streaked shade. Natalie shrieked, Sam laughed; it was that kind of afternoon.

They brought Natalie home, put her down for her nap, then sat on the porch with drinks—the usual for him, Chablis for her. The sun beat down on the freshly watered lawn, a hot desert wind rustling the leaves of the imported elm trees.

Surveying the grounds, he said, "Nice place. Mind if I ask your monthly nut?"

"Frankly?"

He chuckled. "Sorry. Professional curiosity. I was just doing the math in my head, tallying costs, wondering what kind of return the developer's getting."

She smiled wanly. "I don't like to think about it." That seemed as good a way as any to change the subject. "So, Nick says you wanted to ask me something."

Suddenly, he looked awkward, a hint of a blush. It suited him.

"Well, yeah. I suppose . . . You know. Sometimes . . ." He gestured vaguely.

She said, "Don't make me say it for you."

He cleared his throat. "I could maybe use an eightball. Sure."

There, she thought. Was that so hard? "Let's say a gram. I don't know you."

"How about two?"

It was still below the threshold for a special felony, which an eightball, at 3.5 grams, wasn't. "Two-forty, no credit."

"No friend-of-a-friend discount?"

"Nick told you there would be?"

"No, I just—"

"There isn't. There won't be."

He raised his hands, surrender. "Okay." He reached into his hip pocket for his wallet. "Mind if I take a shot while I'm here?"

She collected her glass, rose from her chair. "I'd prefer it, actually. Come on inside." She gestured for him to have a seat on the couch, disappeared into her bedroom, and returned with the coke, delivering the two grams with a mirror, a razor blade, a straw.

As always, a stranger in the house, one of the cats sat in the corner, blinking. The other hid. Sam watched as Jimmy chopped up the lines, an old hand. He hoovered the first, offered her the mirror. She declined. He leaned back down, finished up, tugged at his nose.

"That's nice," he said, collecting the last few grains on his finger, rubbing it into his gums. When his hand came away, it left a smile behind. "I'm guessing Mannitol. I mean, you've got it around, right?"

Sam took a sip of her wine. He was referring to a baby laxative commonly used as a cutting agent. Cooly, she said, "Let a girl have her secrets."

He nodded. "Sorry. That was out of line."

"Don't worry about it." She toddled her glass. "So—will there be anything else?"

She didn't mean to sound coy, but even so she inwardly cringed as she heard the words out loud. The way he looked at her, it was clear he was trying to decipher the signal. And maybe, on some level, she really did mean something.

"No," he said. "I think that's it. Mind if I take one last look before I leave?"

And so that's how they wrapped it up, standing in the doorway to Natalie's room, watching her sleep.

"Such a pretty little creature," he whispered. "Gotta confess, I'm jealous."

Back in his car, Jimmy horned the rest of the first gram, then drove to the Roundup, a little recon, putting faces to names, customers of Sam's that Nick had told him about: card dealers, waitresses, a gambler named Harry Thune, homely Brit, the usual ghastly teeth.

After that, he drove to the strip mall on Charleston where the undercover unit had its off-site location, an anonymous set of offices with blinds drawn, a sign on the door reading "Halliwell Partners, Ltd."

He logged in, parked at his desk, and wrote up his report: the purchase of one gram Cocaine HCL, field tested positive with Scott reagent—blue, pink, then blue with pink separation in successive ampoules after agitation—said gram supplied by Samantha Pitney, White Female Adult.

He invented an encounter far more fitting with department guidelines than the one that had taken place, wrote it out, signed it, then drove to Metro tower, walked in the back entrance, and delivered the report to his sergeant, an old hand named Becker, who sent Jimmy on to log the gram into evidence. Jimmy said hey to the secretaries on his way through the building, went back to his car, moved $120 from his personal wallet to his buy wallet to cover the gram he'd pilfered, then planned his next step.

The following two buys were the same, two grams, and she seemed to grow more comfortable. He got bumped up to an eight-ball, and not long after that he rose to two. He always took a taste right there at the apartment, while they were talking, one of the perks of the job.

Later, he'd either log it in as-is, claiming the shortage had been used for field-testing, or he'd pocket the light one, chop it up into grams, then drive to Henderson—or, on weekends, all the way to Laughlin—work the bars, a little business for himself, cover his costs, a few like minds, deputies he knew.

He found himself oddly divided on Sam. You could see she'd tried to cultivate an aura: the wry feminine reserve, the earth tones, all the talk about yoga and studying for her real estate license. Maybe it was motherhood, all that scrubbed civility, trying to be somebody. Then again, maybe it was cokehead pretence.

Regardless, little things tripped her up, those selfless moments, more and more frequent, when she let him see behind the mask. Trouble was, from what he could tell, the mask had more to offer.

He'd nailed a witness or two in his time, never a smooth move, but nothing compared to bedding a suspect. As fluid as things had become morally since he'd started working undercover, he'd never lost track of that particular red line. That didn't mean he didn't entertain the thought—throwing her over his shoulder, carrying her into her room, dropping her onto the bed, watching her hair unfurl from the soft thudding impact.

Would she try to fight him off—no, that would just be part of the dance. Soon enough she'd draw him down, a winsome smile, hands clasped behind his neck, a few quick nibbles in her kiss, now and then a good firm bite. And was she one of those who showed you around the castle—how hard to pinch the nipples, how many fingers inside, the hand clasped across her mouth as she came— or would she want you to find all that out for yourself? Playing coy, demure, wanting you to take command, maybe even scare her. How deep would she like it, how slow, how rough? Would she come in rolling pulses, or one big back-arching slam?

Then again, of course, there was Natalie. Truth be told, she was the one who'd stolen his heart. And it was clear her poor deluded mother loved her, but love's not enough—never is, never has been.

He remembered Sam asking, in their first face-to-face, about his marriage, about kids. You're not a cop till your first divorce, he thought, go through the custody horseshit. Lose. Bobby was his name. Seven years old now. Somewhere.

When he found himself thinking like that, he also found himself developing a mean thirst. And when he drank, he liked a whiff, to steady the ride, ice it. And so soon he'd be back at Ms. Pitney's door, repeating the whole sad process, telling himself the same wrong stories, wanting everything he had no right to.

Six weeks into things, he asked, "What made you get into this business anyway?"

She was sitting on the sofa, legs tucked beneath her, wearing a new perfume. From the look on her face, you would've thought he'd spat on the floor. "No offense, but that came out sounding ugly."

He razored away at three chalky lines. "Didn't mean it that way. Sorry."

She thought about it for a moment, searching the ceiling with her eyes. "The truth? I wanted to be a stay-at-home mom."

He had to check himself, to keep from laughing, and yet he could see it. So her, thinking that way. "Why not marry the father?"

Again, she took her time before answering, but this time she didn't scour the ceiling, she gazed into his face.

Admittedly, he was a little ragged: His mouth was dry, his eyes were jigging up and down, his pupils were bloated. And his hands, yeah, a mild but noticeable case of the shakes.

"Some men are meant to be fathers," she said. "Some men aren't."

Sam let one of the Claudia's Persians settle in her lap, pressing her skirt with its paws. The other cat lay in its usual spot, on the cushion by the window, lolling in the sun. Natalie sat in her stroller, gumming an apple slice, while Claudia attended her ferns, using a tea kettle for a watering can.

"I usually charge thirty, which is already low, but I'd trim a little more, say twenty-eight." She was talking in thousands of dollars, the price for a pound—or an elbow, in the parlance.

"That's still a little steep for me."

"You could cut your visits here by half. More."

"Is that a problem?" Secretly, Sam loved coming here. She thought of it as Visiting Mother.

Over her shoulder, Claudia said, "You know what I mean."

"Maybe I'll ratchet up another QP. I don't want any more than that in the house."

Claudia bent to reach a pot on the floor. "The point is to get it *out* of the house."

Well duh, Sam thought, feeling judged, a headache looming like a thunderhead just behind her eyes. She was getting them more and more. "There's something else I'd like to talk over, actually. It's about Natalie."

Claudia stopped short. "Is something wrong?"

"No. Not yet. I mean, there's nothing to worry about. But if anything ever happened to me, I don't know who would take care of her."

A disagreeable expression crossed Claudia's face, part disdain, part calculation, part suspicion. "You have family."

"Not local. And not that I trust, frankly."

"What exactly are you asking?"

"I was wondering if she could stay with you. If anything ever happened, I mean."

Claudia put the tea kettle down and came over to a nearby chair, crossing her legs as she sat. "Have you noticed any cars following you lately?"

"It's not like that."

"Any new neighbors?"

"That wasn't what I meant. I meant if I got sick, or was in a car accident." She glanced over at Natalie. The apple slice was nubby and brown, and both it and her fingers were glazed with saliva.

Claudia said, "I couldn't just walk in, take your child. Good Lord."

Her voice rippled, a blast of heat. Sam said, "I'm sorry, I didn't mean—"

"A dozen agencies would be involved, imagine the questions." She rose from her chair, straightened her skirt, shot a toxic glance at Natalie that said: Your mother can't protect you. "Now what quantity are you here for? I have things to do."

Sergeant Becker called Jimmy in, told him to close the door. He was a big man, the kind who could lord over you even sitting down. "This Pitney thing, I've gone over the reports." He picked up a pencil, drummed it against his blotter. "Your buys are light."

He stared into Jimmy's whirling eyes. Jimmy did his best to stare right back.

"I'm a gentleman. I always offer the lady a taste."

"She needs to sample her own coke?"

"Not sampling, indulging. And there's always some lost in the field test."

"Think a jury will buy that? Think I buy that?"

"You want me to piss in a cup?"

Becker pretended to think about that, then leaned forward, lowering his voice. "No. That's what I most definitely do not want you to do. Look, I'll stand up for you, but it's time you cleaned house. You need some time, we'll work it out. There's a program, six weeks, over in Bullhead City, you can use an assumed name. It's the best deal you're gonna get. In the meantime, wrap this up. You've got your case, close it out."

Jimmy felt a surge of bile boiling in his stomach—at the thought of rehab, sure, the shame of it, the tedium, but not just that. "Like when?"

"Like now." Becker's whole face said: Look at yourself. "Why wait?"

Jimmy pictured Sam in her sundress, face raised to the light, hand in her hair. Moisture pooling in the hollow of her throat. Lipstick glistening in the heat.

He said, "There's a kid involved."

Becker stood up behind his desk. They were done. "Get CPS involved, that's what they're there for. Make the calls, do the paperwork, get it over with."

"For chrissake, don't over-think it. Sounds like the last nice guy in Vegas."

It was Mandy talking, Sam's old best friend at the Roundup. She'd stopped by on her way to work, a gram for the shift, and now was lingering, shoes off, stocking feet on the coffee table, toes jigging in their sheer cocoon. They were watching Natalie play, noticing how her focus lasered from her ball to her bear, back to the ball, moving on to her always mysterious foot, then a housefly buzzing at the sliding glass door.

"Dating the clientele," Sam said, "is such a chump move."

"Rules have exceptions. Otherwise, they wouldn't be rules."

Natalie hefted herself onto her feet, staggered to the sliding glass door, reached for the fly—awestruck, gentle.

"He's got a bit of a problem." Sam tapped the side of her nose.

"You can clean him up. Woman's work."

"I don't need that kind of project."

"If you don't mind my asking, how long's it been since you got laid?"

Admittedly, sometimes when Jimmy was there, Sam felt the old urge uncoiling inside her, slithering around. "To be honest, I do mind you asking."

They weren't close anymore, just one of those things. To hide her disappointment, Mandy softly clapped her hands at Natalie. "Hey sweetheart, come on over. Sit with Auntie Man a little while."

The little girl ignored her, still enchanted by the fly. It careened about the room—ceiling, lamp shade, end table—then whirled back to the sliding glass door, a glossy green spec in a flaring pool of sunlight.

"She doesn't like me."

"She can be persnickety." Sam glanced at the clock. "Don't take it personally."

"You think if you let this guy know you were interested, he'd respond?"

Sam felt another headache coming on. Each one seemed worse than the last now. "It's not an issue."

"You're the one playing hard to get, not him."

Jimmy's last visit, Sam had almost thrown herself across his lap, wanting to feel his arms around her. Just that. But that was everything, could be everything. "I've given him a few openings. Nothing obvious, but since when do you need to be obvious with men?"

Mandy crossed her arms across her midriff, as though suddenly chilled. "Maybe he's queer."

Once Mandy was gone, Sam tucked Natalie in for the midday nap with her blue plush piglet, brushing the hair from the little girl's face to plant a kiss on her brow. Leaving the bedroom door slightly ajar—Natalie would never drop off otherwise—Sam fled to her own room and took a Demerol. The pain was flashing through her sinuses now, even pulsing into her spine.

Noticing the time, she changed into a cinched sleeveless dress, freshened her lipstick, her eyeliner. Jimmy had said he'd stop by, and she still couldn't quite decide whether to push the ball into his end of the court or abide by her own better instincts and let it go.

Running a mental inventory of his pros and cons, she admitted he was a joy to look at, had a soldier's good manners, adored Natalie. He was also a flaming cokehead, with the predictable sidekick, a blind thirst.

Those things trended downward in her experience, not a ride she wanted to share. Loneliness is the price you pay for keeping things uncomplicated, she thought, pressing a tissue between her lips.

She heard a shuffle of steps on the walkway out front, but instead of ringing the bell, whoever it was pounded at the door. A voice she didn't recognize called out her name, then: "Police! Open the door."

To her shame, she froze. Out of the corner of her eye she saw three men cluster on the patio—shirtsleeves, sunglasses, protective vests—and her mouth turned to dust.

The front door crashed in, brutal shouts of "On the floor!" and shortly she was facedown, being handcuffed, feeling guilty and terrified and stupid and numb while cops thrashed everywhere, asserting claim to every room.

When they pulled her to her feet, it was Jimmy standing there, wearing a vest like the others, his police card hanging by a thong around his neck. The Demerol not having yet kicked in, her head crackled and throbbed with a new burst of pain, and she feared she might hurl right there on the floor.

"Tell us where everything is, and we won't take the place apart," he said, regarding her with a look of such contemptuous loathing she actually thought he might spit in her face. And I deserve it, she told herself, how stupid I've been, at the same time thinking: Now who's the creature?

She could smell the scotch on his breath, masked with spearmint. So that's what it was, she thought, all that time, the drink, the coke. Mr. Sensitive drowning his guilt. Or was even his guilt phony?

She said, "What about Natalie?" In her room, the little girl was mewling, confused, scared.

Jimmy glanced off toward the sound, eyes dull as lead. "She's a ward of the court now. They'll farm her out, foster home—"

Sam felt the room close in, a sickly shade of white. "Why are you doing this?"

Almost imperceptibly, he stiffened. A weak smile. "I'm doing this?"

"Why are you being such a prick about it?"

He leaned in. His eyes were electric. "You're a mother."

You miserable hypocrite, she thought, trying to muster some disgust of her own, but instead her knees turned liquid. He caught her before she fell, duck-walked her toward the sofa, let her drop—at which point a woman with short sandy hair came out of Natalie's bedroom, carrying the little girl. Her eyes were puffy with sleep but she was squirming, head swiveling this way and that. She began to cry. Sam shook off her daze, turned to hide the handcuffs, calling out, "Just do what the lady says, baby. I'll come get you as soon as I can," but the girl started shrieking, kicking—and then was gone.

"Get a good look?" Jimmy said. "Because that's the last you'll see of her."

He was performing for the other cops, the coward. "You can't do that."

"No? Consider it done."

Sam struggled to her feet. "You can't . . . No . . ."

He nudged her back down. She tried to kick him but he pushed her legs aside. Crouching down, he locked them against his body with one arm, his free hand gripping her chin. Voice lowered, eyes fixed on hers—and, finally, she thought she saw something hovering behind the savage bloodshot blue, something other than the arrogance and hate, something haunted, like pity, even love—he whispered, "Listen to me, Sam. I want to help you. But you've gotta help me. Understand? Give me a name. It's that simple. A name and we work this out. I'll do everything I can, that's a promise, for you, for Natalie—everything. But you've gotta hold up your end. Otherwise . . ."

He let his voice trail away into the nothingness he was offering. For Sam knew where this led, she remembered the words exactly: *I have men who take care of certain matters . . . The time will have passed for you to say or do anything to help yourself . . .*

And there it was: her daughter or her life, she couldn't save both. Maybe not today or tomorrow but someday soon, Claudia's threat would materialize, assuming a face and form but no name—the police would promise protection, but the desert was littered with their failures—and Sam would realize this is it, that pitiless point in time when she would finally know: Which was she? One of those who tried to kick and claw and scream her way out, even though it was hopeless. Or one of those who, seeing there was no escape, calmly said, I'm ready. I've been ready for a long, long while.

RETURNING TO THE KNIFE

Let me say first that the knife was not my idea. I don't mean, of course, that I know whose idea it was. Or that—let's be serious—that the knife is just an idea. I'm not, like, crazy.

I know Colette has said some things, why else would you be here? Sure, take out your microphone, turn on your recorder, take notes, be my guess. Guest, excuse me. I have zip to hide. Put it in your paper, post it on the web, scream it from the chimneys. I appreciate the opportunity to slice my face.

Sorry. I meant, you know, state my case.

Sleep's been a bit iffy lately.

I hold no grudges—Colette, Rachel, the little man at the bottom of the well—Christ, we're all prone to a little excess, no? Mindless rants, wild confessions, shrieks of blame. Life gets lonely. The need to grip someone by the lapels and yodel curses in his face can get the better of anybody. Especially Colette, who frankly could use a dog. Maybe a cat. A parrot who quotes Rumi in Arabic. Something to occupy her imagination.

Not that pets benefit from an imaginative owner, of course. Try filling the dinner bowl of a half-starved rottweiler with a groovy idea.

But returning to the knife.

For the sake of argument, let's grant your assumption that I put the dog outside. This would, as you suggest, make it easier for me to approach Rachel—Colette, rather—without being detected. The dog was not just company, he was protection. I mean, this is obvious.

There are those, I'm sure, who see little contradiction in an animal devoted not just to affection but defense. And yet—indulge me for a moment—I can't see a slobbery, lick-his-niblets-then-your-face mutt being much good against an intruder—can you?

Yes, they bark, but so? The neighbors say, "Oh it's that damn yip-yap poop machine again," and they call Animal Control, not the police. As if Animal Control, they see an intruder, they're gonna put a cap in his ass. Unless it's a raccoon.

But the point is, Colette doesn't have a dog. Ixnay on the ogday. As I said, it might be better if she did, but she doesn't. There. So we must be talking about Rachel.

Except Rachel, she has this thing about sharp objects. So a knife? Out of the question. She refuses to have so much as a letter opener in the house. Go on, read her blog if you doubt me. She lives in abject terror that somewhere somebody is in pain. Only in California, huh?

She's *depressed* is what she is. When the days grow short and dark like this, something comes over her. She sits in that voluptuous red chair of hers with her head bowed and she pats her hands together as though keeping time to a train of thought that any moment might tumble off the rails.

She goes days without bathing, wears the same clothes weeks on end—I mean, I find this disgusting, but it's all right there on the Internet, for the world to see—refuses to eat anything but rice cakes and cruciferous greens. Strange word—like she wants to be nailed to a broccolini. Or get scourged at the pillar outside Mollie Stone's. If this is what they mean by a California girl, I'll take the Midwest farmer's daughter. *And her little dog, too.*

I love that movie. *We're not in Kant's ass, anymore, Toto. . . .*

Getting back to Rachel, or Colette for that matter—where do women like this come from—do they just sprout up from the soil out here? And we're talking about a knockout, movie-star cheekbones, Amazon thighs, breasts like the goddamn *Hindenburg.* Well, before it caught fire. But what difference does beauty make when your mind's a mudslide?

So no, given the fact we're discussing a knife, we're most definitely concerned with Colette. You're mistaken about the dog. That's the only way to explain it. I don't care what the neighbors say.

Mother of Christ. The neighbors. Don't make me choke on my kugel. What is so horrible, so monstrous, so bone-chilling and fearsome about a man sitting in his car, listening to his iPod, eating pastry, waiting. Granted, there are only a few houses in her hamlet, no police, too far out, unincorporated area, the boonies. Paradise, if you're a psycho. Or a raccoon.

I had something to discuss with her, we were getting nowhere over the phone—no, no, listen to me—we were getting nowhere over the phone, nowhere by email, Colette cut off payment on her credit card, I responded by filing a lawsuit online, double damages plus legal fees, get her goddamn attention. I told her I knew where she lived, right there off the Pacific Highway, cute little bungalow shaded by eucalyptus trees facing the inlet, she couldn't hide from me. I'd slit her miserable throat—figure of speech, okay? I'm not that kind of guy and besides, like I said, there was no knife.

She responds by calling the local sheriff. Filed a complaint for harassment—have I mentioned the crazy wicked things she said to me? I'm the one who's been harassed, middle of the night, these messages—understand?

Anyway, it was time somebody took the initiative and grabbed his keys, got in his car, drove all the way from his comfy home in San Francisco across the goddamn Golden Gate into the land of sprouts and bulgur brownies and wheatgrass colonics and made an effort. I did this. I made, may I say it, the fucking effort.

What do I get for my trouble? Some arugula-chewing kale-belching bovine neurotic staring out her window like a pothead paranoid, bitching and moaning about the yippy-yap dog next door and then she sees me and Holy Mother of Meltdowns, call the police, I mean the sheriff, call Animal Control, call the wizard—

Excuse me? How do I . . . I *don't* know. Okay, I confess. Jesus Holy Hell—hang me by the nutsack, you want. I do not know for a fact that the neighbor lady eats arugula. Or kale. I *assumed*. So sue me. Figure of speech, sporadic license. I mean, who else but crazy people eat that stuff? Exhibit A: Colette. I mean Rachel.

Back to the knife. By which I mean: There was no knife, okay? As for the dog . . .

Did you know that male walruses in captivity become sexually aroused by the sound of power tools? I'm not making that up. Google it, you don't believe me.

I run a simple business. I sell pillows, throw pillows to be exact, hand-embroidered, designer fabrics, imported from Turkey, or Ireland, very elegant. It seems such a simple thing, but the demand for throw pillows is astonishing. Who knew?

The problem, as you can imagine, is storage. The overhead will kill you, especially in San Francisco, rents are insane, smother your business like a baby in its crib. I can't keep stock hanging around, and that means I'm not big on returns—is that, like, suddenly an indictable offense?

So—just because somebody whines and moans about a refund, an exchange, credit on their account, doesn't mean I take things back. Merchants have rights too, you know. This thing, what people say—*the customer is always right*—what lunatic honestly believes such a thing? Only in California, I swear.

I am no different than one million other guys hustling to shake a buck. The Internet gives me a very tidy way of attracting customers, showing my product, taking orders, collecting payment, mailing delivery. The only difference is, I understand how the whole thing works.

I was a gizmo guru in Silicon Valley before the dot-com crash, I understand ranking strategies, stacking algorithms, how you get noticed on the web—and how you can disappear without a trace, just like that. Creative destruction, that is capitalism. A drowning pig goes down slower than the average business. Make rain while the sun shines, that's my motto.

No. I didn't say I was from Turkey, I said the pillows were from Turkey. Or Ireland. Half my family comes from Kosovo, the other half Ulster, I've never been either place, well maybe once, when I was, I dunno, six? Twelve? Twenty? It's stamped on my passport but that's another thing, my name is not Osman, I don't care what your records show. My name is Archibald. Look it up, you don't believe me.

Getting back to this trick with the search engines, it came to me by accident. I began to get complaints—these loons, these crazy people, you can't call them liars because they believe their own ridiculous bullshit but they order something, you send it to them—zoom, next day, clean as a thistle, I have happy customers too, you know—but some, I won't call them scumbags, they just change their mind, but do they say that?

No, of course not. No one takes responsibility anymore.

They say: You didn't send the right pillow. I ordered satin, you sent chenille. I wanted scarlet, you gave me crimson. I asked for teal, you mailed me turquoise—yadda yadda, lies, all lies, make me want to puke up a poodle.

They call the number on the website—you can see, my office is my home, but they call all hours of the night, I haven't slept in weeks—no, no, listen to me, they are the ones calling me, not the other way around—they call and you wouldn't believe the filthy nasty California things they leave on my machine. It's incredible, never mind the stinking noxious awful stuff they say to my face. On the phone, I mean, when I pick up. They say *I'm* abusive? It's self-defense, okay?

I'd play one of the messages for you but I can't stand to have them around, I just delete them as soon as they come in. But I'm telling you, there are psychos out there. And they all want pillows.

The knife, yes, I'm getting to that. Keep your horses on.

So I realized, once I began to get complaints, and people started writing things on the web about the company, going on these ombudsman websites, complaint boards, make-your-own review pages—Yelp, Get Satisfaction, California Consumer, Better Business Bureau, FBI, Homeland Security, Interpol—more and more, angry and more angry, a dozen, two dozen, a dozen of dozens—what do you know, my site begins to rise on the search engine rankings.

Not just a little. Like Noah's ark lifted by the rain. Like the good witch ascending to heaven. And I get more and more customers. Who needs ads? As long as people are unhappy, I have the win-win.

Search engines, they're like merry little imbeciles, what do you call them—idiot savants—they just count. They don't care if what's said is nice or not nice, they just count count count. And so complaints or compliments, it makes no difference, all publicity is good publicity, you can't keep bad news down.

And there is the secret: The worse I was to these loony-tune bats, the better it was for business. Talk about creative destruction. But hey, that makes me the bad guy. Fine. Sue me. Shoot me. Cut off my—

Did you know that walruses have a bone in their penises? It's, like, three feet long. A yardstick made out of bone. Eskimos use them for pool cues, I'm not making that up.

Don't let these women fool you, they are not Little Red Riding Crop. You have done your homework on Colette? Then you know she works for Regimar Financial, mortgage servicer, just got the bejeebers sued out of them by investors they were scamming—I swear, you want to look into a racket, that's what you should be investigating, leave me alone. But no, of course, I have a penis, I have a funny accent, psychos never lie, I am the big bad wolfman. Fine. Cut off my head, my tongue, my three-foot salami. With a knife. Except there is no knife.

So this Colette, the one with the dog—I told you, Rachel could use a dog, or a bird, something, but she won't have one, allergic she says, too busy eating rainbow chard—or wait, I mean Colette, I was right the first time—anyway, she harasses me day and night, leaves these yodeling banshee messages on my machine, calling me things that would make a Portuguese sailor cut out his molars.

Luckily she's also bitching up a storm on the web, all the other misery-mongers chiming in, a choir of whiners, so I'm making out okay, business is buzzing, except I'm getting, like, not one wink of sleep, my wife is trying to ovulate, and finally I just say: Enough! Fine. Let's meet face-to-face, earth lady, earth mother, psycho demon witch from Oz.

If she's telling you she never agreed to this . . . Jesus in a nut-shell, how can I keep up with the lies?

So I've been waiting for hours, parked along the road beneath the eucalyptus trees, smells like a throat lozenge out there, I see no car in the drive, finally I say: To hell with this. Walk up to the door, ring the bell.

No answer.

I think, maybe she's in the back, she can't hear the chime, I'll go see.

Next thing I know, there I am in the kitchen. Back door was open, no one answered. I'm concerned, I'm not a bad person, I let myself in and yes, the dog went out. Lock the door. Good. Safe. Fine.

Okay, maybe I gave him a little nudge—you seen the thing? Like a Shetland pony, that dog. Anyway, I'm in, he's out, sure I gave him a little boot but he lived, am I right?

Now he's yapping away outside and the fat miserable wretch next door is dialing 9-1-1 because she gets the hives when the dog starts barking—talk about wackos, there's a record of her calls, long as your small intestines, calls about the dog, I mean, or raccoons—and no, she doesn't dial Animal Control this time, she wants the constable, the sheriff, the wizard. Why? Ask her. Blame me. I don't care anymore.

Meanwhile, I'm trying to figure out if Colette is okay—like I said, I'm a nice person—turns out she's been home the whole time—who knew?—and I find her in the living room, like a mummy without the bandages, buried in that monstrous red chair—it's as big as an altar, this chair—and she's gnawing away on raw barley and organic mustard greens and throwing back burdock root tea—may God strike me down if I'm lying—and she looks up at me with those sunken movie star eyes and I have her pillow in my hands, the chenille not the satin, crimson not scarlet, and I hold it up and say—I mean, what else is there *to* say—*Is this what you fucking want?*

You see what I'm saying? There was no knife. I'm a businessman. I have mortgages to pay. My wife wants to have a baby, it's not as easy as it sounds. Why am I the monster?

Now, let me guess, I can imagine what you're about to say. What about Rachel? Talk about a nut job—did you know she works at the zoo, the aquarium, SeaWorld, some such place. Her job? She tries to get the animals to screw. To mate. But they don't want to—again, you don't believe me, check out her blog. The animals are dying out, you can't get them in the mood anymore. Something about not living in the wild, living in the zoo instead, or the aquarium, Marine World, Sex Flags, the place she works, whatever it is. They've tried everything, panda porn, naughty puppets, even piping in Barry White—I'm not making that up. The females ovulate but the males don't care. They're more interested in power tools.

Wait. Maybe it's Colette's blog where I read this. No. I don't think so. You wouldn't believe how much garbage I've read online lately, it's hard to keep it straight. And sleep, Jesus marry Joseph, I can't tell you the last time I had some decent sleep.

Regardless, Rachel, she makes these huge PVC vaginas then pumps them full of warm petroleum jelly or VapoRub or Jiffy Lube, trying to trick the male into shooting his walrus wad, so they can blow-dart the spung into the bazoo of the female.

I ask you—is that a job for a sane person? Should I take it personally if she calls me a thieving sociopath?

Actually, what she called me was a mad dog.

Which finally explains the knife.

Somehow the dog got back in—I think the hefty nasty neighbor woman had a key—and Rachel is screaming at me and I am as serious as cancer all I was doing was holding up the pillow, Mister Nice Guy, coming all the way out to her godforsaken house, Little Hippy Hamlet, middle of I swear-to-God nowhere—Marin housewife my ass, crazy screwball vegan from hell—but there I am, delivering the thing she said she wanted all along, silk not chenille, turquoise not teal, fine, good, I'm happy, she's happy, win-win, go home, you know?

But suddenly this walrus-sized dog is coming at me and there was, maybe, now that I think about it, I can't say for sure but, perhaps, a knife. Or a power tool. Maybe a pool cue. But I had to defend myself—okay? You've seen the pictures, yes, I'm not making it up, the dog was a moose, a mountain with legs. And teeth.

Ever been bit by a dog? Ever had a rabies shot? I'd rather spend a summer in hell with my Uncle Orhan than do that again. And the parrot is going off in Arabic—I'm not making that up—and the neighbor is screaming, *It's a terrorist, Osama bin Haydn. And he's killed the dog!*

But think for a second. None of that, even if it were true—and I admit nothing—but for the sake of argument, assume it's all, every word, cross my heart, hang me by the yardstick, true. It still does not magically make me a wolfman or a madman or a bad man or a California Man or al Qaeda nor am I the walrus ooh-coo-ca-choo.

And like I said, I don't care if she complains, complaints are good for business, and maybe, sure, I show up, scare her—*ooga booga boo!*—she goes on the web, writes a lot more emails or blah-dee-blogs or whatever, all her idiot psycho women friends chime in, screaming heebie-jeebies—and behold: my site just keeps ascending in the Google rankings, like an angel, like the *Hindenburg*. Before it caught fire.

Bile is good for business, what can I say, I'm supposed to feel bad? There's no crime in making a profit, not yet anyway. Except, of course, in California.

So, back to Rachel, or Colette, I might scare her, but harm her? She's like the goose that lays the golden emails. Even if I *was* there to hurt somebody, why would I kill the dog? The dog didn't order the pillow—you see?

All of which proves, of course, that I was never at Rachel's, I was at Colette's, since Rachel refuses to have a dog. Because she has allergies. But Colette, she's a pacifist, animal lover, cannot bear to have knives in the house. So everything you've heard up until now, this minute—it's crazy. Lies. What else can I say?

Maybe now you understand how upset this has made me. I'm the victim here. My life is going to hell in a ham sandwich. My wife wants a child, it's all she talks about, our cycles are off, I can't get any sleep. Babies die in their cribs. Maybe the fat nosy neighbor— talk about a walrus, the blubber on that woman, her arms alone, bingo wings they call them, she's the one belongs in a zoo—maybe she brought the knife. Maybe Rachel and Colette are in cahoots— I love that word—maybe they got together on the Internet, hoping to frame me or do away with me or cut off my—I get these headaches—I'm telling you, there are crazy people out there, this is California, land of fruits and nuts, people say the ugliest things, online, offline, no one takes responsibility, you can't protect yourself, the Internet—

What's that you're holding?

No, not the microphone.

The other hand.

DEAD BY CHRISTMAS

I'll tell you what ruined my marriage, and it wasn't gambling or drink or chasing skirt. Our son, Donny, was walking home from a friend's house when a LeSabre blew the stop sign, ran the poor kid down in the street and dragged him twenty yards, then fled the scene.

Seven years old, Donny was. And he fought, or his body fought, half the night, until the ER surgeon came out to talk with Barb and me with that look on his face.

All I remember of the next two weeks is I went on a mission—horning my way into the loop as every department in the valley tracked down the driver, even tagging along when the arrest came down in Apache Junction.

They put two men on me, to make sure I didn't take my shot as they dragged the guy out. His name was Phil Packer, an insurance adjustor with a DWI sheet ten years long, bench warrants in four counties—he'd been hiding in his girlfriend's trailer.

After that, every time Packer shuffled into court from lockup for a hearing, I was right there, front row, maddogging him and his wash'n'wear lawyer. None of which made a difference, of course, nor was it anything close to what Barb or our baby girl needed from me. That wasn't part of the mission.

My wife called me out on all that one night—it was late, she'd had a few, her face streaked with mascara from sitting in the dark with a bottomless cocktail and her son's ghost. Melodie, the baby, lay asleep in her room. I'd been out in the car, driving around, something I did a lot.

Seeing me there, Barb stood up and tottered closer, into the light. Her eyes were puffy and raw.

"I'm sorry. Do I know you?" She had that tone.

I said, "I had to finish up some work."

"No. I called. You left hours ago."

"A CI called, he wanted to meet." A ready lie. "They didn't tell you?"

She laughed acidly, inches from my face now. "You're such a coward."

Looking back, I think of the things I might've done, might've said, but all I could come up with in the moment was, "How many have you had?"

"Not nearly enough." She shoved the glass into my hand, a dare. "You know, Nick, disappearing isn't the same as dying."

I remember feeling cold all over. "You're not talking sense."

"You're jealous of Donny." Her eyes, glistening in the light, turned hard. "Somehow you think staying away is going to make me miss you. The way I miss him. Christ. Are you honestly that pathetic?"

Some scientist should measure the speed at which shame turns into hate. I'll never forget that sound, never forget the feel of the glass shattering in my hand or the sight of her crumbling in front of me, no matter how much I try. There's some things "sorry" won't cure, no matter how many times you say the word, or even how much you mean it.

It's said that only one in five marriages survives the death of a child, and maybe I should take comfort in the numbers. Regardless, it was my divorce that turned me into a workhorse, not the other way around.

I rotated in to robbery a short while after that, great place to get lost, the numbing paperwork, sixteen-hour days if you want them. There were four of us from different departments—Phoenix, Tempe, Scottsdale, Mesa—meeting once a week to share intel.

We'd had twenty restaurant takedowns around the valley the previous six months, all the same guy. He came in at closing, when the back door was propped open by the kitchen crew—that's when they dragged the rubber mats out to the parking lot for the nightly hose-down. Meanwhile, inside, the money was getting counted and bagged for deposit.

The robber wore dark coveralls, gloves, a ski mask, and he always slipped in and out within minutes, which meant he knew the business. Brandishing a snubnose, he'd prone out the manager, tie him up with plastic cuffs, the kind they use for riot control, then snatch the night deposit.

Right before leaving, he'd grab the manager's wallet, dig out the driver's license. "You're gonna say some wetback did this," he'd whisper. "I know your name. I know where you live." Even after we found out the guy was white, we still had vics swearing to our faces he was Mexican.

Finally, luck stepped in, as it does more times than most cops care to admit.

Two cars responded to a domestic here in Tempe—how's that for poetic? One cop grabbed the husband, the other took the wife, separated them, different rooms. The wife—eye swollen shut, cracked lip—she bawls to the cop there with her, "You know all the restaurant jobs around here the past few months? That asshole in the next room, he's the one you're after."

The woman wouldn't swear out a statement, though, so the uniform tracks me down in robbery at the end of his shift, to give me a verbal. I'm Tempe's case agent on the restaurant spree. You can imagine, he lays out the scenario, I'm cringing a little. Some guy tuning up his wife. Everybody on the force knew my business. Even so, I should've been thrilled, right? Finally, a suspect.

The guy was Mike Gallardi, his wife's name was Rhonda. Together, they ran a hole-in-the-wall called Mike's Place out on Baseline Road in South Phoenix. You could get a coronary just reading the menu but the place was clean, with a small counter and maybe a half dozen booths.

Here's the thing: They catered to cops. You walked in, one whole wall was dedicated to fallen officers. Flash a badge, your kids got free sodas with their meals. Come in on duty and no one's around? Boom, wink, you ate free.

I'd been at their place just once, a couple years before, taken there by a buddy of mine in the vice unit. Rhonda worked the register and counter, a shy, chesty, bleached-out woman in her thirties. Mike was the talker and he came out from behind the grill to toady up, all shucks and gee-whiz.

How to say this—I don't trust people who backslap cops. They always want something. Not that I made much headway on that point when I broke my news to the robbery roundtable.

"No way Mike's the suspect." This from Cavanaugh, the detective from Phoenix. "I can name fifty guys right now, this minute, who'll vouch for him."

"His own old lady handed him up."

"After he batted her around, yeah. Even then, she wouldn't dec up. Go back, now that she's cooled off even more, I'll bet she admits the whole thing's crap."

He had a point, of course, domestics being what they are. But something about the way he said it clued me in to what he really meant: *What would your wife spill about you, Boghossian, if we gave her half a chance?*

Thankfully, the four commanders overseeing the roundtable agreed with me and ordered surveillance. The teams worked in rotation, each department on for three days then making way for the next detail.

Mike was smart, though. He made our guys early and burned them in heat runs, crazy Ivans, every kind of stunt you can imagine to flush them out.

Once he just stopped in traffic, walked back to the unmarked car and said, "Why are you following me? I haven't done anything."

I could just picture him, over one of those free burgers or shrimp baskets he doled out, pumping guys for information on tail jobs: C'mon, tell me, I'm just so doggone curious. And cops—hated by damn near everybody, grateful for anyone who gives a rat's ass—they couldn't tell him their stories fast enough.

It got to me, sure. We were the ones who'd trained this guy—inadvertently, granted, but he was smarter than he should've been because of us. He was pulling out our wallets, whispering our names and addresses. And yeah, like everybody else he'd chumped, I felt ashamed.

Meanwhile, Mike adapted, lying low for a month, wise to how we'd think. And sure enough, the surveillance sergeants pulled the plug, they needed the bodies. Not a week later, Mike hit his next restaurant, and this time he upped the ante.

It happened out in Mesa. The manager saw Mike coming, locked himself in the office, dialed 9-1-1. Mike fired through the door—his first use of actual violence, not just threats. The manager, terrified, let him in.

Mike went for the man's ID first thing, recited the usual, then dug further through his wallet and found pictures.

"Two little girls. You love 'em?"

The rest went fast, Mike barking orders. He was long gone before the responding units arrived. And the manager, he wouldn't say word one till his wife confirmed by phone there was a squad car stationed outside their house. The next day, no notice, he moved his whole family to Denver. Even left the furniture behind.

"I still don't buy Mike's our man," Cavanaugh said at our next get-together. "But I agree renewing surveillance makes sense—nab him or move on, quicker the better."

The commanders chimed in, each department adding bodies, with new directions to lie back. They were sick of taking the burns.

Two weeks later, I got a call from surveillance. "Boghossian, get this. Gallardi and his wife locked up their place as usual but didn't head home. They checked into a hotel on the frontage road along I-10."

I knew the strip, we all did: a line of restaurants flanked that part of the freeway.

As I drove on over I thought about Rhonda's tagging along. It surprised me, I'll be honest. Maybe Cavanaugh had been right—I should've gone up to her early, asked her to confirm what she'd said that night Mike trashed her. And even though I knew that would've tipped our hand, now she wasn't just keeping mum, she was joining in. I felt responsible, like there'd been a point in time when I could have saved her. No surprise, I felt like that a lot back then.

I met the team at the hotel and, sure enough, after eleven, Mike came out of the room in dark coveralls, a daypack around his waist. He walked down a side street to the parking lot of an Applebee's, then hunkered down in a patch of oleander to watch the kitchen crew do its thing. The radios started to buzz—we had our man, no more doubts. After a half hour, Mike eased out of the bushes, retraced his steps and slipped back into his and Rhonda's hotel room.

The next day, when I called the robbery roundtable together to report, Cavanaugh went from looking like he'd lost his dog to acting like he meant to kill somebody.

"Okay," he said, "I'm in. If Mike Gallardi's our guy he'll get no favors from me."

I volunteered for surveillance at Applebee's, even though it meant staying alert for hours on end with the windows rolled up in hundred degree heat, drinking warm Coke and pissing it all back into the empty cup.

At nine, our eyes at Mike's Place reported that Rhonda had left, heading toward home. An hour later, Mike locked up and followed suit. A collective moan went out over the radio. He'd called it off.

Then, not long after, we heard that Mike and Rhonda were on the move again, leaving the house together. They were on their way toward us.

The voices on the radio perked back up—this was the night, we could feel it. And we knew we'd have to watch the whole thing play out, let him go in, rob the place, or it'd come apart in court. But what if he sniffed us out? What if he took a hostage?

Rhonda drove down one of the side streets and parked, then Mike hopped out, headed for the parking lot. I slouched in my seat, a drunk snoring off a bender. Through slit eyelids I watched him saunter toward the back of Applebee's, and for an instant he looked straight at me. It was dark, some serious distance separated us. Even so, I sat stock still, wondering if I'd been made.

He turned away and ducked inside the concrete dumpster

enclosure. Two other men with eyes on the door reported they had visual, and we had a man out front, too, in case Mike tried to run that way. Surveillance units got in position to take down Rhonda when the time came.

At half past eleven, the kitchen crew trooped out, propped the back door open and dragged out their slimy black mats, sudsing them up, hosing them down.

I kept up my ruse, dripping with sweat but not moving, sipping air through the window crack. Mike stayed put, too, even after the kitchen crew vanished again, leaving the door open as they mopped the floors. After midnight they humped on out again, collected their mats and dragged them back inside.

A whisper crackled on the radio, "What's he waiting for?"

Another whisper snapped back, "Off the air."

We were all raw from the heat, testy from sitting still so long.

Over the next hour, the employees came out in ones or twos, lingering for a smoke before driving away. Finally, the manager trudged out, locked up, not carrying a deposit bag—he'd left it in the safe—then got in his car and left.

Mike waited another fifteen minutes before sliding out of the dumpster enclosure. Hands in his pockets, he meandered across the parking lot, shooting one last glance my direction. Minutes later, surveillance confirmed that he and Rhonda were headed back home.

We waited in place another two hours. Mike might come back, I thought, try to burglarize the place, clip the trunk line on the alarm, pop the safe. Finally, I called in to Rooney, the graveyard sergeant, to report. "I want everybody to stay put, Roon. The money's all there, he's coming back in the morning when they open up."

"I'm calling it off," Rooney said. "Your guys have been stuck in their cars for six hours. It's still what, ninety-five degrees outside? Besides, from the sound of it, you got made."

"The sound of what? You're not sitting here."

"I need a team to report to the rail yards. Call just came in. Somebody made off with two dozen cases of Heineken."

I almost spit. "You're pulling my guys off because a pack of kids rifled a boxcar?"

"We've got a squeaky victim."

"Meaning who?"

"Meaning the Westbrook family."

The Westbrooks, wholesale distributors throughout the state, in-laws at the statehouse, a cousin in Congress. Somebody asks you what it's like to be a cop, I thought, tell them this story.

I got home to my apartment about three, showered the sticky grit off my skin and crawled into bed. I still wasn't used to sleeping by myself back then and I lay awake awhile, puzzling the whole thing through.

Get a cop alone, find him on a day he wants to be honest, he'll tell you the cases that bothered him most always involved a suspect who someway, somehow, reminded him of himself. And I knew Mike Gallardi pretty well, I thought.

Down deep, where it mattered, he was weak. That's why he liked power, not just over Rhonda but the people he robbed—gunpoint, the terror in their eyes. *Do what I tell you.* Like a cop, or his bent idea of one: a guy who gets what he wants, even hammers his wife, and never pays.

I was going to change that. I'd be the one who finally made sure Mike Gallardi suffered, if only for the chance to tell myself I was different. I was better.

Eventually, I drifted off and dreamed I stood in the doorway of a house off in the desert somewhere. A wounded dog limped toward me through the moonlit chaparral. As it drew close, I looked into its eyes, and saw my son looking back at me.

Next thing, the phone was ringing.

It was Rooney. "I don't know what to say, Nick. Appelbee's got hit this morning, eight o'clock." Some throat-clearing. "Just like you said."

I rubbed my face, checked my watch. Eight-thirty. "How much?"

"Twelve grand."

Hardly a take worth risking your freedom for, I thought. But this wasn't just about money. I wondered if Mike had driven back alone, or if he'd dragged Rhonda along with him again. And maybe she didn't feel bullied at all. Maybe, for the first time in a long, long while, she felt married.

"We're never gonna catch this guy without a wire." I was laying out my case to John Tally, the county attorney. "He's getting cocky, cocky crooks get sloppy and that's when people get hurt."

Tally tented his hands, rocking in his chair, sunlight flaring in the windows behind him. An ASU man, politician to the bone, he was tan and fit, pompous, cutthroat.

"I'll approve a wire," he said finally. "And a task force, but I want hard numbers on bodies."

"Phoenix and Tempe'll pony up ten men apiece," I said, guessing. "Scottsdale and Mesa half that each, an even thirty."

"You're lead agent," he said pointedly. "Team up with Tom Kolchek for the wire affidavit. And don't be fooled by his looks. He's the smartest guy I've got."

I stood up to leave. "I want to call off the surveillance, make the target think he's in the clear."

Tally glanced up, like I'd already become a bother. "I told you," he said. "You're lead agent."

Tally was right, Kolchek looked like your Uncle Monty—thick all over with thinning hair and sad-sack eyes—but he was one of the sharpest cops I ever worked with.

The affidavit came to a hundred pages and was airtight, detailing every job, how Mike came to be our suspect, the ensuing surveillance, the continuing robberies, everything. We argued that, given Rhonda's new accomplice role, phone communications between the house and the restaurant could prove fruitful.

The judge granted us thirty days for the wire, with a re-up possible for another thirty if the need arose, which would carry us through the holidays. But if we didn't have results by then, tough. We'd have to bag up and go home.

We notified the phone company of our target lines and anticipated start date, so they could build the parallel circuits for the wiretap. Two days later, they called back to tell us Mike had disconnected his home phone. He'd done it the same day we submitted the affidavit.

Kolchek hung up and sat there, thinking it through. Finally, in an oddly sunny voice, he said, "We'll bug his house."

"You don't get it," I told him.

"I get it," Kolchek said. "So? We tighten the circle of who knows what, rewrite the affidavit, wire up his house. Maybe we'll get lucky. You get any better ideas, let me know."

I didn't get any better ideas, of course. And every time I tried to imagine who might be tipping Mike off, I could never convince myself I had the right man.

Cavanaugh was the first and obvious choice, given how long he'd stuck up for Mike, but he was a hard cop and I'd seen the betrayal in his face before the Applebee's job. Besides, like he'd said, fifty cops would vouch for Mike in a heartbeat—any one of them could be our leak.

Kolchek and I reworked the affidavit, kept the wire on the restaurant phone and asked for three transmitters for the residence—one in the living room, one in the dining room, one in the bedroom—sensitive enough, at ten thousand dollars a pop, to catch voices throughout the house.

The judge signed off and Kolchek introduced me to a tech for the county attorney's office named Pritchard, who'd go in and actually set things up.

"I'll go with," I told Kolchek.

"No, I will," he said. "I'm a pretty good lock pick and we only need two men inside."

"What about the dog?"

Kolchek cocked his head. "Dog?"

"A white shepherd," I said. "It's in the surveillance reports."

"Right. I remember. What's your point?"

"I used to work canine. The white ones are unpredictable, you don't want to go in there alone." That was mostly crap, but there was no way I wasn't going with them. I wanted a look inside that house.

The next day, when Mike and Rhonda were at the restaurant, Kolchek walked up their front walk and took a Polaroid, then went to the hardware store, bought an identical door and set it up in his office, practicing till it took only forty-five seconds to pop both locks.

Meanwhile, I scoped the neighborhood for the best spot to place the undercover van. Mike and Rhonda lived in a maze-like community of townhouses grouped in quads, and the geometry of the place was all wrong; there was no place within a hundred yards of their unit to park the van and not stand out.

Then I saw there was a unit for rent one quad over. We could set up the wire room in there, as long as we kept a low profile.

I hit up Tally's office for the rent and two days later, when Mike and Rhonda and most of the neighbors were off to work, we moved our guys in. Me, Kolchek, and Pritchard headed over for our entry to plant the bugs, while a ram car took up position on the street in case Mike or Rhonda came back while we were still inside the house.

When we got to the front porch, though, we found a brand new security gate with two additional locks, barring access to the door. Kolchek just stood there, staring, holding his lockpick tools. "This isn't happening." He glanced at his watch and swallowed hard. Inside, the dog was barking like the place was on fire.

I started heading for the back of the house. "Bet you're glad you brought me along now."

There was a privacy wall around the patio in back and I scaled it, dropping down onto the pavers. A sliding Arcadia door led inside, with an insert for a doggy door. I got down on the ground, reached through and flicked aside the dowel lodging the door in place. The dog realized what was happening then, and as I slipped inside he turned a corner and charged toward me, hackling up, fangs bared.

I reached frantically in my pocket for the syringe of Isoforine I'd brought along to knock him out, only to sink my thumb into the needle. I played air banjo with my hand for a second, saying something original like, "Goddamnmother*fuck*," then glanced up and saw I wasn't the only one to miscalculate.

As his paws hit linoleum, the dog lost traction, sliding toward me helplessly. Stepping forward, I caught him under the jaw with a kick so fierce he cartwheeled backwards.

"Get in the god damn bathroom!"

The dog sulked off, mewling, as I checked my thumb, hoping adrenalin would ward off any grogginess. Suddenly, I remembered my dream from weeks before—the lonely house, the wounded dog.

A chirp from my radio broke the spell.

I clicked on. "Yeah?"

"We heard that, detective." It was one of my guys in the wire room. In the background, laughter. "Punt the pooch—that what they teach you in canine?"

I switched off my radio and searched out the front door. When I got there I found out the security gate was locked from inside, requiring a key. "This nails it," I told Kolchek through the grating. "Somebody's tipping this guy off."

"We'll talk about it later," Kolchek whispered, standing exposed with Pritchard on the porch. "Get us inside."

Kolchek lacked the physique to scale the privacy wall, so I found a window in a small utility room near the back for the two men to crawl through. Once everybody was inside, we headed to the living room to set up shop. Kolchek got busy taking pictures of the room on his phone so we could put it back the same way we found it.

"Look at this," I said, pointing to the couch. There were sheets, blankets, a pillow. "Christ, she's kicked him out of bed. They're in the middle of another fight."

"Get to work," Kolchek said. He was testy and pouring sweat. It dawned on me then that, despite a first-rate mind, Kolchek lacked any serious operational experience. The glitch with the locks had rattled him.

Pritchard hooked up his transmitters to the phone lines. Even though the service had been cut off, the wires still held voltage. We set them up in the three different rooms as planned, and Pritchard asked me to contact the wire room to see if we were live. Only then did I realize I hadn't switched my radio back on after that crack about my dropkicking the dog.

When I flipped the button, a voice came through almost screaming. "Jesus, Boghossian, where'd you go? We've been trying to contact you for ten minutes. The wife's on her way, just west of Pepperwood. You're lucky she stopped for smokes. Move!"

We rushed to test the transmitters through the wire room and got an all-clear. Kolchek's hands shook so bad from nerves he couldn't screw the plates back on the phone plugs, so I took the screwdriver from him, told him to pack up with Pritchard, I'd close up.

They scrambled out the utility room window and I locked it behind them. Turning back to finish up, something caught my eye, something I'd overlooked before.

On a shelf near the door, a small daypack rested among some other odds and ends.

We had no warrant to search the house or its contents, but I took the daypack down regardless and opened it up: A ski mask. A pair of black garden gloves. A .38 snubnose and a dozen plastic cuffs.

There was a desk in the room and I laid the contents out, took out my phone and snapped a picture. This was a trophy, not evidence—I wouldn't even tell anybody about it, let alone show them the snapshot. The whole investigation might vanish down a hole if guys started jabbering.

I packed everything up again and put the daypack back where I'd found it, but then my curiosity got the best of me and I searched the desk. In the bottommost drawer, I found a photograph—Mike with Cavanaugh, up in the mountains somewhere. They were hunting together, carrying shotguns, the best of friends from their smiles. Rhonda, I guess, had snapped the picture.

I took out my phone again. This too, of course, wasn't evidence, and I told myself it didn't really prove anything. It was just a reminder—my reminder—of what I might be up against.

I ran back to the dining room and was just about finished putting things back in place when the voice came through my radio again: "Boghossian, she's at the corner."

I barked into the mouthpiece, "Ram her!"

I was making one last check when I heard the collision outside. It was about fifty yards from the house, some undercover cop plowing into Rhonda's back end at the stop sign.

I opened the bathroom door and told the dog to stay, then headed toward the patio, fit the doggy door insert into place and reached through and slipped the dowel back onto the runner.

Through the glass of the sliding door, I saw the large white dog slink into view. Our eyes met. He flinched a little, tail lodged between his legs. Ashamed, like everybody else.

It was up to the boys in the wire room now. I checked in as often as I could, but the days went by, nothing. Mike knew we'd been in there—tipped off by Cavanaugh, I supposed, something I had to keep to myself.

Besides which, just like I'd thought, Mike and Rhonda were in a tiff, the two of them seldom speaking.

As time passed, though, I felt strangely encouraged. I knew the dynamics of the simmering fight. I heard the cues—the caustic one-liners, the icy silences. Somehow, some night, something would set them off. And the words would come boiling out, things they'd regret forever.

As it turned out, that night came right before Thanksgiving. And the somehow and something of it proved, to my way of thinking anyway, too apropos.

The surveillance team trailed Mike to a porno arcade near the airport. We'd watched him visit smut shops and strip clubs all over the valley, not sure if he was casing the places or had just grown tired of not getting any at home. This time, though, according to the cop watching from the parking lot, Mike came out wobbly.

"I may be wrong," the radio voice reported, "but I think our boy just had himself a little love."

When Mike got home he wasn't inside five minutes before he launched into Rhonda—a fight over nothing, but so blistering everybody in the wire room shuddered. When one of the cops

reached out to turn off the recorder, though, honoring the mini-
mization guidelines, I told him, "Wait."

We'd gotten our first lead in this case after a brawl between
these two. I could justify listening on the grounds there was a
reasonable expectation that, in their fury, one of them would say
something useful. Accusing.

The voices kept rising, more and more shrill and cruel. And
sexual. One Mormon on the wire crew blushed, but everybody
kept listening, each of us wondering what we should do if, at some
point, one of them tried to kill the other.

And yes, finally, we heard scuffling.

I reached for the phone to dial dispatch as I heard Rhonda stam-
mer oddly, "M-Mike, n-no. No!" The yelling turned to muffled
cries, then rhythmic, whimpering moans. Gradually it dawned on
us that Mike had decided on a little show'n'tell, to demonstrate for
Rhonda what had happened earlier that night, during his encounter at the porn hole.

"One good pipe cleaning deserves another," somebody cracked.

"Turn off the machine," I said, knowing we'd get nothing of
any use now. Adding insult to injury, Mike moved back into the
bedroom that night. So that's how you make your marriage work,
I thought, hating him even more.

The first thirty days played out, no results. We got an extension
but none of the departments would pony up the manpower like
before. They put rookies on the line-of-sight details. Once, after
letting one tail car pass him, Mike chased the cop all the way down
Central Avenue, flashing his brights, just to embarrass the kid.

Meanwhile, the wire crew was going batty listening to nothing and more of nothing. We were back where we'd started—we'd
never catch Mike Gallardi except red-handed, coming out the
back of a restaurant. And everything we knew about him said, if
that happened, he'd make us kill him.

"The man's gonna be dead by Christmas," someone quipped,
and it became the unofficial slogan of the whole operation, until I
told everybody to knock it off.

"If you're right, and we take him out, you don't want to have to explain that little mantra to Internal Affairs."

Given where we stood, though, I decided it was time to tickle the wire. I went to Tally again, told him we needed to put some pressure on the couple, inflict a little fear.

I showed up at Rhonda's front door when surveillance confirmed Mike was at the restaurant alone. I came in a marked unit, the strobe spinning out at the curb, and the uniform who'd driven stood with me on the porch. No more avoiding the neighbors—we wanted their attention now.

Inside, the dog went off when the doorbell rang, then went still, dropping his tail, when he saw me beyond the grating.

Rhonda deadpanned, "Gee, if I didn't know better, I'd think you and the dog knew each other."

I pulled the subpoena from my jacket pocket and gestured for her to open the security gate. "Rhonda Gallardi, you're to appear before the grand jury on December 5th. You're not to discuss your scheduled appearance or the subject matter of your testimony with anyone except your lawyer—not even your husband. Understood?"

She looked taken aback but hardly stunned—some fright in her eyes, but a baiting grin too. I wondered if that was how she looked right before Mike hit her.

"What if I don't open the door?"

"I'll just set it down on the porch here. Either way, you're served."

The grin faded a bit, her fear quickening into anger as her eyes checked the cop behind me, then slid back. "This is harassment."

"Guess how many times a day I hear that."

"Because you're a prick?"

I nodded for the cop to head back to the car. Once he was out of earshot, I said, "Know what I think? You've been trying hard for a long time to make things work—your restaurant, your marriage. I admire that. But the point where things were gonna change is gone for good." I stuck my hands in my pockets, to look harmless. "You want to turn that around, now's the time."

Women who've been hit more than once have a look—sad and yet defiant, almost mocking, but defeated all the same. Come on, I thought, invite me in, talk to me. I knew, given the chance, I could open her up, end this thing. But her eyes turned hard and faraway again. "Leave your papers on the porch," she said, then shut the door.

In the wire room, we listened when Mike came home that night. Apparently, what I'd said registered, at least a little, because the good wife unloaded.

"No more! I'm done."

"Shut up, Rhonda."

"I'm not gonna lie under oath for you! I never wanted—"

"I said shut the fuck up, Rhonda!"

The sound of scuffling came again. I grabbed the phone to dial dispatch. But a minute later, they were outside the house, walking the dog. The perfect couple—Mike with his arm around Rhonda's shoulder, holding her close, loving, protective, whispering into her hair.

Rhonda got coached well for her grand jury appearance. All her answers reduced to: I don't remember. I'm not sure. I don't think so. I don't know.

"He beat us," I told my guys afterward, like I was confessing to some crime of my own.

A week later we went in to pull the wires, and I was hardly shocked to see they'd put a three-piece console in front of the wall socket where we'd planted the living room transmitter. They'd been a step ahead of us the whole time. Took us an hour, though, to take the knickknacks down, drag the big thing away, claim our bug then push the monster back and make sure all the junk was in the right place again, even smoothing the carpet so you couldn't tell anything had moved.

The operation got bagged, departments couldn't justify the manpower any more. We went around to restaurants, schooling them on smarter ways to close up at night—it was all we could do at that point. Maybe Mike would decide his luck had played out. Or maybe he'd get reckless, hurt somebody, and the whole thing would heat up all over again.

On Christmas Eve, I visited Barb and our daughter for the annual holiday torture—unwanted presents, forced smiles. And no talk of Donny, as though the only thing that could keep the pain at bay was a punishing silence.

Walking to my car, though, I heard the front door click open behind me. Turning, I saw my daughter—she was five then—running toward me in her red velvet dress and green tights. Behind her, Barb waited in the doorway, a silhouette.

Melodie scooted up, gripped my hand and pulled so I'd bend down. In a solemn whisper, she said, "Don't be sad, okay? It's Christmas."

"I'm not sad," I lied, but she'd already dropped my hand, spun around and fled back toward her mother who let her back in, then closed the door.

Later at my own place, drinking scotch as I flipped through the channels, I got the call from dispatch. A steak house up in Paradise Valley got hit right at closing. I was on my way to the scene when the second call came in. Shots fired. The address made my stomach drop.

By the time I got to the condo the place was alive with cops, strobes spinning around the complex, mingling eerily with the Christmas lights. I got out of my car and pushed through the crowd of neighbors outside. The cop with the entry/exit log took my name and badge number, then waved me in.

Techs and detectives ambled about. A spindly tree stood in the living room, sagging with ornaments and tinsel. One of the guys from homicide pointed me back to the kitchen.

In the breakfast nook, I found a uniformed cop standing guard over Cavanaugh, who sat gripping his head. He glanced up just long enough to catch my eye, his gaze frantic with calculation.

To the uniform, I said, "Do everybody a favor and stand back a little. He makes a grab for your gun, you may both wind up dead."

From the kitchen I made way toward the utility room. A body sheet covered a sprawling form on the floor, a pool of drying blood trailing out from underneath. Spray patterns hazed the walls. An eerie handprint smeared the doorframe.

In the bedroom, wearing an undershirt and cargo shorts, Rhonda sat with hollow eyes, stroking the shepherd, who lay at her feet whimpering. A female officer stood guard, one hand on her sidearm, as though she intended to shoot the dog if it so much as moved.

It took a second for Rhonda to sense I was there in the door-way. Glancing up, she blinked, took me in. Her hair was a mess. She looked ashen and lost.

Cavanaugh would take the fall, pleading out to manslaugh-ter. His story—I can't say whether it's true or not, though I tend to believe more than I doubt—was that he and Rhonda, his cop-crazy buddy's wife, were lovers. The night Mike found out, he knocked Rhonda around a while, then went out, got coked up and took down his first restaurant. He'd been pumping Cavanaugh for information on robberies for ages, claiming he just wanted to know how to protect his own place.

Mike came back from that first job in an odd heat, feeling invincible—the man he was meant to be—and told Rhonda that, if he ever went down, he'd hand up her lover as the man who'd taught him everything. Cavanaugh had to protect him then, to protect himself, protect Rhonda. He began tipping Mike off on the rob-bery investigations, staying away from Rhonda once the surveil-lance began but getting messages through by using the guy who washed dishes at their restaurant as a go-between.

That went on until Rhonda's grand jury appearance, after which she told Mike she'd dime him out herself if he didn't stop, she didn't care who got hurt. And Mike obliged her—until Christ-mas Eve.

He missed it, that nervy heat when he slipped in, pointing the gun. The fear. The begging.

As soon as he left the house for Paradise Valley, Rhonda picked up the phone, dialed Cavanaugh, told him she was leaving for good, she'd had it. He told her to wait, he'd be right over. They meant to be gone by the time Mike got back but—here again I'm not sure what to believe—he surprised them, slipping into the house unnoticed. It was self-defense, if you looked at it right, though Cavanaugh knew better than to take that to trial.

But all of that was yet in the telling as I stood there in the bedroom doorway. The dog ignored me for once, still whimpering, its ears pricked up. It was Rhonda who stared right at me.

"You're the one whose wife walked out," she said finally. She left the rest hanging, but her voice was accusing. She wouldn't be gloated over, not by the likes of me.

I don't know how to explain it. Despite her contempt, despite everything, I felt for her. And I could afford to be gracious, not because I was different or better or even because it was Christmas. I remembered my daughter's words, whispered in my ear: *Don't be sad, okay?* I had a piece of something back I'd thought was lost for good.

"My wife had good reason to leave," I said, thinking: Why lie?

But Rhonda just turned away. With a soft, miserable laugh, she said, "Like that's all it takes."

BABYLON SISTER

Swaying a bit atop her stool as she nursed a fourth whiskey, Sister Rita Donovan gazed across the packed hotel bar, admiring furtively (so she hoped) the British thriller novelist Jon Carleton: raffish, handsome, bespectacled, tall. He stood in a crush of fans beyond the leather banquettes and dark oak tables, framed deftly between two vintage Tiffany lamps, pumping hands in grip-and-grins amid camera flash—ever the professional, she thought, marveling at his shrewd and tireless charm.

They'd spoken earlier, idle hallway chatter. She'd felt a bit like a schoolgirl, fixed in his gaze. Now, from some warm but shadowy place within her, a wistful sigh gathered, a little heated ball of air pushing upward like a mood balloon.

Oh, what a wickedly delicious confession I'd gladly make, an irksome but familiar voice within her said. *If, if, if . . .*

Shush, she thought, fearing for a moment she'd said it out loud.

It was Mayhem by the Bay, a San Francisco conclave of mystery enthusiasts—writers, publishers, booksellers, fans—and six o'clock, the hour when everyone thronged the bar.

People had come from as far away as Copenhagen and Perth to attend, and many were whip-smart, with an almost encyclopedic capacity for rattling off titles and authors, even quoting whole passages from their absolute-favorite-you-*must*-read-this book.

Rita had found the conversation daunting at times; it seemed she'd spent much of the day with the same gnomish smile plastered across her face, nodding along.

There were a number of bookish stay-at-homes in attendance

as well, of course, out for their one lark of the year—painfully shy, physically unmemorable, hovering in the background until a sudden boldness surged within, at which point they'd emerge from their anonymity, corner someone not too intimidating—Rita, for example—and latch on like barnacles.

Speaking of which, the voice said, *let's not neglect our two blatteroons.*

Rita returned her misty gaze to the near-at-hand. A pair of Franciscan sisters were talking to her—about her, at her—mystery buffs, both of waddling girth and jackhammer mind, one sipping ginger ale, the other knocking back a lager.

Leave it to you, Rita thought, to get trapped by a pair you could just as easily have met on retreat. Though well-meaning, they prattled on with such breakneck oblivion she wished they would just buzz off.

"But then again, some do say your book is derivative of the Father Brown stories." This from the graying one with her ginger ale—corkscrew curls, tiny eyes in an ample face. "And Father Dowling."

"Oh crap," the other barked. She was a stout Celtic broad—backbone of the faith—cropped red hair, blotchy freckles. "Father Dowling, Father Brown, they're apples and orangutans." She threw back some beer, a belch slipped out. "Ralph McInerny, bless his soul, was a saint. Chesterton? A smug, sanctimonious anti-Semite. With a spanking fetish."

"That's been blown out of all proportion," the first one said.

"Oh, yes, those touchy conniving Jews."

"I meant . . ." a sigh, deep from the belly, "the other thing. And that was C. S. Lewis, not Chesterton."

"Right. Spanker of Narnia."

"Getting back to *Rita*." The first one pointed, using her glass, as though there might be some question as to who "Rita" was. "I meant merely that, here and there, of whatever consequence, certain people at the conference have suggested that Sister Killian—you know, Rita's heroine—reminds them somewhat of Father Dowling's Sister Steve."

The redhead cocked an eyebrow. "You're talking the TV series, not the books. McInerny had zip to do with her."

"I realize—"

"And the TV series was crap."

"Sister, that word—"

"Crap in a basket."

"I was simply trying to say that there are those who think Rita here—"

"For God's sake, stop *picking* on her." Another belch, this one a ripper. "She *won.*"

Ah yes, Rita reminded herself: I won. Her Mistress of Mayhem Award for Best First Novel rested atop the bar for all to see. All of whom, she thought tartly, casting a glance about. No one but the two Franciscans paid her any mind. Meanwhile, the statuette sat there like a totem of bad taste.

Ghastly little eyesore. Looks like the shrunken head of a Cubist.

"I'm not trying to quarrel, sister, I'm merely—"

"Give the little thing some *credit.*"

Rita eyed them through the sensual gloom of her buzz, the gray blinky one clutching her ginger ale, the other gathering a fistful of pretzels from a dish on the bar.

Sister Rotunda. Sister Mary Porcine.

Don't be uncharitable, she thought, addressing the voice, or rather the darkness from which it emerged.

It had first come to her at age eighteen, just once, a dramatic moment in her life. She found herself in a room at the Homewood Motel with three snoring boys she did not remember meeting. The room stank of liquor, and she was naked.

On that occasion, the voice said simply, *Get dressed and go home.*

The next day, it wasn't just guilt that paralyzed her, but fear. How could she ask forgiveness or do penance for a sin she couldn't remember? What would it mean to live a whole life like that?

After a long and unflinching examination of conscience (since her memory was unavailing) she went to her mother two days later and announced her belief that she had a vocation, and wanted to enter an order known as the Handmaidens of the Word Incarnate.

Anne Marie Donovan responded by clasping her youngest daughter's hands and saying through tears that she'd just been made the happiest mother alive.

The woman was the family rock, a widow at thirty-three when her husband caught a patch of black ice on the Illinois side of the Julien Dubuque Bridge. She raised her three girls, Rita and her two older sisters, alone thereafter, the one constant mainstay, her faith—morning Mass, nightly prayer, Friday novenas, altar society, rosary society, baking pies for bingo.

Whenever a movie she considered suitably Catholic came on TV, she'd shepherd everyone into the den, plying all three sisters with popcorn and Seven-Up floats, the four of them cocooned together beneath blankets on the sofa, dappled by the flickering light from the screen: *Brother Orchid*, *The Sound of Music*, *Going My Way*, *Quo Vadis*, even Hitchcock's *I Confess*.

Sometimes, Rita blamed her annoyingly persistent sexual longings on her girlhood fascination with *Heaven Knows, Mr. Allison*—if she were half as fetching a nun as Deborah Kerr, she thought, would it justify her lifelong crush on Robert Mitchum?

Her mother attended every ceremony as Rita climbed the spiritual ladder from postulate to novice to perpetual vows, always beaming with gratitude and hope.

Then, after all that devotion and faithful sacrifice, she fell sick at age fifty-two to advanced anaplastic thyroid cancer. By the time she was diagnosed, tumors had already spread to her throat and lungs. First order of business, a tracheostomy. For the few months remaining to her, she would breathe through a plastic tube.

As often as she could, Rita traveled back to Dubuque to help her sisters care for the woman who defined their notion of sainthood, each visit more heartbreaking than the last. Near the end, a ghost of her former self, her mother turned demented from the chemo and morphine—paranoid, wandering the hospital corridors in terror of every nightfall, confusing daughters and nurses, days and years—what next? Death. A relief. For everyone.

Well, not quite everyone. A woman from the parish, Mrs. Mastronardi, pronounced during one of her cloying vigils how glorious it was that God would crown their mother's life with suffering, just as he did with his own son and his most cherished saints—Francis of Assisi and Catherine de Ricci with the stigmata, for example.

It took every ounce of strength Rita possessed not to slap the old bat right there in the oncology ward.

That was when the voice returned. It said: *Take comfort in a dying woman's misery, will you? Here, let me take some comfort in yours.*

The voice began speaking to her regularly after that. It sounded different than it had that first time, almost twenty years before. It bore no resemblance to her dead mother's voice, either, so she didn't feel particularly haunted. Badgered, more like it.

Guardian angel? Hardly. Conscience? Please. To her ear, it sometimes sounded like Tracey Ullman impersonating Maggie Smith stoked on gin.

Meanwhile, bit by bit, a light went out in her soul. She'd tried everything to rekindle it—vigorous prayer, intensified devotions, renewed obedience to her superiors. Someday, she hoped, substance would follow form. But the hope was dwindling.

And now?

She slid off the cushion of the towering stool and gathered her balance, tottering momentarily in her sensible shoes.

"Excuse me, sisters," she murmured, only the hint of a slur, despite the tricky sibilants. "It's been a very, very long afternoon."

The two plump nuns shot acid glances back and forth. Rita collected her statuette, lifting it from the bar with difficulty, its ugliness equaled by its heft. In her small hands, the thing brought to mind a murder weapon.

Tragedy struck this weekend when two garrulous Franciscan fatsos . . .

Rita offered a smiling farewell nod, then shambled tipsily through the bustling lounge, feeling the damning stares of her fellow sisters scalding her back like wagging tongues of fire.

◆   ◆   ◆

As she neared the group surrounding Jon Carleton, she caught her distant reflection in a lobby mirror: charcoal calf-length skirt, simple white blouse with Peter Pan collar, blue cardigan sweater. Only the cross around her neck, hanging by its thin gold chain, marked her as a nun. Sandy shoulder-length hair, bangs across the brow. Sad eyes in a longish face with a longish nose, paprika freckles, thin lips.

Pretty in a drab way, she thought, or drab in a pretty way—that's me.

You want to flirt with him, you filthy little minx.

As though he'd somehow managed to overhear her thoughts, the British author glanced up suddenly and offered a welcoming smile. Following the direction of his gaze, his circle of fans turned in sympathetic unison.

Suddenly, all eyes were on Rita. She felt naked, gripping her homely little bronze, and wobbling just a tad.

Christ in socks, you're lit to the gills.

"Congratulations!" Jon Carleton reached out a hand past several people, offering it to her. She shifted her trophy to her left arm, clutching it to her body, in order to extend her right. His grip, engulfing and warm, melted her.

He said, "You must be terribly chuffed."

She smiled, hoping the word meant proud, not blotto.

Instantly, the crowd around him echoed his graciousness, showering Rita with praise of such cheerful and generous exuberance she felt ashamed at having thought unkindly of the stammering bookish ones earlier. Why do I judge people so harshly, she wondered, shaking their smooth soft hands. What makes me so petty and ungracious?

You're unhappy. And, where it matters most, insincere.

No, she thought, standing up for herself. Well, unhappy, granted, but this has nothing to do with questioning my vocation, loss of faith, any of that. I've got every reason to be disappointed today.

◆   ◆   ◆

Earlier that afternoon, while Rita was still flush from the thrill of having won her award, her editor, Jean Virdell—a canny New Yorker of brisk disposition, bright red lipstick, and the attention span of a cat—had invited her to the bar for the first of the day's cocktails.

A celebration, Rita supposed, not knowing then where the discussion would lead. She ordered champagne, thinking it wise to pace herself, only switching to whiskey later.

"Sales weren't as brisk as we would have liked," the editor remarked, addressing a spot two inches to the left of Rita's head. "And, unfortunately, in today's market, a slow start never turns into a gradual build. You end up where you begin and, regrettably, our beginning was . . . uneventful."

"But the prize." Rita was stunned. "Doesn't that count for anything?"

The woman smiled as though that were the most pitiable thing she'd heard in years. A heartfelt sigh, deftly executed. "I'm sure you're very proud."

"There must be some way you could publicize—"

"We gave you everything in the way of publicity we give any start-up author." Her tone turned scolding. She gestured for the check. "Don't take it personally, Sister."

But it's not just about me, Rita thought. There are so many other people affected by this, relying on me. I need these silly little books to sell for the sake of my convent, the older sisters who need medical care, the work we do.

"But the second novel's just about to come out. Are you saying—"

"We've trimmed the marketing budget a bit." She handed the waitress a pair of bills, shooed her away, then clicked her small purse shut. "You'll still tour locally, here in the Bay Area. And anything you can pay for yourself, of course, you're free to do."

Pay for myself, she thought. I'm a nun. Perpetual chastity, perfect obedience. Voluntary poverty. "I don't know what to say. . . . "

The editor's attention, however, had already focused elsewhere. She fluttered her hand to a distant someone. Her eyes shone. "Some things can't be helped," she said, getting up to leave.

The surge of congratulation from Jon Carleton's fans finally ebbed and Rita thanked everyone again, acknowledging the handsome Brit's courtliness with particular warmth.

Taking her leave, she drifted across the lobby until she reached the elevators, where she waited alone as a Haydn horn concerto burbled from an overhead speaker.

The heavy brass doors slid open and she entered, pushing the button for her floor. A wave of leaden fatigue swept through her, tinged with dejection.

The shiny doors were nearly closed when a male hand reached through, jamming itself into the breach. The doors trembled, a rattling metal thud.

"Mind terribly if I share your lift?"

No sooner did the doors close than he turned to her with that knee-wobbling *je ne sais quoi*.

"An impressive debut," he said, nodding toward the homely statuette. "And now you have the hardware to prove it."

Rita could feel the blood warming her cheeks. It was just the two of them. There. Together. She wondered if he could smell the alcohol on her breath, oozing out her pores.

Get a grip. He's a Brit, not a beagle.

The overhead panel chimed, the doors slid open. They'd reached her floor.

Stepping aside to hold the door, he said, "By the way, my dinner plans appear to have gone tits up, if you'll excuse the vernacular." A puckish smile. "Figure I'll just bang up to the old home-away-from-home, switch on the telly, ring down for room service. Simple enough to order for two, if you'd care to join me." His eyes met hers. "I'd be so terribly honored if you would."

Six hours later, not long before midnight, they spoke from opposite sides of the locked bathroom door. Rita stood within, the tile floor cold against her stocking feet. She took heart from the fact that otherwise she'd managed to remain fully clothed.

Jon Carleton uttered a lowing sigh. "I really do wish you'd come out. I feel badly as it is, and this is hardly improving my spirits."

"I'm sorry." Rita meant the phrase in every conceivable way. Pressing her cheek against the smooth white door, she added, "It isn't you, it's me."

"There is such a thing, you know, as innocent human touch."

Not with me, Rita thought. Not with you, I mean. And me. "I realize—"

"Seriously, I'm feeling a right cad at the moment. Couldn't we manage this face to face?"

Face to face is exactly how you couldn't manage it.

"Oh, leave me alone."

"I'm sorry?"

"Not you. I mean, give me a moment. Please."

The evening had proceeded swimmingly up until eleven or so. When he first let her in, she discovered, to her profound relief, that he had a suite, the bedroom discreetly invisible beyond a closed door.

Quite an improvement over the Homewood, eh?

The sitting room, furnished with staid elegance, looked out upon Union Square, lit up for the early evening crowds. It being early January, post-Christmas sales still drew the bargain hunters. A cold drizzle soaked the storefront lights. Trolleys clamored damply up and down Powell.

"The last great hope of western civilization," he quipped, standing very close behind her at the window. "Shopping."

She declined a pre-dinner cocktail, hoping to hold on until dinner, when food in her system might help the slow trek back to sober. With a shrug and a smile he poured himself a snifter of aged Barbados rum from a decanter.

They began to chat and it wasn't like two strangers feeling each other out at all. They were colleagues, two like minds, two (dare she think it) *writers* sharing thoughts on aesthetics and craft.

They talked opera and film noir, Mark Twain and Aristophanes and Kurt Weill. When the discussion turned to teenage favorites, she confessed to Chesterton, he to Graham Greene.

"Both Catholics," he remarked. "Imagine that."

They dined at half past eight—she, skillet-roasted barramundi with wok-fried greens and rockmelon salsa; he, roast lamb rump with sweet potato rösti and port wine jus—and with dinner and its web of aromas came champagne, Billecart-Salmon 1996 Cuvee, then further talk of such dizzying digression they could sometimes not remember who'd made which point.

Blithering on, he called it. She was in heaven.

Agreeing to the champagne, perhaps, had been reckless, but he intended to celebrate her success, as he called it, and she lacked the heart (or the nerve) to tell him the truth, that her success was a sham, her career kaput when only half begun. Besides, the crisp pink bubbles cheered her. She relaxed.

Two hours later (and after but another bottle of Billecart-Salmon, delivered by a judiciously unobservant room-service waiter), they finished their dessert of three milk cake and hazelnut mousse with chocolate biscotti, and Rita plopped onto the sofa, slipped off her flats and tucked her legs beneath her, an overly feminine pose, perhaps, and thus needlessly provocative.

Try slutty.

If he noticed, he hid it well. He just continued with the discussion, sitting there beside her, leaning over to top off her crystal flute from time to time, his eyes always fastened on hers.

It was deft, how he did it, reaching over to lay his hand on hers in agreement of a point she made—something to do with Flannery O'Connor, one more tortured Catholic—and then the hand lingered.

Secretly, she savored the touch. A vow of chastity was one thing, forsaking affection quite another.

She'd not come to the convent inexperienced, few if any of the sisters in America under forty had—not that her tortured misadventures, above and beyond whatever happened with those boys in the motel room that night, would qualify as a sex life. But here and now, the simple warmth of his hand, enveloping hers, filled her with a murky heat. She had the sense that, if he wanted, he could somehow make her disappear.

Very slowly, he withdrew his hand, only to collect her stocking foot, which he held tenderly for an instant, as though caressing a wounded bird. Then he speared his thumb into the sole with an artful pressure and her entire musculature uncoiled.

The next thing she knew, both feet lay in his lap, he was kneading them like a crazed baker, *blithering on* about the existentialist hero and the Continental Op, until the heat of her blood made her head pound, the room started dancing, the lights played tricks.

"Excuse me for just a moment," she whispered, disengaging herself and fleeing to the bathroom where she locked the door behind her. A quarter of an hour later, the door remained locked, with each of them on opposite sides.

Splashing water on her face, she glanced up into the mirror and regarded her reflection with dismay. The thing they never tell you about sin, she thought, is how it returns you, over and over, to the same terrible place, a precursor of eternity in hell.

And so here she was, once again, like almost twenty years ago, blind from drink, in a room with a man—narrowing it down to one, was that progress? You failed as a daughter, you've failed as a writer, are you trying to fail as a nun as well? To prove what?

She toweled dry her face and hands, then finally mustered the courage to unlock the door and come out.

"I feel foolish." She padded to the couch, poked her feet into her shoes, and took a slow deep breath.

"Pardon me if this is overly personal." He came up behind her gingerly. "But if your vows require of you such theatrics when you're simply alone with a member of the opposite sex, could it be that it—celibacy, I mean—is the problem, not you or me?"

"I didn't say you were a problem," she replied. And what to make of "simply" alone?

"Making a vice of sex is itself a bit depraved, don't you think? You've got priests laying on hands when anything under thirteen prances by, but none of the men in the funny hats thinks that maybe, just maybe, vows of lifelong chastity are unnatural. No. Better the Vatican puts its mind to abolishing limbo."

She turned to face him. "Jon?"

"Can't tell you how relieved I am *that* one's finally settled. Now Jews and Buddhists can get into heaven. Pity none of them believe in it."

"Jon—"

"Do you really think all those parsons and rabbis shake hands with the bloody devil when they—"

"Renouncing sex doesn't prevent me from loving. On the contrary, it allows me the freedom to express many other kinds of love, for many other people, in many other ways."

He shifted his weight uneasily, as though an itch had struck an odd spot. "Please excuse my saying this, but that came out just a wee bit practiced. And half-hearted."

"That may be." She ventured a cautious step forward. "But it's not with half my heart that I thank you for the lovely dinner, the wonderful conversation, and wish you goodnight."

When she entered her room, she found it immaculate, everything prim and tucked away, courtesy of housekeeping. The accommodations had been generously provided by the conference. "In the event you need somewhere to freshen up," they'd said innocently.

For a moment, as the door clicked shut behind her, the utter anonymity of it all made her feel that she'd somehow wandered into the wrong place. This wasn't her room. It wasn't her life.

The effect of the champagne lingered but that wasn't it. She felt a blurring of the edges of everything, even her own body, as though existence itself—what Chesterton called "the mystical minimum"—was dissolving.

So different from the warm dissolution she'd felt at the touch of Jon Carleton's hand. This was pernicious, impersonal, as though to remind her that the stuff of life is just a dream, vivid but meaningless, over too soon.

She'd devised a ritual for dispelling this creeping sense of unreality, which came over her when she felt particularly alone. And she'd felt alone a great deal since her mother's death.

She sat down at the dressing table. Opening the drawer, she removed the items she'd shoplifted from nearby drugstores earlier in the day, after her meeting with Jean Virdell, anticipating there might be a need tonight.

Her students bragged about how easily it was done, thinking they could scandalize her, not knowing she'd been quite the little thief herself when she was their age.

The Three Holy Terrors, they'd called themselves: Rita, Molly Napolitano, Jan Smulski. After school, they'd wander downtown Dubuque, especially the winter-scarred back alleys from St. Patrick's to Cable Car Square, playing scissors-paper-rock to determine who would create the diversion, who would serve as lookout, who would get to do the actual stealing.

Rita always envied the designated thief, and felt thrilled when she earned the right herself—cherishing the way her heart pounded like a fist inside her chest when her eye fastened on what it was she intended to take.

They'd started with candy and gum, then moved up to magazines or cigarettes (Molly's obsession), only turning to cosmetics once boys entered the picture. None of them were beauties, and each had suffered the ultimate teenage insult: Lesbo. All the more reason to get with the program, they'd told themselves, accentuate the positive.

Booty in hand, they'd scurry up Iowa Street to Madison Park, then smoke menthols as they tutored one another on the intricacies of how beauty got done, what colors worked best with whose complexion, how much was too much and why, tricks learned from their mothers or older sisters.

How curious, the way things turned out. Molly had taken a job with Allstate and moved to Sioux City, where she'd screamed her way through two marriages and now silenced her regret by pursuing the title of Life Master in contract bridge. Jan had gone off to college in Madison, where she confirmed everyone's suspicions by taking up with one of her professors, a woman, and hadn't set foot in Dubuque since.

Rita, of course, had found her vocation, the success story of the group. Everyone said so. But what does anyone know about such things? How can you look at someone, even someone you've known from birth, and weigh their heartbreak or fathom their secrets?

Enough with the brooding. Get on with it.

She started with powder, enjoying the comforting softness of the puff gliding across her skin.

Next came rouge, a touch of rust-and-rose for her cheeks, then she penciled in eyeliner and darkened her lashes with mascara, savoring the airy tingle of the brush.

She finished up with lipstick, a color called Cherries in the Snow.

Bit by bit her plain features took form, highlights and shadow, her pale eyes acquiring a wistful intensity, her meager lips turning sensual and bold.

Sitting back to appraise her handiwork, she gave in to a sense of defiant surrender, thinking: The face only God's allowed to see. Assuming he bothers to look.

She did not notice the note slipped under the door until she went to turn out the light in the entry. Hotel stationery, both the envelope and the single slip of paper inside.

Dear Rita:

As we talked tonight, you mentioned that your convent is in serious need of money. The older sisters, whom you clearly admire, require considerable medical care, while the diocese is strapped due to all the abuse litigation. As one of the only younger nuns in your order, you feel a special obligation. That is why you wrote your book—which I've read cover-to-cover twice, by the way, and think is marvelous. Please don't doubt that. My praise was entirely sincere.

I happen to be in a position to lend a hand. Here is what I propose: I will begin to champion your novel in every interview I have, every article I write, every appearance I make. I will do everything in my power to get the word out until your publisher realizes the gem that lies in their hands. I also am fortunate in that I possess the means to do the obvious: write a generous check.

Please understand, none of this is motivated by guilt. I don't believe either of us did anything even remotely wrong. Rather, it is my admiration and fondness for you that compels me to reach out and help.

I hope this is acceptable. If not, well, try and stop me.

All the very best,
Jon

Come morning, she still lay awake, staring at the single page of folded paper resting on her nightstand. And like the refrain of a song that she couldn't get out of her head, one of her mother's expressions—a favorite, right up until the end—kept repeating over and over within the tumble of her thoughts.

Only cowards close their hearts to the miraculous.

ACKNOWLEDGMENTS

Most of the stories in this collection first appeared, sometimes in slightly different form, in various magazines, anthologies, or collections: "Pretty Little Parasite" in *Las Vegas Noir*, edited by Jarret Keene and Todd James Pierce (it was also selected for inclusion in *Best American Mystery Stories 2009*, edited by Jeffery Deaver and Otto Penzler); "Are You with Me, Doctor Wu?" first appeared in *Crime Plus Music*, edited by Jim Fusilli; "Stray," in *The Smoking Poet*; "It Can Happen" (a Macavity Award nominee for Best Short Story), in *San Francisco Noir*, edited by Peter Maravelis; "Untamed Animal" in *Needle Magazine*, edited by Steve Weddle; "What the Creature Hath Built" in *Scoundrels*, edited by Gary Phillips; "Dead by Christmas," in *Phoenix Noir*, edited by Patrick Millikan (with a special word of appreciation to Det. Jay Pirouznia (ret.), Tempe PD); "The Axiom of Choice," in *The Strand Magazine*; "The Ant Who Carried Stones," in *Kwik Krimes*, edited by Otto Penzler; "Returning to the Knife," in *West Coast Crime Wave*, edited by Brian Thornton; "A Boy and a Girl," in *Out of the Gutter 8*, edited by Matthew Louis, Joe Clifford, Tom Pitts, and Court Merrigan.

Also, five of the stories included here appeared in a predecessor collection, *Killing Yourself to Survive*, also published by Mysterious Press in conjunction with Open Road Media.

ABOUT THE AUTHOR

Before becoming a novelist, David Corbett spent fifteen years as an investigator for the San Francisco private detective agency Palladino & Sutherland, working on several high-profile cases. In 1995, he left to help his wife set up her own law firm, and in 2000 he sold his first novel, *The Devil's Redhead*, a thriller about a reformed pot smuggler trying to save his ex-girlfriend from the deadly consequences of her own misguided sympathy.

Corbett's second novel, *Done for a Dime* (2003), begins with the murder of a blues legend and turns into a battle for the soul of a small town. It was a *New York Times* Notable Book and was nominated for a Macavity Award from Mystery Readers International. Next came *Blood of Paradise* (2007), which was nominated for the Edgar and numerous other awards. It was named both a *San Francisco Chronicle* Notable Book and one of the Top Ten Mysteries and Thrillers of 2007 by the *Washington Post*. Corbett's fourth novel, the critically acclaimed *Do They Know I'm Running?* (2010), tells of a young Salvadoran-American's harrowing journey to El Salvador to retrieve his deported uncle. It received the Spinetingler Award, Best Novel: Rising Star Category. Corbett's fifth and most recent novel, *The Mercy of the Night*, appeared in 2015, along with a companion novella, *The Devil Prayed and Darkness Fell*. He has also contributed chapters to the two Harry Middleton serial novels.

Corbett's most recent book, a collection of short stories titled *Thirteen Confessions* (2016), is offered exclusively through Mysterious Press and Open Road Media.

DAVID CORBETT

FROM MYSTERIOUSPRESS.COM
AND OPEN ROAD MEDIA

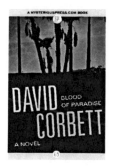
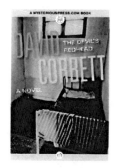
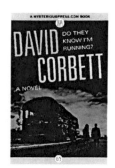

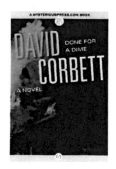
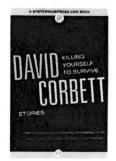

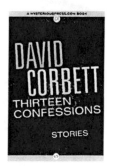

MYSTERIOUSPRESS.COM

OPEN ROAD
INTEGRATED MEDIA

MYSTERIOUSPRESS.COM

Otto Penzler, owner of the Mysterious Bookshop in Manhattan, founded the Mysterious Press in 1975. Penzler quickly became known for his outstanding selection of mystery, crime, and suspense books, both from his imprint and in his store. The imprint was devoted to printing the best books in these genres, using fine paper and top dust-jacket artists, as well as offering many limited, signed editions.

Now the Mysterious Press has gone digital, publishing ebooks through **MysteriousPress.com**.

MysteriousPress.com offers readers essential noir and suspense fiction, hard-boiled crime novels, and the latest thrillers from both debut authors and mystery masters. Discover classics and new voices, all from one legendary source.

FIND OUT MORE AT

WWW.MYSTERIOUSPRESS.COM

FOLLOW US:

@emysteries and Facebook.com/MysteriousPressCom

MysteriousPress.com is one of a select group of publishing partners of Open Road Integrated Media, Inc.

THE MYSTERIOUS BOOKSHOP, founded in 1979, is located in Manhattan's Tribeca neighborhood. It is the oldest and largest mystery-specialty bookstore in America.

The shop stocks the finest selection of new mystery hardcovers, paperbacks, and periodicals. It also features a superb collection of signed modern first editions, rare and collectable works, and Sherlock Holmes titles. The bookshop issues a free monthly newsletter highlighting its book clubs, new releases, events, and recently acquired books.

58 Warren Street
info@mysteriousbookshop.com
(212) 587-1011
Monday through Saturday
11:00 a.m. to 7:00 p.m.

FIND OUT MORE AT:

www.mysteriousbookshop.com

FOLLOW US:

@TheMysterious and Facebook.com/MysteriousBookshop

OPEN ROAD

INTEGRATED MEDIA

Find a full list of our authors and
titles at www.openroadmedia.com

FOLLOW US
@OpenRoadMedia

CPSIA information can be obtained
at www.ICGtesting.com
Printed in the USA
FSOW01n0949140916
25002FS

9 781504 035958